What was Mercy running from?

It could be his imagination, Spencer supposed. Maybe it was just fright at being stranded on the lonesome stretch of highway, a woman and child alone in a strange place, that put that glaze of terror in her expressive dark eyes. Maybe tomorrow some handsome husband and father would show up to kiss and claim them both.

But Spencer didn't think so. It was more than his odd reluctance to connect the mysterious woman to another man. It was a gut feeling. The kind a man in his position developed over the years in order to survive.

Something wasn't right about Mercy Royce and her little girl, and Spencer couldn't stop wondering what it was.

Dear Reader,

Welcome to another month of fabulous reading here at Silhouette Intimate Moments. As always, we've put together six terrific books for your reading pleasure, starting with *Another Man's Wife* by Dallas Schulze. This is another of our Heartbreakers titles, as well as the latest in her miniseries entitled A Family Circle. As usual with one of this author's titles, you won't want to miss it.

Next up is *Iain Ross's Woman* by Emilie Richards. This, too, is part of a miniseries, The Men of Midnight. This is a suspenseful and deeply emotional book that I predict will end up on your "keeper" shelf.

The rest of the month is filled out with new titles by Nikki Benjamin, *The Wedding Venture;* Susan Mallery, *The Only Way Out;* Suzanne Brockmann, *Not Without Risk;* and Nancy Gideon, *For Mercy's Sake.* Every one of them provides exactly the sort of romantic excitement you've come to expect from Intimate Moments.

In months to come, look for more reading from some of the best authors in the business. We've got books coming up from Linda Turner, Judith Duncan, Naomi Horton and Paula Detmer Riggs, to name only a few. So come back next month—and every month—to Silhouette Intimate Moments, where romance is the name of the game.

Yours,
Leslie Wainger
Senior Editor and Editorial Coordinator

Please address questions and book requests to:
Silhouette Reader Service
U.S.: 3010 Walden Ave., P.O. Box 1325, Buffalo, NY 14269
Canadian: P.O. Box 609, Fort Erie, Ont. L2A 5X3

FOR MERCY'S SAKE

NANCY GIDEON

Silhouette®
INTIMATE™ MOMENTS®
Published by Silhouette Books
America's Publisher of Contemporary Romance

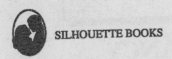 SILHOUETTE BOOKS

ISBN 0-373-07648-7

FOR MERCY'S SAKE

NANCY GIDEON

attributes her output of over twenty-six novels to a background in journalism and to the discipline of writing with two grade school-aged boys in the house. She begins her day at 5:00 a.m. when the rest of the family is still sleeping. While the writing pace is often hectic, the Southwestern Michigan author enjoys working on diverse projects. She's vice president of her local RWA chapter and a member of a number of other groups. And somehow she always finds the time to stay active in her sons' Cub Scout pack. Fans may know her under her pseudonyms Dana Ransom and Lauren Giddings.

For my friends and fellow members of
Mid-Michigan Romance Writers of America:

Proof that perseverance pays off!

Chapter 1

He saw the car the minute he crested the hill. It was pulled over at an awkward angle halfway off onto the steep gravel shoulder. Rear flashers beckoned rhythmically for aid, reflecting as bright smears of red in the puddles on the road.

Frowning, Spencer Halloway snapped on his own signal and pumped his brakes. Waves of water swept the dark stretch of highway, turning it into a treacherous ribbon as slick as black ice. The wide tires of his four-by-four skated across the standing water with a roaring whine. What kind of crazy person would be out on the road at eleven-thirty on a Sunday night with the rain coming down like an honest-to-God monsoon?

All the weekend vacationers had long since headed south. It wasn't one of the locals, because he didn't recognize the car. And he knew every car in Pine Creek and the outlying lake areas. That was part of his job. And as miserable as the night was, and as tired as he was, stopping to help a stranded motorist was part of it, too. After all, he was sheriff of Pine Creek.

He eased his Chevy S-10 in behind the crippled Pontiac and opened the door of his truck. Rain blew in to pepper the light gray of his uniform slacks with dark, spreading blotches. A cold knot of tension started in his belly, the kind he always felt when he approached an unknown situation. Experience had taught him that what looked the most innocent could turn deadly in an instant. Only a fool took things for granted.

He swung down from the seat into the inhospitable weather and hunched over to the driver's side of the car. Instinct had his hand reaching up to unsnap the flap of his holster but his hand grew damp as it lingered there at the ready. Easing up to the door, he muttered a brief prayer. *Don't let this be anything I don't want to get into.* He took a slow breath, trying to control the ache of apprehension tightening about his chest. *Do your job, Spencer. Do it smart.*

He startled movement from behind the foggy glass when he tapped on the window. Someone rolled it down a wary two inches.

A woman was in the driver's seat. Her face was as pale as the obscured moon above. As he always did in such circumstances, he flicked the glow of his flashlight over the front of his uniform shirt, letting it pick up the metallic glint. He knew the minute she saw the badge pinned to his chest. An alarming stillness came over her as she stared. A man in a police uniform should have been seen as a savior to a motorist lamed on this lonely patch of highway. Should have, but in this case, wasn't. The lovely features of the driver screwed up into a mask of obvious dismay. And his initial relief became caution again.

"Evening," he called. "Having some car trouble?"

The stabbing beam of his flashlight fanned across a pair of wide brown eyes. The woman in the car squinted and turned her head slightly, giving him a view of exquisite cheekbones. She seemed reluctant to answer and he was about to ask again, when she said in a breathless voice, "It just quit on me. I couldn't get it started again. I think I might have flooded it."

No normal fluster of frustration edged her words. He could swear he heard the strain of fear. To subdue it, he made his tone firm and competent as he suggested, "Why don't you pop the hood and I'll see if I can spot the problem."

Wordlessly, the woman complied.

As he moved around the front bumper and groped for the catch of the hood, he considered the woman's reaction. It was odd. Damned odd. The rain pounded down on him as he tucked himself into the engine compartment, making it difficult to concentrate on anything other than getting the car mobile and himself back where it was dry. But a part of him was alert and edgy, ready to jump aside if the engine suddenly growled to life. It never hurt to be prepared for anything. And on this cold, wet night, he sure as hell didn't want to become a statistic in anyone's book.

After a minute of tinkering, Spencer slammed down the hood and came around to the side. The window had been rolled up tight. To protect against the weather? Or him? As his hand slid back to the holster he wore on his belt, he tapped the rim of his flashlight on the glass and it gave those few cautious inches, not far enough for him to see past her to whatever else the car might hold.

"Sorry, ma'am. Looks like it's the water pump. I can't do anything to get you going again. It'll have to go to a garage. I'm afraid there are none open around here at this time of night."

Her distress magnified in those deep dark eyes and, wise or not, a dose of male protectiveness crept up inside him to battle caution.

"I'd be glad to give you a lift back into Pine Creek. They've got a fairly decent motel where you can put up for the night." He shivered as the wetness of the evening stuck his shirt to his back. Raindrops beat down on the brim of his silverbelly-tan Stetson hat as he waited for her reply, gauging her response.

"No, thank you, officer. I'm not going that way." Her voice was a low purr, calmer than before, sounding like the vibration of a well-tuned motor. A man couldn't help wondering how sweet it would rumble if revved up in earnest. Ordinarily he would have, if the better part of his passions hadn't already been soaked clear through. She hesitated, unwilling to volunteer the information, then finally told him, "I've got a cabin on Big Bear Lake. It should be only a few miles farther."

"That it is. I'm going there myself. Why don't you grab what you need and I'll give you a lift." Again, the hesitation on her part. "It might be a good long while before anyone else passes this way tonight," he added for good measure.

"All right," she murmured in heavy resignation. "Thank you, officer."

He heard the latch pop on the door and he opened it for her, anxious to get a quick look inside the car at what she might be anxious to hide behind that overly cautious attitude. It was then he got his first glimpse of her—all of her. She must have been a tall woman from the way she was wedged beneath the wheel. A snug beige-colored skirt was hiked up to expose an incredible length of shapely leg. He stared in a helpless moment of masculine appreciation, and as he did, he leaned toward her. His head tipped to follow that clean line and all the rainwater collecting in the curve of his Stetson rushed forward to funnel off the front of the rolled brim. Right into the woman's lap.

She gave a gasp and brushed ineffectively at her skirt from where she was trapped behind the wheel.

Oh, damn! "Sorry," he muttered inadequately, feeling hot color seep up his cheeks.

He'd meant to rescue, not drown her. His reserve momentarily scattered in the face of his embarrassment. "Let me give you a hand."

When he pulled out his handkerchief and automatically reached to blot up some of the dampness, she struck his hand away. From the brusqueness of that move, he expected to see irritation in her features, not the apprehension he found there.

"It's all right. Really," she stammered anxiously. "No harm done."

Only when he straightened and moved back did her anxious pose ease. Then she twisted on the seat and when he followed the supple curve of her body with his flashlight beam, he saw for the first time that she wasn't alone in the car. On the seat beside her, wrapped in a quilt, was a sleeping child, a girl he guessed to be about six or seven. A real dangerous pair—mother and child.

Feeling foolish for his earlier apprehension, Spencer resnapped his holster. His relief made him eager to please.

"I'll help with her if you want to go on and get in the truck."

"No!"

She dropped into a protective crouch over the child. The sharpness of her tone set him back. As if realizing how she'd sounded, she managed a tight smile of apology that was as strained as the moment.

"I'll carry her. It's been a long day and she's exhausted. If she should wake up, I don't want her to be frightened by the sight of a stranger."

She could have been telling the truth. But instinctively, Spencer knew she wasn't. The woman simply didn't want any part of him or his help. She'd made it clear she was accepting the ride with the utmost reservation, probably only for the sake of the child. His wary nature working overtime again, he stepped back to let her ease out of the car with the burden of the little girl in her arms. It was a nice view, her cute rounded bottom wiggling toward him as she backed out of the interior. It took all his willpower to keep from placing a helping hand on that nicely curved fanny—to assist her, of course. All part of the job. But nervous as she was around him, he was afraid she'd bolt back into the car and lock the doors. And he didn't want to be responsible for the two of them shivering the night away on the shoulder of the deserted highway.

The woman straightened. She was tall. He was over six foot and she nearly topped his shoulder. An enticing amount of that height was made up of trim calves and sleek thighs. His gaze moved up from there in lingering appreciation, stopping dead at the expression on her face. Under his detailing scrutiny, she looked like a doe caught in the glare of headlights.

"Do you need anything out of the car?"

She blinked and some of the glaze faded. "If you'd just grab that case in the back seat for me," she said, as she struggled to hold the girl and maneuver the quilt so it covered her against the downpour. The woman froze when Spencer tugged the edge of it up over the child's head, as if she expected the gesture to hold some threat. Then, she ran quickly toward the shelter of his truck.

He watched them go with a slightly pensive frown on his face, then, anxious to get out of the weather himself, Spencer pushed up the bucket seat to retrieve the single bag in back. As he straightened, he noticed she'd left her set of keys in the ignition in her haste. He palmed them, wondering what had flustered her enough to make her forget something so basic.

When Spencer climbed up behind the wheel of his four-by-four, he was surprised to find she'd placed herself between him and the girl. Because the back seat had been taken out, there was no choice but for all of them to squeeze into the front. It seemed an awkward arrangement, her long legs twisted to accommodate the hump on the floor. But nice, he noted, as an assessing gaze followed the smooth bend of her knees. Real nice. When his hand moved toward them, he heard her suck in a quick breath.

"Thought I'd get a little heat going in here," he told her as he slid the appropriate levers on the dash. She tucked those gorgeous legs of hers nearly up under her chin to avoid the brush of his forearm. Only when a sigh of warmth started blowing from the vents and Spencer had settled back into his seat to click his shoulder harness into place did the woman relax to any degree.

Huddled against the opposite door, the well-cocooned child slept on, seemingly dead to the world.

Spencer eased the truck out onto the highway and started the wipers on high to keep up with the rain. He could almost hear the heartbeat of the woman at his side echoing that same frantic tempo. Most people wouldn't equate a ride from the local law with being picked up by a possible madman.

Yet she was afraid. Of him. Despite the uniform. Or because of it.

"You say you're headed for Big Bear?"

The sound of his voice startled her. He felt her flinch nervously away from him as her big eyes darted in his direction. And he heard her draw in a long breath, pausing to carefully phrase her reply.

"Yes."

That was it. Not a particularly gabby female.

"Buying or renting?" he prodded.

"Borrowing. From a friend."

"For how long?"

"The summer." An edge had crept into her voice and that spark almost made him smile. Spencer could hear *Mind your own business, buster* in her tone. She had some spunk, afterall, he thought with satisfaction. Well, weren't policemen supposed to be inquisitive? It came with the territory.

"Which place? So I know where I'm going," he qualified rather pointedly; the model Good Samaritan. She sounded suitably chastened in her response.

"It belongs to a family by the name of Cheswick. On the east side of the lake."

"Oh, yeah. I know which one. I'm just on the other side of the cove. We're neighbors, you might say."

She made no sound that would indicate her pleasure in that arrangement. It was going to be hard being neighborly with this one. But worth the effort, he decided with another glance at those bared legs canted his way. He'd bet the payoff on his truck that she was a knockout in a swimsuit.

"I'm Spencer Halloway." When a long silence followed that disclosure, he prompted, "And you are—?"

"Um, what? Oh. Mercy. Mercy . . . Royce."

That bit of information was offered so unnaturally, it was immediately suspect. Mercy Royce. Sure she was. He wondered if that was how her driver's license read. It came out too stilted to be a name she was familiar with. Why? Was she lying or just reluctant to volunteer anything about herself? Again, why? His instincts were quivering. Just as his interest was simmering.

Mercy gave him a sidelong glance, noting the way his lips pursed in thought, then quickly, she looked away, turning her attention back to the sleeping figure beside her to make sure the seat belt was snug but not tight.

Now that was handled real well, Mercy.

She held her groan of frustration as their reflections briefly appeared on the windshield as a semi roared past, making the smaller truck shudder. She was shuddering, too, at the clumsiness of her words. If he wasn't already suspicious, she was pushing him toward it. She was no master at deception. Lies didn't come easily to her lips, especially when she was so frightened, every tendon in her body ached.

Of all the terrible luck. First to be stranded when they were so close to their goal. Then to be rescued by the last person in the world she wanted to see—a policeman. How could he miss the guilt stamped upon her features? She might as well have confessed all while staring at his badge in horror. How could she expect to maintain the lie all summer when she couldn't support it for the first few minutes under the probing eyes of a lawman?

A cop for a neighbor. Great. Just great.

For long minutes, only the shush of the windshield wipers sounded in the steamy interior of the truck. Words appearing wavery through the sheets of water proclaimed Big Bear Lake on a road sign. Mercy felt a rush of relief. Almost there. She smiled with grim satisfaction, her hand rubbing the small shoulders of the sleeping child. Again she glanced furtively at the lawman behind the wheel.

In the glare of the mercury lights irregularly spaced at some of the lakeside cottages, she could form a clear picture of him. He had a nice profile; clean, fine, strong. Before, she'd seen only the badge set between broad shoulders. She supposed women would find his chiseled features attractive. They would see his easy smile as roguishly charming, the way it lifted one side of his mouth with a lazy tug, then coaxed the other to follow. It was a smug, confident smile, spelling out Male and Proud of It with one brief flash of white teeth. She'd seen the interest warm in his eyes when he looked at her. She was used to the response and wasn't flattered by it the way she figured most women would be; the way he expected her to be. And that could spell trouble with a man as arrogantly sure of his appeal as Spencer Halloway. The last thing she needed was a lawman sniffing about her door.

The road had gone from smooth blacktop to washboard gravel. The four-by-four jounced over the water-filled cavities as if trying to shake her from her stiff posture. It was impossible not to bump against the man at her side while she reflexively steadied the little girl. No matter how hard Mercy gripped the dash and braced the awkward angle of her feet, she came in continual contact with his lean, hard form. The spareness of male muscle beneath his water-stained dress shirt didn't incite appreciation. It quickened apprehension inside Mercy. She gritted her teeth to still their sudden chattering.

Finally, the truck slowed and made a cautious turn into a narrow, tree-lined drive. It was too dark and rain-drenched for her to get a good look at the cabin, but its silhouette had a comforting solidity. Shelter against the weather. Shelter against the storm of her emotions. An escape from their rescuer.

The sound of the rain heightened as Spencer shut off the engine. She looked to him in alarm. Why had he stopped the truck?

"Have you got the key handy?" he was asking.

"Wh-why?"

"I'll unlock the door for you so you won't get soaked."

The thought of him going inside woke a thinly veiled panic. "No. Thank you, but I can manage."

She could see the brightness of his smile against the dim interior. "It's no problem. It's the least I can do after nearly drowning you earlier." There was a pause and when she refused to surrender the key, he added with a smooth logic, "Besides, you don't want your little girl to get wet."

Mercy bit down on her indecision. She wanted to scream out, "Just go away and leave us alone." But she couldn't very well do that, could she? Finally, she forced a sigh. She was being silly. She was tired. Her nerves were raw. It was a friendly gesture. She shouldn't act like it was more than that. She fished in her handbag and silently gave him the single key that would unlock their sanctuary.

He was gone for only a minute. Mercy could make out the outline of his bunched shoulders as he passed in front of the truck's low beams. She closed her eyes for a moment, lost in the relief of reaching their destination undiscovered. At last, she could get a good night's sleep.

Mercy gave a start as the passenger door opened. Before she could protest, Spencer gathered up the slumbering child to his sturdy chest and started for the cabin. She had no alternative but to rush after him in a flurry of anxiety, their lone bag clutched in her trembling hands.

He was arranging the little girl on a shadowy sofa when Mercy entered. The interior of the cabin smelled musty, damp and unused; a clammy welcome.

"I'll get you some lights."

"No, you don't have to do..." Her objection trailed off as Spencer's flashlight beam disappeared down a narrow hall. She was fast learning that he did pretty much whatever he wanted, regardless of her feelings on the matter. He had a take-charge manner, and for the moment, she was forced to endure it. At least, he seemed to know what he was doing. She should have been grateful. She had no idea how to turn on the power and water to bring civilization to the primitive surroundings. She hadn't thought that far ahead.

Maybe running into him on the road was more a godsend than a curse.

She was more convinced of it as a pool of yellow appeared beneath a dusty lampshade on a corner table. Looking pleased, Spencer emerged from the back rooms with a cold flashlight and a warm smile.

"Let there be light," he announced.

"Thank you for your help, Officer Halloway—" Her dismissal was left dangling as he strode into the small kitchen area and abruptly dropped out of sight. Cautiously, she circled the breakfast bar and was surprised to find him down on the chipped linoleum floor, head and shoulders lost beneath the sink.

"What are you doing?" she asked anxiously.

"Getting you some hot water. The place has been shut up since last summer and everything's still winterized. Michigan winters do a number on the pipes if you don't flush them out. It'll take a while to get the hot water tank up to temperature but the shower will be ready by morning."

With that, he scooted out from under the cabinets, and Mercy instinctively took a few steps back. He stood, brushing his hands off against the swell of his thighs, and finally face-to-face with him, she was able to take the full measure of the man. And was thoroughly intimidated.

He was bigger than she'd first assumed. Taller, broader, with a tensile strength his easy smile couldn't relieve. He'd taken off the water-spattered hat, but it had left the crease of its band upon his tawny-colored hair, leading her to believe he was more often with than without it. Sort of a northern Michigan cowboy. It fit, that ideal of rangy toughness and gosh-golly-ma'am manners, and she was sure the image would have pleased him. His eyes were gray, she noticed with a sudden clarity. Steel gray, like cold gunmetal in contrast to the warmth of his expression. His aura filled the small space, making her feel totally engulfed. Smothered. She retreated farther, moving back into the open living area.

As if unaware of her agitation, Spencer gave the cabin's interior a slow inspection. "Looks like everything's in good shape. If you have any problems with the pump or anything else, feel free to holler. I'm pretty good with my hands." The corners of his eyes creased with a hint of humor. She wasn't amused so he added in casual explanation, "We tend to take care of one another up here."

As he made the offer, he opened the old-model refrigerator, taking out the stick of wood that held the door slightly ajar and adjusting the temperature-control knob in back.

"Thank you, but I'm sure we'll be—"

"I'm just on the other side of the cove," he went on as if she hadn't been speaking, neatly severing her claim of capability. "The log home. You can see it from the back porch. If I'm not there, just tuck a note in the door. I've got a phone if you need one and a TV if the little one gets lonely for the Saturday-morning cartoons."

Mercy offered a stiff smile. The picture he was painting was growing too intimate for her liking. She made her tone cool and very final. "Thank you, Officer Halloway, but we'll be fine. We came up here to get away from those things."

But Spencer wasn't daunted. He grinned and picked up his silver Stetson. "Just yell out. I'll hear you. We're neighbors, after all."

That was far from a comforting fact.

She stood, gesturing to the door with her gaze. It was as effective as giving him a push toward it. Finally, he took the not-so-subtle hint.

"Well, I'll be on my way so you can get settled in." He clapped the hat down on his head so it tipped at a rakish angle. For effect, she was sure. "Don't worry about your car. I'll call in for a tow."

"Thank you," Mercy repeated with a trace of exasperation creeping into her voice. Would she never be rid of him? She moved toward the door, feeling him following on her heels. How quickly he overwhelmed her with his nearness. She opened the door and with her hand on the knob, turned to him. He was standing so close, they were toe to toe. His shiny badge was at eye level. She could read the numbers on it and the word *sheriff*. Sheriff Halloway. She repressed a shiver. This was no time for her to act out of the ordinary. She forced a smile. "Good night, Sheriff."

"Ma'am." He made that polite title glide like a caress. Then, he tipped his hat brim to show no offense intended. And finally, he was gone.

Mercy shut the door behind him and slid the bolt. Rivers of relief rippled through her. For a moment, she could do no more than lean weakly against the wall and shake. They were safe. For the moment, they were safe.

Because her knees felt too watery to support her right away, Mercy used the long, strength-gathering minutes to assess the cabin. Despite the dampness and grit of disuse, it was a cozy place within its wood-paneled walls. The small, L-shaped living room was large enough for a round dinette next to the kitchen. There were no separating walls to enclose the areas from one another. The furnishings were an old collection of garage-sale refugees, each adding to the rustic decor; an odd chair at the table, a crocheted throw cover over a tattered platform rocker, rag rugs scattered over cold tiles. A potbellied iron woodstove crouched in one corner as the mode of heat. It wasn't a fancy retreat. No phone. No television. Just an ancient gas range and a tiny fifties-style icebox. But Spencer had said there was a shower. And if there were beds, a lock on the door and a roof that didn't leak, it had everything she needed at the moment. What she needed was seclusion. What she needed was rest.

Thinking along that line, Mercy moved wearily toward the back hall, turning on lights as she went. There, she found a compartmental bath with just the bare necessities, and two small bedrooms, each with a double bed, an antique dresser and little room for movement. She tossed back the patched and repatched quilt on one of the beds to find it already made up in a set of faded sheets. They would do. Her own were in the trunk of the stranded Pontiac.

Thinking of that, she froze in panic. The car keys. He must have taken them. Would the sheriff look through her car? Had her fearful actions alerted him enough to go to that extreme? She recalled the sharp curiosity of his gaze. A natural part of his job? Or had she done something to make him suspicious? Was there anything in the hurriedly packed bags in the trunk to give them away? No. She didn't think so. She'd been very careful. And besides, there was little she could do about it now. No use worrying without reason. She let out her suspended breath and forced the panic to subside.

The little girl was still asleep on the sofa. Mercy considered waking her to get her out of her traveling clothes but decided against it. She needed the sleep, deep and undisturbed. Besides, the bed would be cold enough without slipping bare skin in between those clammy sheets. Mercy lifted the slight figure to carry her into the first bedroom. Without shedding more than her shoes, Mercy placed her on the too-soft mattress. The girl stirred only long enough to burrow into the covers of the bed they would share.

Tonight, she wanted the child close. In case she woke in the strange place. Just for the comfort of having her near and the knowledge that she was safe. Tonight, she was safe. And that made Mercy smile when she finally switched off the light and drew the warm little body into the curve of her own. Tonight, they could both sleep well.

Who was she?

On the other side of the quiet cove, Spencer Halloway took another swallow of his beer and studied the blaze of lights within the Cheswicks' cabin.

What was she running from?

After twelve years of police work, Spencer knew the look. He'd seen it in the eyes of kids he'd caught joyriding in a "borrowed" car. He remembered it from the faces of young runaways when he'd worked the big-city beat. It was an instinct that prickled along his spine when he pulled over a speeder who just happened to have hit an area gas station hours before. They all shared that glaze of panic flickering like a desperate flame behind the eyes, just like the woman behind the wheel of the disabled car. They all managed that tense smile, torturing stiff lips into an unnatural upward bow. And they all brought a sweat of warning to his hands and an acceleration to his heartbeat.

What was she running from?

It could be his imagination, he supposed, as he flicked the lengthening ash from the end of his cigarette. Maybe it was just the fright of being stranded on the lonesome stretch of highway—a woman and child alone in a strange place—that had put that glaze of terror in her expressive dark eyes. Maybe tomorrow some handsome husband and father would show up to kiss and claim them both. But he didn't think so. It was more than his odd reluctance to attach the mysterious Mercy Royce to another man. It was a gut feeling. The kind a man in his position developed over the years in order to survive. And those gut feelings had only failed him once.

Something wasn't right about Mercy Royce and her little girl, and Spencer couldn't stop wondering what it was.

Carrying the beer and smoldering-but-as-yet-unsmoked cigarette with him, he strode to his phone and made a call.

"Pine Creek Sheriff's Department. How may I help you?"

"Judy, this is Spencer."

"Oh, hi, Sheriff." The sleepy voice immediately brightened and distracted him for a moment from his brooding thoughts.

He could picture the pert twenty-year-old on the other end of the line. Judy Alcott made no bones about her interest in him. And he'd done nothing drastic to discourage it. Though he would, eventually. He didn't mind the playful banter, but he wouldn't allow the girl to be hurt by her expectations.

Most of the eligible women in Pine Creek knew he wasn't in the market for more than the noncommittal enjoyment of their charms. As much as he liked their company, he'd posted his heart as strictly off-limits. He made sure they knew that, right up front. He wasn't lonely in his bachelor status. The influx of summer swimsuits provided ample entertainment during the warm months and when the season ended, there were always plenty of encouraging smiles turned his way from the local ladies. He had no desire to tamper with the innocence of youth or test the parameters of love.

Not again. Never again.

As if in rebellion, his mind conjured the image of Mercy Royce unwinding gracefully from the seat of her car.

"Did I wake you up?" he asked into the phone, forcing his thoughts with a mental jerk back into the present.

A giggling was his answer. "Of course not, Sheriff," Judy lied cheerfully. "What can I do for you?"

There was no mistaking the open invitation in that breathy drawl. Spencer grinned wryly. He'd have to have that talk with her sooner than anticipated. "You can start by waking up Kevin Hobbs. I've got a car out on 37 that needs to be picked up."

"In this weather?"

He knew she was anticipating Hobbs's sentiments. "It's a favor to me, Judy. There was no way to get it safely off the highway and I'd like him to start on it as soon as he can. If he grumbles too much just tell him I could start calling Virg over at the 76 station with my business."

"Sure thing, Sheriff. Anything else?"

"Yeah. I want you to run a DMV check for me." He recited the plate number off Mercy's car. "I want that information A.S.A.P."

"Sure, Spence." She sounded disappointed. "I'll get it right out."

"You're an angel, Judy. You can go back to sleep now."

He set the receiver down and made a pensive face. Soon, he would know Mercy Royce's secrets. Why it was so important, he wasn't sure. Maybe because things had been slow in town and she offered a little excitement. He thought of her long, long legs and smiled. Oh, yeah. She was exciting, all right. Then his expression sobered as he recalled the fear shining in her eyes.

What else was she?

With the warm . . .

Chapter 2

Except for the heavy weight of the cool morning air, it was hard to believe a storm had raged the night before. The sun lifted from a vivid pool of colors into the promise of a clear sky and warmer temperatures. It was a beautiful view; the spill of oranges and reds over the still lake, the lush green fringe of oaks and pine. The occasional cabin nestled near the water. Such peace, such serenity.

Mercy felt her soul sigh.

The cement floor of the open porch was cold beneath her bare feet. The area had been built with the intention of it becoming all-weather, but the owners had stopped short of installing screens. It had an unfinished charm with its wafting breezes and old platform glider nestled against the faded siding of the cottage. And a lot of assorted spiders nesting in its corners, she noted with an internal cringe. She would take the broom to them later. Each evening she could watch the sun set while rocking on the swing. She couldn't imagine a more peaceful end to the day.

With a cup of strong coffee brewed in the ancient automatic drip machine she'd found in one of the cupboards warming her hands, Mercy was content to let the crisp cool of morning chafe her skin. There was a lot of it to chafe. All she had with her were the toiletries from her overnight case and the baggy T-shirt she usually wore to bed. Beneath its mid-thigh hem, her legs were bare. The rest of her things, even changes of underclothes, were in her suitcase. That brought her thoughts back to the disabled car. And Sheriff Halloway.

Her suddenly restless gaze scanned the edge of the opposing beach across the narrow cove. Which cottage was his? she wondered. She felt a chill move along her arms. She would have to be extra careful where the lawman was concerned. He could have no reason to think she was other than she pretended; a woman seeking a restful summer. Alone. She would have to make it immediately clear that she was not out for a summer romance or companionship in any form. She was here at Big Bear Lake desperately seeking a respite, not new complications. And Sheriff Halloway had the look of a major complication.

Enough about the sheriff. Worries in that direction were self-destructive. She would concentrate on optimistic things, like how well she'd slept and how good she'd felt looking down upon Casey's freckled features when she'd awakened. If her earlier doubts about doing the right thing had been close to overwhelming, they were fading fast. This place was the perfect answer. They couldn't have found a more beautiful or a more isolated spot. Big Bear Lake was miles from the nearest town and Pine Creek was definitely of the one-horse variety, a place where they could blend in silently with the tourist crowd and wait out the summer in anonymity. Just perfect for her plan.

"Morning."

She jumped. Coffee splashed over the edge of her mug, burning her hand and splotching the cement about her bare feet. With alarm, she turned toward the issuance of that husky masculine voice. It was a moment before she could get the rapid palpitations of her heart under enough control to gasp for a shaky breath.

"You nearly scared the life out of me, Sheriff Hallo-way." She tried to smile as if she'd just received a mild star-tle instead of a major shock.

"Didn't mean to," he said with an answering smile.

Of course he did. Otherwise, she would have heard him moving up through all the bits and pieces of fallen limbs about the yard. He must have placed his feet very carefully to have been so soundless in his stalking. The image made her frown and left her feeling uncomfortably vulnerable.

"What is it you want, Sheriff?" That came out more sharply than she intended, but it was hard to be polite with her heart doing jumping jacks at a high aerobic level.

He'd come around to the front of the porch by then, and she could see he was toting two suitcases. "I ran into town to drop off the keys to your car at the garage and thought you might need your things this morning. You couldn't have been carrying much in that itty-bitty bag you had last night."

Mercy stared at the large hands curled around the han-dles of her suitcases. Distress knotted inside her, forming a huge ache. She swallowed hard and managed to say, "How very thoughtful of you."

He shrugged it off with an easy roll of his broad shoul-ders. "I pulled some strings with Kevin Hobbs, the garage owner. He said he'd have your car for you this morning." He waited for her to respond with the proper degree of gratitude.

"I guess it helps to have friends among the police." She smiled wanly, not truly convinced.

His grin was wide and white against his tanner skin, and faintly predatory. "I've heard it said that we can be your best friend or your worst enemy."

Which will I be to you? was the unspoken question. *A threat?* Mercy felt herself pale. No, Spencer Halloway seemed too sure of himself as a man to resort to cheap in-timidation. He was the type to woo, not bully. But the last thing she wanted was indebtedness, especially if it gave the tall intruder the notion that he could come and go as he pleased. That, she wouldn't allow. The thought of him soft-footing it around her foundations spun her overtaxed nerves into fine threads of glass.

"A comforting thought," she remarked coolly. Before he could step onto the porch, she set down her cup, came forward to form a bodily barrier and took both bags from him. Their hands brushed accidentally in the exchange. Mercy was instantly aware of the warm roughness of his skin. A workingman's hands. She wondered distractedly what he did to have such calluses. Obviously, he wasn't the type to stay indoors tied to a desk chair. She could tell that much from his bronze coloring and the ripple of athletic grace betrayed whenever he moved. He was a man of the outdoors, a man of action. Again, she repressed a shiver.

Spencer Halloway was deceiving. Despite his slow smile and good-old-boy manner, there was nothing lazy about him. Particularly in the mind working behind his slate-gray eyes. She could see the continuous line of questions forming there as he glanced beyond her into the cabin, as he looked her slowly up and leisurely down. Then that all-business gleam took on a different glimmer, one of male admiration.

Suddenly, Mercy was very aware of how she was dressed, or rather, of how she was undressed, with her bare legs and baggy T-shirt. She fought the instinct to cross her arms protectively against his simmering gaze.

"I won't detain you any longer, Sheriff," she said curtly, in hopes of offsetting the warm caress of his assessment. "I'm sure you have work to get to."

Spencer grinned. For someone knock-down gorgeous as she was, the lady sure didn't appreciate a complimentary look. He didn't plan to be rude, but it was hard not to stare at her. There wasn't a single spot on her where he could rest his eyes and not be stirred to lusty speculation. Beyond those long, lithe legs that had danced seductively through his dreams, there was the tease of pale cotton jersey. The morning's cool air detailed an enticing pucker where it stretched in snug contour over her generous breasts and set it fluttering about the narrow nip of her waist. And if a splendid figure wasn't enough, her face was perfection. Waves of burnished hair cascaded to her shoulders, framing artfully crafted features—well-spaced dark eyes, a slender nose and lush lips—in a manner no man was meant to ignore.

Then there was the surprising scatter of freckles across high cheekbones, a warming contrast to the cool sophistication she exuded. Even her low, rumbly voice was enough to put a fellow's heart through its paces. It was his experience that beautiful women liked to be recognized as such. But not this one. Her cool gaze posted a No Trespassing sign spelled out in capital letters and reinforced it with barbed wire. But hell, he was never much for reading, anyway.

"Since your car will be ready in a few hours, I thought you and your daughter might like a ride into town to pick it up."

She frowned and he could see refusal written all over her expression. Again, he chose not to take the warning literally.

"Of course, you could choose to walk, I guess. Nice day for it. It's only—oh, eight miles or so. Half of it uphill."

He waited for her to mull that over. This wasn't the big city. There was no public transportation or even a cab for hire. From the look of her, she might be stubborn enough to set off on foot, but he doubted that she'd subject the little girl to it. And from what he'd seen of her protectiveness, he knew she wouldn't leave the child alone. He liked that quality about her. He let his offer dangle and watched her nudge it with obvious suspicion before she reluctantly gave in and bit.

"All right, Sheriff. Thank you. As long as you're sure we're not putting you to any extra trouble."

"Oh, no, ma'am. It's on my way. I'll be by for you around ten."

He lounged in the open doorframe, his solid form filling it quite capably. His gaze touched on the coffee cup she held and lingered there meaningfully. Mercy took his hint and pointedly set the mug aside again in a statement he couldn't mistake.

"We'll be ready, Sheriff."

So much for the invitation to join her for the fresh brew he could smell steeping inside. But it was a long ride into Pine Creek. Lots of time to get better acquainted. Smiling, he tipped his hat and ambled back around the house.

After he'd gone, Mercy carried the bags inside and hurried into the empty bedroom. She laid them atop the faded chenille spread and studied them for a long moment before slipping the catches. Had the contents been disturbed? Impossible to tell.

Had Sheriff Halloway rummaged through her belongings before bringing them to her door? Anxiously, she searched through the contents; through the clothing, the shoes, the children's games, the books, looking at them as he might have, for a clue to her identity. And with relief, she found nothing that would give her away.

Mercy gave a soft laugh at her own behavior. Why would the sheriff of this small lazy town go to all that trouble? She was the one being overly suspicious, not him. She had to relax and act the part of tourist before he started wondering what else she might be.

As she dressed herself in comfortable jeans and a striped pullover sweater, she heard Casey stirring in the other room. It was a precious sound, the childlike snufflings and sleepy grumbles. Warmth stole about her heart and squeezed tight. It was worth it. Everything was worth it to hear the simple pleasure of a child waking gradually and without fear. Mercy was smiling as she carried a change of clothes to the girl engulfed beneath the tattered quilt.

Spencer was right on time. Exactly at ten o'clock, he pulled his muddy four-by-four up to the front door. With an agile ease, he swung down from the cab and approached the two standing at the door.

"Ladies, your ride is here."

They came out and Mercy conscientiously locked the door while the little girl tucked back behind her shyly. The child was adorable and Spencer, who had a soft spot for small members of any species, felt his heart at immediate risk. All those freckles and that tangle of strawberry-blond hair softened the somber look in her big brown eyes. She would be a beauty, just like her mom.

"Why, hello there, Miss Royce," he said with the offer of an engaging smile. She observed him as suspiciously as the woman, he noted with some chagrin. He'd really never thought of himself as an ogre. Perhaps it was the uniform. And that opened the way to all sorts of puzzles.

Both mother and child stood stiffly as he neared them, their every tendon taut and ready for flight. He slowed his step and widened his smile until his cheeks hurt, doing his best to look harmless. "I'm Spencer Halloway, your neighbor," he told the child as he squatted down to her eye level. "We weren't really introduced last night but a friend of yours was telling me all about you."

The girl looked up at Mercy in surprise and the tall woman returned the question with her slight frown. Then, the child's features lit as he brought a well-loved stuffed monkey from behind his back.

"Mr. Stubbs!" she exclaimed in delight.

"I found the little fellow on the floor of my truck. He was pretty upset about being left behind."

The little girl forgot her shyness as she reached for her favorite companion and snuggled it close. She never slept without him, and Mercy had been so stressed the night before, she hadn't thought to miss it. But Casey would have. The reappearance of Mr. Stubbs would save on gallons of tears and many a fretful night to come. It was a sweet thing to do. Mercy was touched by his consideration.

She began to smile her thanks as Spencer looked up. Then her expression froze. Mercy watched his big hand tousle the child's bright curls and her insides twisted. The gaze he brought to hers was warm and expectant. Sweetness or pure calculation? What was he up to? Wariness lanced through her. Was he using the trusting affections of a child to wriggle into their lives? He could have given Mercy the toy when he brought the luggage over, yet he'd chosen to wait to make this grand presentation. To win Casey over. Her features tensed. Sheriff Halloway was very smooth. And she began to fear him even more.

"Let's get going, shall we?" he announced, straightening. His hand was still on Casey's head and he couldn't miss the way Mercy's stare riveted to it. She looked as though she would like to sink her teeth into his wrist. The woman was a bristled she-wolf when it came to protecting the little girl, and every bit as cautious. He'd seen the moment when she began to doubt his motives. The attractive half-smile shaping her lips had firmed to granite. The eyes that had softened toward him for just an instant hardened into an impenetrable glaze. Hiding what? Annoyance? Anger? Fear? What had happened to this woman and child to put such a jaded brilliance into eyes so deep and velvety? Mercy was too tense, too overly sensitive for it to be him triggering the response.

Spencer's curiosity was piqued as Mercy took the child's arm and led her quickly out of his reach. When he went around the truck and hopped up into the seat, he noted once again that Mercy had placed herself in the middle. And he was darned sure this time it wasn't to be closer to him. She was making herself into a barrier. His eyes swept over her. A very attractive barrier. One he would enjoy overcoming. He smiled and made the engine growl to life.

There was a lot more to see on this trip to Pine Creek without the deluge of water to obscure it. The little girl bounced within the restraint of her seat belt, commenting upon the woodsy sights, and Mercy merely smiled in answer. They were an interesting pair, Spencer mused as he watched them together from the corner of his eye. The love between them was a warm, palpable thing and he experienced a second of wistfulness. And just as quickly quashed it. That kind of family picture was definitely not in his future plans.

"I forgot to ask your daughter's name."

Mercy gave a start. "My—?" She looked at him blankly for a moment, then caught herself. "Casey."

He leaned ahead to view the child around the mother. "How do you like the north country, Casey? Ever been up here before?"

She shook her head, setting the vivid curls in motion. "Uh-uh. My mom and dad were always talking about camping, and they were going to take me, but—" Her words fractured, as if in suddenly remembered surprise and pain.

"This is our first trip," Mercy put in quickly. Her arm went around the little girl's shoulders in a gesture of comfort.

"Is your daddy joining you here?" he prodded gently. He didn't like it, taking advantage of the girl's obvious distress, but it was information he would never drag out of the mother. And it was suddenly vital for him to know where the man in their life fit in.

In a little voice saturated with hurt, Casey said, "I don't have a daddy."

"We're divorced," Mercy concluded brusquely. She cuddled the child close and shot him a withering glare. *Are you satisfied now?* it seemed to say.

Sorry, his contrite gaze returned.

Mercy's angry features didn't ease. Instead, she turned her attention back to the girl. "This is our first vacation together, isn't it, Casey? Just the two of us girls off on our own." She said that pointedly, hoping he would take the hint and quit pushing so hard. For a moment, he did.

Divorced. Spencer stared out at the thread of southbound blacktop. That would explain the edginess, the caution, the protectiveness. But not the fear. Had Mercy Royce run illegally with the child? He glanced at her briefly, noting the tenderness in her expression, the love steeped in her embrace of the little girl. He couldn't imagine any court taking custody from her. If she was on the mend from a bad divorce—and how well he could relate to that—she wouldn't be receptive to his charm. In fact, she would probably be scornful of any member of the male species. Well, he would just have to change her mind. He could be a good friend, a good listener.

Then his gaze slid over her again, lingering on the supple fit of denim and the gentle tug of yarn. "Friend" didn't in any way encompass all he wanted to be to Mercy Royce. But it was a start.

Slow, he cautioned himself. *Slow.* There was a fragility to her hard shell that spoke of vulnerability. Had he been thinking beyond the sensual way her sweater molded to her superb figure, he would have paid more attention to it. Vulnerability suggested involvement and care. Those two things he'd avoided like the plague these past years. Suddenly, he seemed to forget why.

If Mercy Royce was on the mend, he had just the medicine for it. If he could persuade her to take it.

Pine Creek wasn't much of a town. Spencer glanced at Mercy to see how she perceived it. He knew she was a big-city type. He could tell by the expensive brand of clothes they couldn't get in any of the local stores and noted the reserve of her manner. Townsfolk were more open, more naturally gabby. She would probably be like most of their summer visitors; used to shopping malls and corner convenience stores. The little girl would be spoiled by cable television and video arcades. How would they adjust to this step back into a simpler life? Some people never did. He remembered that lesson most cruelly. Would they chafe and mourn the loss of those pampering commodities? Or could they appreciate the crisp beauty and slower pace of his hometown? He didn't know why it should matter to him one way or another. Except that maybe Mercy reminded him just a little of Paula, the cool blonde who'd hated the lack of civilized pleasures and grew to despise him for his need of the simplicity found here in Pine Creek.

It was small. Mercy saw everything the town had to offer at first glance down the main street. Those three blocks contained the basics: three hardware stores, a five-and-dime, a pharmacy, a card and souvenir shop, coffee shop and res-

taurant, barber shop, ancient town hall, and a homemade
ice-cream parlor. The last made Casey sit up and take notice. On the side streets, Mercy could see newer businesses;
a substantial lumber company that guaranteed growth, a
post office, a bowling alley, even an old-fashioned drive-in
fast food-joint. And a small but modern jail.

Spencer had slowed to accommodate the drop in speed
limit from fifty-five to twenty-five in the space of a block—
obviously a fine means of stocking the town's coffers. The
citizens of Pine Creek waved to him from the sidewalks and
from the doors of their establishments. And he smiled and
returned each greeting. As he did, he seemed to be watching her with an intensity she didn't understand, as if waiting for her response to some unasked question. She looked
away from his penetrating stare to study the clean sun-
washed sidewalks and friendly faces. She almost expected to
see Andy Taylor and Aunt Bea from Mayberry in the homey
setting. But it didn't leave a corny feeling. The whole atmosphere had the intimacy of a friendly embrace. And she
liked it.

Kevin Hobbs's garage was at the south end of the town.
It was one of the two gas stations; the other being a shiny,
modern self-serve with an air-conditioned deli directly across
the street. He couldn't compete at the pumps but the locals
came to him with confidence to tend their ailing automo-
biles. He always had at least one up on the rack and two
waiting. Mercy's Pontiac was parked out front and she began to frown. She'd hoped it would be ready so they
wouldn't have to linger in town any longer than necessary in
Sheriff Halloway's overzealous company.

At the ding-ding of Spencer's Blazer pulling in, Hobbs,
himself, emerged from the office, wiping greasy hands on
his rear-pocket red rag. Mercy couldn't tell which was putting more oil on the other.

"Howdy there, Spence. Looks like you need some air in
that right rear. Fix 'er up for you?"

"Later, maybe," the sheriff called as he swung down to the gas-puddled pavement. "Have you got that Pontiac ready yet?"

"Said it was a rush job, didn't you?" He sounded hurt that Spencer would question him. "A personal favor, I think, was the way you put it." He canted a knowing glance toward the four-by-four, trying to get a look at this fair "favor." And raised an appreciative brow. "Nice," he muttered to the lawman.

Spencer circled the truck and opened the passenger-side door. The girl hesitated only an instant before sliding down into his upraised arms. He twirled her easily to the ground, marveling at her near weightlessness. Kids that age were all legs and elbows, he mused. Then he turned toward Mercy to offer a hand. And immediately took back the gesture. Her glare would have frozen milk in the cow. He took a few steps of retreat to give her the space to scoot from the high seat with dignity. He'd meant to be polite. He prided himself on his manners where the weaker sex was concerned but she was having none of his generously offered chivalry. Until her slick sneaker bottom slid on a pool of oil and sent her skidding into him.

"Whoa, there," he called out, catching her by the forearms as she tottered for balance. The rescue brought her up against his chest and snug between the spraddle of his thighs. The innocent bump of contact ignited a flare of response in both of them. Spencer sucked in a quick breath and tightened his grip. Lord, she felt good pressed up to him like that. Mercy also drew an abrupt gasp and went as rigid as stone on the inside.

"Thank you, Sheriff. I'm fine now," she snapped out curtly. She pulled back sharply and he immediately released her.

Noting the exchange with the lift of a single bushy brow, Hobbs fished into his soiled shirt pocket. "Here are your keys, ma'am. How you fixin' to take care of the cost—check or charge?"

"Cash."

He produced a grimy bill of services and unfolded it for her inspection.

Wordlessly, Mercy took out her wallet. Inside, Spencer got a glimpse of a whole lot of money. Twenties. A stack of them so thick, the billfold could hardly bend. Didn't the woman know it was foolish to flash so much green around in front of strangers? Of course, he wasn't in the least bit worried about Kevin Hobbs's honesty, but she should have been. She didn't know anyone in Pine Creek from Adam, and a woman in her position, alone with a child, should have known better.

She turned to him suddenly and he could see her taken aback by his grim expression. Gingerly, she offered, "Thank you for the ride, Sheriff. You've been very kind."

"Part of the job, ma'am."

She didn't think so. She didn't think the sheriff of Pine Creek would take such a—how did the mechanic phrase it?—such a "personal" interest in every newcomer in town. He'd gone out of his way for the two of them. A generous gesture she prayed came without strings attached. He grinned—that slow, one-sided smile that provoked an image of deceivingly sinister laziness—and she hoped he wasn't planning to stop in later, thinking to collect on a favor owed.

"Come on, Casey. Get in the car," she said with an unnecessary crispness. The girl scampered to comply. "Thanks again, Sheriff, and to you, Mr. Hobbs, for getting the job done so quickly."

"Any friend of the sheriff's . . ." He let that trail off significantly.

Mercy's smile stiffened.

Once they were driving on the main street, she released a sigh of relief. She remembered seeing a small grocery store off the highway. It would be a good place to stop to stock their larder. The cabin came with only dry-goods necessities. She didn't want to make any more trips to Pine Creek than she had to. A strictly low-profile summer; that was the way she'd planned it.

"He's nice," Casey concluded.

"Who? You mean Sheriff Halloway?"

Casey nodded.

Mercy frowned at that. *Nice* wasn't how she would term him. *Dangerous* seemed the more appropriate word. But because she didn't want to frighten the child, she made her reprimand gentle. "He's asking too many questions. Be careful what you say around him, Casey. Any little slip could start him snooping around in our business. And you know what that could mean."

The child's face tightened into a mask far older than her tender years. Yes, sadly she did know. But she was still a child and, in the enthusiasm of youth, tended to speak before she thought.

"I still think he's nice," Casey repeated quietly.

The subtle rebellion struck a quiver of fear into Mercy's heart. "Dangerous" didn't begin to describe what Spencer Halloway could be if he found out the truth. The law wouldn't be understanding of what she'd done. It wouldn't make allowances for her panic and her impulsive decision to flee north with Casey. The child's safety wouldn't be their primary concern. But it was hers. And so she would keep a cautious distance between him and the impressionable child.

"Where are we going?"

"To the store," Mercy answered distractedly. Her brow was lined with worry and her voice reflected it. Seeing the taut evidence of Mercy's concern, the little girl slipped her small hand over the woman's and squeezed.

"I'll be careful," she told her soberly. Then she was animated once more. "Can I get some gum at the store? And a couple of picture books? I've looked at all the ones I brought with me."

"We'll see," Mercy replied, a smile melting her sternness. She found the child's enthusiasm contagious and the urge to spoil her shamelessly almost impossible to resist.

"And some hot dogs. Maybe Mr. Halloway could come over for a cookout some night. To thank him for being so nice to us." Purposefully, she looked out the window to avoid Mercy's scowl.

Mercy stared at her freckled profile for a long moment. Perhaps she was being naive to think a child so young could grasp the seriousness of their situation. It would be up to her to see that Casey was careful.

Just one slip would be all it took to ruin everything.

Mercy looked back to the road, her features firming.

Damn Spencer Halloway for being so nice.

Chapter 3

Mercy took her time drying the dishes, letting the silence of early evening lap over her senses like a soothing breeze.

The cupboards were stocked, their stomachs were full, and now she was looking forward to rocking on the glider with the last cup of coffee of the day. The aura of peace was thick enough to wallow in and that's what she meant to do. After the weeks of dread and tension, she would wallow. This was the reward for all those sleepless nights, all those terrible, never-forgotten dreams. She and Casey deserved this chance to luxuriate in the sweet sensation of peace.

After the last glass was tucked away and the damp towel hung to dry, Mercy filled her cup with steaming water from the kettle and stirred in a large spoonful of instant decaf. The aroma rose, rich and tantalizing. Sighing in her contentment, she walked toward the porch. There, she would relax and watch Casey collect stones at the water's edge.

The child had been intrigued by one of the bedroom lamps, its wide base made from an old Seagram's bottle filled with buffed lake pebbles, and she wanted to make one like it for her own room. She decided to gather her own

collection of colorful and unique stones from the sandy
shallows. It would keep her busy and free from gloomy
thoughts, so Mercy encouraged her. Together, they would
go to the small lakeside party store and pick out a suitable
bottle and she would take pleasure in leisurely emptying it
on the long, quiet nights ahead. She only hoped the child's
enthusiasm for simple things would last.

They were far from anything or anyone Casey was familiar with, but that couldn't be helped. They had no television, no stereo, not even a radio. No treasured friends to
play with. Mercy realized that was a mighty sacrifice for a
child Casey's age. Isolation was a small, necessary price to
pay and they'd had no chance to gather the luxuries together. Casey would get used to it. She was an imaginative
and resilient child. And as the summer lingered, perhaps
families with kids her age would fill the neighboring cabins
to provide her with the frolicsome play she'd been long denied. She was just beginning to emerge from the cycle of
grief for her parents and was ready to reach out to others.
That was good. It gave Mercy hope that the child could recover from the trauma. That things could be normal for her.
And Mercy would watch and let the dormant feelings
crowding her heart finally have full rein. To enjoy those
things she'd been denied.

The air was still too cold for late-afternoon swimming.
The temperature dropped along with the sun. But Casey had
rolled up her pant legs and, with bucket in hand, had
marched down to the water as soon as they'd finished their
meal. Smiling to herself at the image of the six-year-old
wading like some tropical bird on spindly legs in the shallows, Mercy stepped out onto the porch to look toward the
beach. And froze.

A shock of paralyzing horror seized up inside her, bind-
ing muscle, halting breath for one long, terrible moment.
The sight woke a host of primitive emotions; surprise,
mouth-drying fear and a rage of protective anger.

Before she was consciously aware of making the decision, she was running down the gentle slope of the yard,

mindless of the hot coffee sloshing over her hand. To where Casey stood in congenial conversation with a man.

The child glanced up to greet her rampaging charge with an innocent smile of pleasure. And then, her companion straightened from his crouch and turned. Mercy skidded to a stop, panting, her heart chugging against her ribs. She must have looked like a madwoman to win such an expression of discomposure from the laid-back Spencer Halloway.

"I was just showing Spencer my stones," Casey chatted happily. She had no idea of the turmoil her conversation had shaken up inside the woman. Or that Spencer's unexpected arrivals had taken a measure of ten years off Mercy's life since this morning. Instead, she beamed up at the sheriff as if he were her new best friend.

"Are you all right, Mrs. Royce? You look—" *A fright* described it, but he was too polite to say that to a lady.

Mercy gasped for breath and coherent thought. Good Lord, she had to get a hold of herself. Spencer was staring at her in questioning alarm. If she didn't start to make some sense, she would never be able to convince their insightful neighbor that nothing was amiss.

"I'm—sorry," she wheezed with difficulty. "I don't allow Casey to—speak to strangers. I didn't recognize you without your uniform on."

Spencer looked thoroughly intrigued by that idea and began his lazy smile.

It took a moment for the double edge of her words to penetrate her frenzied brain, then Mercy scowled fiercely in the face of his amusement. The annoyance returned her claim to sanity. She purposefully slowed her breathing and panicked heart rate.

Recognizing Casey's companion in no way lessened the danger. What had the two been discussing so intently? Casey's rocks? She hoped that was all. Or was the silky-tongued sheriff coaxing answers from the guileless child to questions best left unresolved? Spencer, Casey had called him. Not Sheriff. Not Mr. Halloway. Spencer.

How disturbingly familiar.

"Just passing by, Sheriff, or are you some sort of closet rock hound?" she asked. Casually, she angled herself between him and the girl. Casey had gone back to her search for the perfect pebbles, seeming to ignore them.

Spencer grinned at the tang in her voice and replied easily, "Just out on my daily run. I usually do it in the mornings but today, I got distracted." He let his gaze slip over her to show the interruption of his schedule was not an unwelcomed one.

"Running where?" She tried to keep the suspicion out of her tone. Surely he wouldn't have her believe he was out for a jog along the edge of the highway.

"I do a five-mile lap around the lake before breakfast. Well, most of the time," he amended. "Generally somewhere along the way, I get invited in for coffee and a decent meal. Sort of a business-combined-with-pleasure outing. Better than dry flakes in a bowl at home alone."

He was single. She had wondered even though she wouldn't admit it to herself. That, instantly, made him more appealing, and more intimidating. Was he expecting her to provide one of those morning stops? Sheriff Spencer Halloway at the breakfast table was a most disconcerting thought.

He seemed to be waiting, glancing as he had that morning at the coffee cup in her hand, angling for an invitation to—what? She was afraid to entertain the idea. A man with Halloway's looks wasn't a man long without a companion. Was he lining her up for a little fun in the sun? Her jaw firmed. And her stomach quivered.

"Well, we won't keep you from your exercise, Sheriff." A cool suggestion that he be on his way.

"Actually, I'm all done. Just doing my cooldown when I saw Casey playing amateur prospector." To emphasize his point, he moved quite naturally through a series of stretches. Mercy's gaze followed in fascination.

Against the waning brilliance of the day, Spencer didn't look like a lawman, which was why she hadn't recognized him right off. The officially pressed gray uniform had been supplanted by scanty attire suitable for jogging. Beaten track shoes and sagging socks were topped by two long stretches of tanned leg, each nicely delineated by toned runner's muscles. They were shown off to their best advantage by a pair of denims cut so scandalously short, the pockets hung down farther than the frayed hem. A navy blue University of Michigan sweatshirt had suffered similarly from the scissors, minus sleeves and chopped off at midriff level. A patch of flat and lightly furred middle was visible between the teasing gap of his top and bottoms.

Afraid he'd find her staring at the expanse of rock-hard belly, Mercy jerked her gaze upward. His hat was gone, replaced by a twist of red bandanna tied to keep damp hair out of his eyes. The sweat of exertion dappled his lean features and glimmered on his neck and arms. All in all, Spencer Halloway had the look of a sleek, fit male animal. The lazy stretches he was doing accentuated it, whether he was conscious of it or not.

Mercy was mesmerized. And alarmed by her own reaction. She caught herself wondering how the taut flesh of his bared middle would feel against her palms. Hot and slick. Like the sensations sliding through her. And because it was unlike her to consider men in such a bold manner, she was confused. And angry. At him for showing up in her backyard in the tantalizing shorts. At herself for getting dry-mouthed looking at them and wondering if he wore anything under the snug fit of denim. She took a nervous step back, her hands clutching the coffee cup with what little remained inside after her panicked run from the house. Spencer Halloway was becoming more of a danger than she'd anticipated.

Spencer saw her flustered fury and guessed at the cause. She wasn't a woman who liked to be shaken up by her own sensuality. How long had she been divorced? he wondered. He hoped to lead the little girl carefully into that topic but it looked like it would have to wait for another time. Mercy was a relentless watchdog where the child was concerned.

And she had her hackles up every time he was near. What was she afraid of? Him? Or herself? Or of life in general? There were a lot of warm summer days ahead. And as many sultry nights. On one of them, he determined right then and there, he would discover all there was to know about Mercy Royce.

"Well," he drawled out at last, "guess I should get on home to my soup. If you ladies need anything, just give a yell."

Mercy's thin smile was noncommittal.

"Maybe you could come over for a cookout sometime this week," Casey suggested. "We got hot dogs at the store, but I've never really cooked anything over a fire. I bet you have, haven't you, Spencer?"

"Lots of times. I'm a real Boy Scout when it comes to making campfires. I'd love to join you," he told her honestly.

Oh, yes, he would. Dinner with Mercy Royce conjured up images of a fire and a good bottle of wine. The chance to sink his fingers into that mass of gorgeous red hair, so like flame, itself. To work that too-often-narrowed mouth into a willing bruise of passion. The chance to heat her luscious body into a willing flush of desire. The chance to run his hands along those long, long legs and have them wrap around him. A powerful sense of want stirred through him, the first to reach beyond mild uncomplicated interest in a good long while. That surprised and enticed him.

Yes, he wanted to come to dinner and to stay for breakfast. He wanted a leisurely taste of the cool Mrs. Royce. And he suspected that once having sampled, he would want all. But was she ready to entertain him on that intimate level? He studied her pallid features. She looked embarrassed by the child's bluntness. More than that, she looked stricken. As much as he sympathized with her dismay, there was no way he was going to let her off the hook. But neither did he want her to squirm in misery.

To the child, he said, "Dinner sounds great." To the apprehensive mother, he added softly, with all the meaning in the world, "But after you've had a chance to settle in. I have a feeling it's too soon to invite company over." *Especially of the male gender,* his understanding gaze concluded, much to Mercy's obvious relief. She actually managed a real smile. Weak. Strained. But genuine.

"See you later, short stuff." He rumpled Casey's unruly curls and with a last tempting smile for Mercy, he started down the beach at a loose lope.

The cutoffs looked even more revealing from the back, hugging his flanks the way the cup of her hands might.

" 'Bye, Spencer," Casey called out after him.

Mercy stood rooted to the spot, watching him trot around the narrow cove to his cabin. She'd forgotten to reprimand Casey for using his first name and for issuing the impossible invitation. She'd forgotten to breathe. If there was a term for the tight, skittery feeling in her chest, she wasn't sure she wanted to know it.

Spencer let the glass door sigh closed behind him. Even that slight sound brought up the ever alert eyes of May Walker from her command-post reception desk. Her initial smile of greeting faded as he drew near. After offering a suspicious frown, her features puckered in disgust.

"Is that a cigarette I smell on you, Spencer Halloway?"

Without breaking stride or congenial expression, Spencer crossed to the small table at the end of her desk to pour a cup of coffee, then rummaged through the pasteboard box beside the pot. His voice was as innocent as a choir boy's.

"Why, May, how could you ask such a thing? You know I gave up smoking three months ago. Bad for the health."

"So are those," she pronounced staunchly, pointing her pencil tip at the sweet roll in his hand. But that didn't stop her from bringing in a box each morning. Nor did it keep her from finishing off the leftovers to keep them from the terrible fate of going stale and therefore, being wasted. He grinned, trying to tease her out of her glower.

"Man's got to keep up his strength."

"You need more than nicotine, caffeine and sugar. What you need is a woman to look after you." A familiar argument, one she never tired of springing on him at the most inconvenient times.

"You volunteering, May?"

He winked as her rosy blush deepened, then ambled back into his glass-partioned office, coffee and roll in one hand and a stack of paperwork in the other. As was his habit, he left the door open. There was an intercom on his desk but he never used it. He could never remember which button to push. It seemed easier just to yell out for what he needed.

"May, you got that DMV report Judy sent for the other night?" he hollered around his first bite of breakfast.

"Just a second, Sheriff. It's around here somewhere."

Somewhere meant exactly that. For all her skill at typing, dispatching and handling the general mayhem that occasionally went with the job, May Walker hadn't a clue how to file or organize. Her desk was one big In basket and the Out was overflowing on the floor beside it. Amazingly, nothing ever got lost in that vast mound of material.

"Has Chet come in yet this morning?" he yelled across his desk after he'd gotten comfortable.

"Been and gone. I saw him lying in wait for unsuspecting motorists behind the billboard on 37." What she thought of the young deputy's unscrupulous police methods was clear in her derisive tone.

"Now, don't be too hard on him, May. He brings more revenue into the office than your yearly bake sale."

He could hear her indignant "Humph," and smiled as he sifted through his half-finished reports. Before he could take the first sip of his coffee, she was standing at the door, a sheet of paper in her hand.

"Here you go, Sheriff. Something important?"

"Uh-huh," he murmured with irritating neutrality. "Close the door on your way out, would you, May?"

Before she could question that unusual order, he'd swiveled his chair away from her to study the DMV sheet. May gave the door an extra-loud bang, muttering something about Mr. High and Mighty suddenly needing his privacy.

Spencer was oblivious to his girl Friday's chagrin. He was puzzling over the information in his hand. The Pontiac was registered to an Amy Cheswick, the same Cheswick who owned the cabin Mercy and her daughter were staying in. The sheet was a clean one, with nothing suspicious, no hint that it was a stolen vehicle. Perhaps Mercy was borrowing it, just as she was the cabin. But he found it hard to believe that a woman displaying the outward and wallet-wise wealth of Mercy Royce had no car of her own.

He was distracted from his broodings by the arrival of his deputy. Glass shivered in the frames whenever Chet Allen entered a room and let loose his booming voice. This morning there was an eerie silence from the other room. Spencer looked up from his desk to see May and Chet both staring at his closed door as if he had suddenly gone stark raving mad behind it. Finally, he was moved to get up and swing it open into its regular position, without the offer of an explanation or apology. May resumed her seat looking satisfied but in an agony of curiosity. And Chet went for the box of doughnuts.

"Didn't your mother ever tell you too many of those were bad for you?" May was busy scolding.

"No," the surly deputy mumbled with his mouthful. "She taught me to mind my own business. Morning, Spence."

Chet Allen was stocky and perpetually sullen. He was the type of policeman who would retire bemoaning the fact that he'd never gotten to shoot anyone instead of rejoicing in it. At twenty-six, his one ambition in life was to be accepted by the state police so he could blow out of Pine Creek and never look back. Spencer Halloway had shot that hope all to hell when he'd suddenly applied for the job Chet had thought would be his. Spencer, with his big-city credentials, was one big roadblock to his own advancement.

Chet had little respect or understanding for a man who'd had it all and had given it up without regret. Spencer had once worked the mean streets of Detroit and now, he was content sucking up to the tourists in Hicksville, U.S.A. And he seemed proud of it. Chet thought he was just plain nuts. But then he'd seen the sheriff take on four well-armed motorcyclists bent on robbing Maxine's Diner with nothing more than a two-by-four in his hand. Chet had gotten there just as he was mopping up the floor with the last of them.

For that reason, Chet kept his opinions to himself and was careful not to challenge the sheriff of Pine Creek too overtly.

"May, I need you to do something for me. Hiya, Chet," the sheriff added as a brief sidebar. Then he was back to business. "I want you to check out a Mercy Royce. Go through the usual channels. No…better go beyond them on this one. I want to know when she got her first polio vaccination and where. I want to know if she buys her shoes with MasterCard or Visa."

"Trouble, Sheriff?" Chet leaned in with a look of sharp interest, hope that there was, etched all over his face.

Trouble? Mercy Royce? Spencer had to think on that one a minute. Yes, he was suspicious of her behavior. No, he didn't think she was some gangster's moll or a bank robber on the lam. But she sure as hell was something. Something wasn't right about her and he didn't like to think of her as a woman in distress. Knowing she wouldn't turn to him with any confidence prompted his casual inquiry. He wasn't sure exactly what she was. And he wanted to know.

Legally, he had no cause to pry into her affairs and demand answers. She'd done nothing wrong in borrowing a car and staying in a cabin on his lake. But he was used to being on top of everything that went on in Pine Creek, and being kept in the dark on this intriguing matter provoked him something fierce.

And then there was the way she had his professional instincts buzzing, that feeling fed by the fear in her eyes. He didn't want to admit to himself that he was issuing the unofficial background check because he didn't think he could get the truth out of the lady herself. That would mean admitting there was a limitation on his charms. And he wasn't at a standstill on that point yet.

Not after seeing her dazed appreciation of his cutoffs.

But so far, Mercy Royce continued to hold the upper hand, and he didn't like being off-balance. Maybe that was it; the irresistible challenge to discover what was purposefully being kept from him. He was at heart a fierce competitor, and Mercy touched off all the right kinds of provocation.

"No trouble that I know of," he confessed at last. "Just a fine-looking lady. I want to make sure she doesn't have a boyfriend dangling around somewhere." He grinned to throw them off and sauntered back into his office.

Neither of his co-workers believed him for a second. Spencer Halloway wasn't the type to abuse his authority for personal reasons. If he was checking out Mercy Royce, they could bet he had cause. And Chet was on the scent like a hungry hound dog sniffing around a sealed trash bag. He knew something good was wrapped inside, he just wasn't sure what it was. And he didn't like secrets, either.

For the remainder of the day, Spencer was too busy with the everyday details of his job to give his mysterious new neighbor another thought. He waded through a Mount Everest of paperwork to earn May's scowl at his request that she file it, intimidated the socks off a youthful shoplifter at the five-and-dime, filled out his Publishers Clearing House Sweepstakes forms and mediated a property-line dispute before fists were made. A full, meandering day of work in Pine Creek. Just the way he liked it.

As he was getting ready to go home, May called him over with a perplexed look on her face.

"Spencer, you know that woman, Mercy Royce, you wanted me to run through the system?"

"Yeah. Get something back already? What did you find?" He made his tone casual as he settled his hip on the corner of her cluttered desk and lowered his lids to disguise the sudden hot glimmer in his eyes. A sense of anticipation rose inside him, as if he were about to receive the keys that unlocked the doors to the secrets of the universe.

Only to find that door had a dead bolt, too.

"Nothing."

"You mean her record is clean?"

"No. I mean nothing. I ran her through Motor Vehicles, credit history, social security, voter registration, the works. I can't find one single fact to prove that a Mercy Royce ever existed."

Chapter 4

The sun rose, a proverbial ball of fire, lifting the mercury with it until the cool of overnight became the promising warmth of summer. Telling herself it was that heat that drew her out onto the porch, Mercy stood at the framed opening but her traitorous gaze didn't linger on the glorious sunrise. It strayed along the edging of sand where crisp waves made last night's footprints this morning's memories.

She was watching for Spencer Halloway.

He was an amazing creature of habit. Six o'clock on the nose, he would come loping around the curve of narrow beach, all long, powerful strides and teasing flashes of toned flesh and white teeth. His gaze invariably canted up toward the cabin as he trotted along their one hundred fifty feet of frontage. If he caught sight of her, he would raise a hand in greeting, then grin all the wider when she would pretend not to see him; but since that first evening, he hadn't stopped again. And Mercy hated to consider that what hovered in his wake was disappointment.

She told herself that she was just being careful. Spencer warranted watching. He was dangerous to her plan and un-

settling to her peace of mind. It was better to know where he
was than to be taken by surprise. True, he hadn't intruded
upon their privacy under the guise of being neighborly but
just the same, she felt his presence. Awareness of him was
as palpable as the clammy chill of a north woods night. It
hung heavy in the air like the aftermath of a storm, stroking along her bared arms, raising gooseflesh and a strange
restlessness as it clung to shadowed places in defiance of the
light. She shivered in an anxious reaction as she strained her
gaze along the empty stretch of sand. And as she waited, a
betraying warmth rose inside her, a flush that spread as
slowly and surely as that conquering sunrise.

She could call it what she liked but that didn't change it
from being what it was: anticipation.

And that confused her mightily. For beyond the worry of
him being sheriff was a greater threat—the very basic threat
of him being a man. That was usually enough to make her
put up her guard behind barbed wire. So what in her instinctive defenses was failing her now, when the need for
caution was critical? How had one handsome sheriff managed to slip through her protective pattern of distrust?

Over the past two weeks, she and Casey had settled into
the easy lake pace. Still too early for the rush of vacationers, there was a balm of quiet rather than the later roar of
power boats and summer teen music. Anchored rafts
bobbed listlessly on the clear blue surface and aluminum
vee-hull boats dotted the hidden coves where sunrise fish-
ermen hoped to snag the big one. Newly greened oaks and
lush pines muted sound from the nearby highway and occasional voices carried across the water from spottily pop-
ulated seasonal cottages. All in all, a verdant paradise with
but one distracting element.

And he was late. It was close to six-thirty.

"Looking for Spencer?"

Mercy gave a guilty start, words of denial springing to her
lips. She didn't speak them as Casey came up to loop a thin
arm through hers. Too many lies lived with them already.
Instead, she made her tone light.

"I'm used to setting my watch by him."

"It's Saturday. He doesn't have to go in to work today so he's probably sleeping in. That's what I do when I'm in school."

Saturday? She'd lost track of the weekdays with one blending so serenely into the next. It was surprising how quickly her workweek routine was forgotten when it had once made up the foundation of her life. Work was all she'd had—until Casey. Now it seemed unimportant and as distant as all the other daily stresses. Now there was only this precocious mop-topped child and the need to provide stability in her reeling world.

"Maybe Spencer can come over for a cookout tonight," Casey suggested cheerfully.

The idea gave Mercy an instant shock of panic. She made herself smile and reply sensibly. "Well, I don't know about that, Casey. He's probably pretty busy."

"No, he's not," she piped up. "He told me he didn't have a single thing to do all weekend."

"And just when did he tell you that?" It was hard to keep the edge of alarm out of her voice.

"Yesterday. He pulled his boat in while I was out looking for rocks. You were washing the dishes."

Mercy's anxiety quadrupled. Casey and Spencer were having conversations without her knowledge. Couldn't she turn her back for a second without fear of his subtle intrusion into their private lives?

How had she missed him?

"Anyway," Casey continued in blissful ignorance, "I asked him if he was doing anything, just in case we wanted to start a fire, and he said no, just to give him a yell." And she smiled at that, obviously pleased at how things worked out.

Thank you very much, Spencer Halloway.

Mercy hung on to her smile even though it made her cheeks ache. "I'm sure he was just being nice."

At that news, Casey looked so crestfallen, Mercy felt the need to bolster her bruised heart with a quick distraction.

She was quickly learning how to juggle her moods for the sake of Casey's peace of mind. But her own was getting fairly frazzled.

"Maybe it will be warm enough to go swimming this afternoon. Then you and I can cook those hot dogs. I'm sure we could get a fire going. Doesn't that sound like fun?"

"I guess."

Glum resignation sighed from the child, filling Mercy with a sense of frustration and inadequacy. She'd known it wasn't going to be easy at the onset. At six going on seven, Casey was too young to be constantly reminded of the reason for their isolation. It was Mercy's job to try to fill the child's hours with a substitute for normal life. At least until they could begin to build one together. Mercy had precious little experience to draw upon but if determination counted, she was more than qualified.

"I was hoping Spencer would come over," the moppet mumbled with the pain-filled honesty of youth. "I miss having someone to talk to."

Anguish swelled up like a water balloon in Mercy's throat, the child's miserable confession making her feel ridiculously slighted. "I'm someone."

Casey's smile was sweet and at the same time, dismissing. "But you're family. And Spencer is—fun."

Fun. Mercy couldn't remember how to be fun. It had been ages since she'd done a spontaneous thing for the sheer sake of enjoyment. Not since she had been Casey's age. After that, there had been no real joy left in her life, just a desperate day-to-day struggle with the pain of living. She'd been forced too fast into a grown-up existence where everything was serious and sinister. Casey would not know that same bleak helplessness. Not if Mercy could do anything about it.

"I'm sorry if things are kind of boring for you, Casey. I'm doing the best I can." Did that sound as plaintive to the child as it did to her own ears? She hoped not. But then tears were suddenly all too close to the surface. "Maybe you can spend the summer teaching me how to be fun."

Casey looked up at her for a somber moment, then grinned. "Maybe, I will. And maybe I'll get some help."

Before Mercy could question that concluding phrase, Casey was off the porch, dashing toward the beach, her thin arms pin wheeling in waves of welcome.

"Hi, Spencer!"

Mercy followed with her stare. A rush of expectation collided with the plummeting of her peace. All balled up in confusion somewhere between the sudden race of her heart and clench of her belly.

"Hey, short stuff," Spencer called back as he trolled his pontoon boat up into the shallows so she could wade out to it. He was dressed for sun and surf with battered deck shoes, nylon swim trunks, baggy T-shirt and Detroit Pistons ball cap. It should have been less alluring, less alarming attire than what he wore jogging, but as a breeze off the water molded the cotton and nylon against the hard contours of his body, Mercy realized her mistake. There was nothing safe about this man. His penetrating eyes were hidden behind dark, polarized glasses. She couldn't tell if he was looking at Casey or staring up at her, and that made her uneasy. Spencer Halloway was a sleek cat crouched casually before a mouse hole. Why did she have the feeling she was the one he was waiting for?

"Perfect day for some fishing," Spencer began. Then Mercy didn't need to see beyond the dark glasses. She could feel the scorch of his gaze. The lazy smile slid across his face as if any minute he'd be licking his lips with a smug anticipation of being well fed. "I've got a jug of coffee, soft drinks, sandwiches, and loads of sunscreen, if I could coax you ladies to take up a couple of my extra poles. I'll even bait your hooks for you. What do you say?"

Both he and Casey were looking up at her expectantly. Mercy felt paralyzed with dismay. Go out on that small craft with Spencer Halloway? Alone, just her and Casey, with his probing stare and lethally harmless questions? With his potently male vibrations? She'd have to be crazy to consider such a thing. Crazy!

"Sounds like fun, doesn't it?"

Casey's statement was filled with a provoking challenge—put your money where your mouth is.

Fun? Mercy eyed the subtly malevolent figure crouched down at the bow of his boat. All ready to pounce. Anxiety had her palms cold with a rush of moisture. Fun like poking a rattlesnake with a short stick. Fun like playing chicken on a dark stretch of road with another car rushing toward her. Deadly consequence was all but inevitable.

Then Spencer drawled with his tone all silken persuasion, "Come on, Mercy. It'll be fun."

"Yeah," Casey echoed. "It'll be fun." Then the child's expression became one of big beseeching eyes. Hound-dog eyes. Doe eyes. Eyes too recently haunted by sorrow. Mercy swallowed hard, emotion clutching her chest like a cruel fist. Fun. How could she deny this little girl a chance at fun?

"Casey's not much of a swimmer." She was grabbing at straws but Spencer brushed her excuse aside with that devilish grin that all but said, you'll have to do better than that.

"I've got a life vest that should be about a perfect fit. And one for you, too, Mrs. Royce, if it's drowning you're so afraid of."

"I'm a very good swimmer, Sheriff."

His grin widened with the taste of triumph. "Then go put on your swimsuit. You're about to get all wet."

Casey stood poised there in the shallows, her hand on the edge of Spencer's boat, her gaze on Mercy, waiting, asking for a sign from her. There was such tender hope in the child's face.

"Well, I guess..."

Casey gave a whoop of excitement and bolted toward the cabin. "I'll get my suit on. You wait right here, Spencer. Maybe we can have a fish fry!" She had a dazzling smile for Mercy in passing and that made the risk worthwhile.

Until Mercy glanced back down at Spencer and saw him unwinding from his crouch like a smooth panther. Then she was questioning her sanity.

* * *

For such an awkward-looking craft, the pontoon boat knifed through the clear waters of Big Bear Lake with a roar of power. Mercy sat on one of the inward-facing seats, her fingers curled about the rail behind her. A bulky cable-knit sweater concealed her modest one-piece bathing suit but stretch terry shorts left her legs bare to the warmth of the sun and Spencer's gaze. Casey perched on the bench seat opposite, bouncing on the hard cushion as if reluctant to sit still. She was all but engulfed in the safety vest and above it, her bright curls rumpled wildly in the wind. As their pilot, Spencer was at the sleek console, looking competent and in control; of both the craft and the situation. A far-from-comforting thought. Mercy redirected her gaze outward, into the damp chill blowing at them as they cut through the crystal lake surface, and she vowed to concentrate on the beauty of the day. It was a chance to soak up a bit of summer tan and the sight of Casey's pleasure; to enjoy the warming glow to both skin and spirit. Spencer would require some watching but she refused to let anxiety rule the day. He could be charming. Casey adored him. Maybe it wouldn't be so bad, after all. She made a grim face into the wind.

From his position at the wheel, Spencer watched the play of subtle emotions upon Mercy's face, wondering what to make of them. If he'd been any kind of gentleman, he would feel guilty about using the child to coerce Mercy into doing something she was so averse to. He didn't. In fact, he was enough of a cad to guide the boat against the chop of the tide so that the slap of aluminum upon gentle waves created a rhythmic bounce to both the unbound red hair and enticingly rounded sweater front. He contained a wolfish grin as she reached up to capture that tangle of mane at the nape of her neck, her uplifted arm accentuating the snug curve of ramie cotton over generous breasts. No, sir, he was no gentleman—not if his thoughts were any measure.

But beyond that purely male attraction was the purpose for his invitation: the tantalizing chafe of mystery that had been driving him slowly toward obsession. Who was she *really?*

When the roar of the motor shifted into a more sedate purr, Mercy glanced back at him in question. There was no mistaking the wariness in her eyes. No sense alarming her too soon, he decided.

"This looks like a good spot. I'll drop anchor and rig you up something a big bass can't resist for breakfast."

Casey grinned. "Then maybe we'll be having them for breakfast."

Spencer smiled back. "Could be, if we're smarter than the average fish."

He went about securing the boat in a shaded cove where the shoreline was dappled with lily pads and partially submerged branches. The only sounds were the whir of water bugs and the occasional frog clearing its throat. He put together a simple system for Casey: a sit-and-stare rather than the rig and reel he preferred. She was all wide-eyed when he explained the rudiments of tempting a pan fish to sample the forbidden fruit—in this case a fat brown night-crawler that the child studied with admirable interest as it did figure eights about the hook. He didn't miss Mercy's delicate shudder. She was definitely a candidate for artificial bait. After setting the depth and the drag, he gave an expert flick of the wrist to set the reel whizzing. There was a distant plunk as the bait disturbed the glimmering surface. He took up the slack until the far bobber popped upright like a signal buoy.

"You just keep an eye on that bobber. When it goes under, you jerk back on your pole and reel in for all you're worth."

"Okay, Spencer." Casey settled on the seat cushion, her gaze intent and as serious as a professional angler's.

And that left Mercy.

She eyed him suspiciously when he turned to her with a smile.

"Want a big juicy worm or a harmless length of rubber?"

"I think I'll just help Casey watch her line."

"That sounds exciting."

"I thought the idea of fishing was to relax," she challenged mildly.

"I like to think of it as a competition, a sort of man-against-nature thing."

Her smile thinned like a three-pound test line with an eight-pound bass on the end of it. And she looked about that relaxed. He could feel her stare as he rigged his own pole, then carefully selected the right lure from his well-stocked tackle box.

"You look like an ad for *Michigan Outdoors,*" she observed.

"Fishing is a science," he explained without looking up, not sure if she was the one baiting him with her dry remark. "It's a matter of calculating the water pH and temperature, the cycle of the moon, the weather and picking the right color and motion to the lure." He risked a glimpse at his audience to find her frowning doubtfully. He flipped on the liquid crystal display of his fish finder and pointed at the dark graph. "That's the contour of the bottom and these little blips are our breakfast."

"All computerized," Mercy commented flatly. "That doesn't seem all that fair to the fish."

"Cane poles are a thing of the past. I like to catch what I go after and I'll take every advantage I can get. That's what sets the eater and the eatee apart."

Mercy retreated behind an impenetrable glaze. She seemed uncomfortable, as if they were no longer talking about fish. Maybe they weren't.

"Squirt on a little attractant to get their taste buds tingling and..." He gave a smooth cast right beneath one of the bobbing logs. Almost immediately, he hauled back and cranked the reel furiously. "Bingo!"

With a squeal of delight, Casey abandoned her rod to champion his struggle to bring the fish abreast of the boat. Even Mercy was craning forward as he leaned over the side and brought up a wiggling trophy.

"You caught one! It's a monster!"

Spencer grinned proudly at Casey's enthusiasm. "Not quite. About three pounds, I'd say." Gently, he worked the hook free, then dipped the bass back into the water, shaking it briefly before letting it go. It glided motionlessly for a moment as if playing dead, then darted down out of sight.

"You let him get away!" Casey sounded disappointed, then confused. "Why did you do that?"

"The fun's in the contest. If I kept everything I caught, I'd run out of challengers. This way, that big boy will still be there tomorrow, maybe a little wiser for the experience. Makes it a little more fair, don't you think, Mrs. Royce?"

"Only if the fish can learn from its mistakes, Sheriff."

"That's up to the fish."

Mercy didn't smile back. She couldn't decide if his release of his prey was a merciful prolonging of its life or a cruel continuation of a deadly game.

As if he understood her reservations, Spencer went on to say, "The match is a lot more even than you think. Bass are wily opponents. They don't get that size by being easy to catch. It's once in a lifetime that a man brings in something worth tacking up on the wall. No other game fish fights as hard or takes as many lures."

"Maybe it just thinks it has the right to survive, Sheriff."

And that put an end to his casually offered fishing philosophies.

Casey went back to her pole and Spencer took his time selecting another from a glittering array of skirted and colorful baits.

"Have you known the Cheswicks long, Mrs. Royce?"

The question snapped her spine into a stiff column. He could see a flash of something behind her suddenly opaque stare. Anger or fright? Either way, it was hardly a natural response to a normal point of conversation.

"I went to school with Amy. She's letting me use the cabin while she's on her honeymoon in the Caribbean."

"So Amy went and got married. I haven't seen her up here in years. What is she now? A doctor?"

"Lawyer."

"Oh, yeah. Now I remember. You say you went to school with her? Was that law school?"

"No. Just junior college before we decided what we wanted to become."

"And what—"

"What about you, Sheriff?" she interrupted. "Why did you go into law? Your love of the chase?"

He chuckled at that wry summation. "Something like that."

"Pine Creek seems a little tame for a big-game hunter like you. I'd think you'd want someplace more exciting."

Suddenly, all traces of humor were gone from his look and his tone. "Believe me, I've seen enough excitement in my life. Pine Creek suits me just fine."

Mercy had turned the topic in his direction to keep his questions from her past, not out of any desire on her part to learn more about him. But she'd have to have had the sensitivity of a stump not to catch the raw snag in his voice. And then the curiosity tables were turned.

"Where?" she asked softly, wondering what could have put such intense compression into a mouth so quick to smile.

"Detroit's inner city. Five years and enough action to last anyone a lifetime." That was all he said, but the unspoken text behind it told of gritty volumes. He'd been tying on one of his fancy lures and found himself staring down at his fingers as if he'd forgotten what he was doing and how to finish what he'd started. After an awkward moment, he laid it aside. "How about some coffee? I could use some about now."

Mercy nodded. The sight of the laid-back sheriff so discomposed acted upon her strangely. Perhaps it was because she understood inner pain so personally that she could sense his own. It was like a cancer, never healing, eating away at a surface confidence, destroying what had once been healthy. He didn't have to say more. She recognized the symptoms. They mirrored her own. And like him, she was unwilling to leave it alone.

"This must seem like a paradise after that."

He passed her a thermal cup and for a moment, their stares engaged and held in a brief but shockingly intimate communion. He withdrew his hand quickly, as if he wished he could pull back the words, as well. "Paradise? Yeah, that about sums it up. No two o'clock calls to mothers to say their son has been involved in a senseless shooting. No kids on the street corners so pumped full of dope and bitterness that hell looks like a good place to go. No grade schoolers packing a handgun along with their peanut-butter and jelly sandwiches. No smell of garbage and despair and hatred. When I left the metro force, my enthusiasm as fried as an egg, this was the first place I thought of. My family used to vacation here when I was a kid. Yeah, this is paradise or at least as close to it as I've been able to find. Not everyone thinks so. Some would look at it as a different kind of life sentence."

Someone, who? Mercy caught back the question before she actually spoke it. Had there been someone else in Spencer Halloway's past? Someone who didn't share his view of heaven? She didn't want to pry. She didn't want to admit the need to know consumed her. But there was still the fear that if conversation lagged, he would turn it back upon her. Better he was in the defensive mode.

"I can't imagine anyone not loving it up here."

His gaze jumped to her, all surprise and skepticism. "No cable TV, no designer stores, no place to wear glamorous nails. Some would see it as a cultural wasteland. Some would rather die than give up a high-powered profile to live in Sherwood Forest."

"Like who?"

He stared at her for a moment because she delivered that question like a bullet fired unerringly for the heart. But he didn't try to avoid the impact. "Like my ex-wife. She wasn't what you'd call thrilled about the change of scenery. Pine Creek isn't exactly a Mecca of volunteer projects and fund-raising dinners. She would have been like one of those pioneer women who went completely crazy out on the prairie. She's better off in her own environment. I couldn't argue that. But I couldn't stay there. It was just one of those things.'' He shrugged eloquently to put a period to it.

"I'm sorry," she said, meaning it.

"Don't be." His smile was full of bittersweet memories and wounded strength. "She's remarried now. It didn't take her long to find what she was looking for."

"And did you?"

He spread his hands wide, swiveling to encompass everything around him. "All this. Who could ask for anything more?"

Then why did his tone sound so wistful, as if he knew there was something he was missing yet couldn't quite put his finger on it? Wasn't his Andy Taylor, Mayberry-sheriff life all he'd hoped it would be? What could be lacking—except the void she felt in her own life? Family. That topic was too volatile to open even for safety's sake. She didn't want to know what longings lay in Spencer Halloway's heart. That would make him easy prey for a tender spirit such as her own. She had a hopeless habit of bringing home strays to nurture. Spencer wasn't some helpless creature she could take under her wing. It wouldn't do to forget that.

Just then, Casey let out a shriek.

"I got one! Spence, what do I do?"

"Get your rod tip up. That's it." He came up behind Casey, wrapping his arms around her so he could guide her through the motions of landing her six-inch sunfish. She gave a cry of accomplishment as it came out of the water, flapping and glittering in the sunlight.

"Oh, look! Mercy, look what I caught! It's a monster!"

Mercy came to admire the slippery creature with a proud, "Yes, it is." She was so tuned in to the child's excitement, she hadn't noticed that she'd been called by her given name.

But Spencer had.

"What do you want to do with it, honey? Shall we have it for breakfast?"

Casey looked from her to Spencer, then handed him the fish. "I think we should let it go so someone else can have the fun of catching it tomorrow."

That small gesture tugged at Spencer's heart, distracting him from what she'd called her mother. "I think that's a fine idea. Maybe he'll grow up to be a whale."

Casey giggled and scooted up close beside him to watch as he carefully worked the hook free.

"Don't hurt him."

"He'll be just fine. Do you want to let him go?" At Casey's nod, he made room for her next to the rail. "Hang on tight. He's a squirmy one."

Together, they leaned over the side so that the child could release her prize into the water and have the pleasure of seeing it shimmy away. They were both smiling as if they'd done something important. It was a heart-touching moment, Casey nestled within the curl of his arms, almost like father and daughter. Having her close sparked all sorts of soft and dewy-eyed sentiments inside the jaded bachelor, a swell of paternal instinct he hadn't known he possessed. The idea startled him.

But not as much as the shock he received upon looking up at Mercy.

Mercy's face was a twist of anguished horror, laced liberally with outrage. Her hands were clenched at her sides as if she was controlling her desire to pull the two apart. Obvious tremors shook through her as she beheld the two of them together, as if it were something unwholesome, something vile. He released the girl at once, recognizing the danger like one who'd been bitten by a protective female dog hunched over her unweaned pups. He moved back slightly to reduce the threat, saying, "Casey, why don't you see if you can find another big old night crawler in my bait box?"

"Okay, Spencer." She darted to comply, oblivious of what had passed between the two adults.

What, exactly, had been exchanged? A warning, certainly. A clue, probably.

Who had hurt Mercy Royce and her child enough to put that glaze of terror in her eyes? Or more specifically, what man had?

Chapter 5

The day went entirely too fast for Casey and Spencer, but seemed to linger interminably for Mercy. Midafternoon, after stale sandwiches and cold soda combined with warm sun, Casey fell soundly asleep curled up on one of the forward seats and Mercy was relieved to call the outing at an end. Spencer didn't argue. He maneuvered the pontoon boat up against the shore and handed down the slumbering child into impatiently extended arms. Then, with a brusque word of thanks, Mercy headed up to the cabin, never once looking back.

Spencer followed her retreat with a perplexed study. The harder he tried to discover what lay behind the brittle shell of Mercy Royce—or whatever her name was—the more confusion piled upon the rest. The wildness of her glare when he was close to Casey haunted him. Nothing he'd done had put that panic there.

Someone had. He wanted to know who. Was it the man she'd been married to, Casey's father?

Spencer felt an irrational need to punish that individual for putting such a dreadful fear into eyes that could warm so wonderfully with feeling. He'd gotten a brief glimpse of the compassionate soul she so zealously guarded. That surprisingly tender empathy had slipped through his own barriers with unsettling ease. For all his clever planning to draw out her own story, he'd found himself spilling his past, something he never did, not even to his most trusted friends. His earlier days in Detroit were strictly off-limits to those who knew him. But somehow, he'd come close to unburdening all to a total stranger. Not to gain her trust, not in an attempt to coax her into similarly confessing her own past, but because her unspoken understanding cracked the surface of his personal reserve.

"How did you learn so much, Ms. Royce?" he asked the blank face of the uninviting cabin.

Something about the way pain mirrored back in her big dark eyes let him know that she could comprehend the frustration and guilt he'd hoped to leave behind when he'd left the city—which, of course, had not been the case. For one crazy moment he'd wanted to purge his troubles, and that scared him. Because he wasn't the one who was supposed to lose control. He wanted her to trust him, not the other way around.

He knew better.

He started the boat's motor again, cursing his own internal engine that refused his command to idle. He'd spent two entire weeks trying to stay away, trying to tell himself that the Royces were none of his concern. Mercy gave no sign of encouraging his pursuit of her. But as he'd told her, it was the chase that made things interesting, the challenge he couldn't resist. Was that what it was? Some misguided urge to run after the unobtainable because he was afraid of the commitment that came with pursuing a woman who wanted to be caught?

"A coward," he muttered to himself over the drone of the outboard. "A coward and an idiot to boot, that's what I am. What would I do with her if I did catch her?"

Annoyingly, his agile mind was quick to provide many varied and quite erotic examples. And he'd never gotten to see her in that swimsuit.

He guided the boat back and across the cove, kicking himself for wanting to linger and wondering when he dared risk seeing her again.

It didn't matter that her eyes were melting soft, that her lips were sweetly ripe, that her whole luscious figure held a snag of vulnerability that went straight to the heart. He refused to let that tempting package lure him out to test romantic waters. Those waters could glimmer with deceiving promise and still contain a treacherous undertow. He'd nearly drowned in them once before. Not again. He'd believed those loving waters would support him and he'd sunk like a stone. No way was he ready to get his feet wet again.

And if he ever found himself prepared to take that dip a second time, he told himself sternly, it wouldn't be with a woman wrapped up tight in secrets and shadowed by fear. It would be with someone safe, someone nonthreatening, someone *he* could trust.

So why was he allowing himself to get so dangerously close to the edge, well knowing what disaster awaited if he should slip and plunge in headfirst?

There was only one answer he could come up with. It was time he started treating the lovely and mysterious Ms. Royce more as a professional investigation and less like a personal interest.

He was dreaming of long, long legs wrapped around husky laughter, the sound of which he had yet to hear.

At first, Spencer thought the rapid pounding was a part of that dream, an amplification of nocturnal heartbeats stirred to a hungry calypso pace. But as the hazy sensations of passion faded, the reality of someone at his door broke through. He squinted at his clock, groaning when the luminous green glow told him it was just past midnight. Grumbling at the untimely interruption, he jerked up a pair of jeans and shuffled barefoot to the front door. And once there, he blinked rather foolishly at the sight of Mercy Royce under the yellow glow of his porch light.

Threads of his erotic dream confused the fact of her standing there until he focused on the fright darkening her wide eyes. When he pushed open the outer door, her panic rolled in on a tidal wave of tears.

"I'm sorry to wake you, but I didn't know what else to do."

All his alarm bells going off at once, Spencer was immediately the calm professional. "It's all right. What's wrong?"

"It's Casey."

A fist of anxiety struck him square in the gut. He was grabbing for his coat. "What's the matter with her?"

"I don't know. She can't catch her breath."

"Is she choking?"

"No. That's the first thing I thought of. She was just sitting up in bed, gasping, like she was suffocating. Oh, Spencer, if anything happens to her..."

He brushed off the rest of that because he couldn't bear to think beyond it. "Nothing's going to happen. Where is she?"

"In the car."

For the first time, Spencer noticed the Pontiac pulled up in his drive, still running. He started for it at a jog, not bothering with his shoes. Mercy was right behind him, clutching at the back of his leather jacket. She was babbling in her agitation.

"I didn't know what else I could do for her. She needs a doctor. I don't know where to take her. We don't have a phone."

"It's all right, Mercy. I'll take care of things. We've got a medical center about five miles away."

He heard her shaky sigh of relief even as he pulled open the passenger door. The sound of the child's wheezing was terrible, like a crosscut-saw blade rasping through dry wood. No wonder Mercy was in such a state.

"Hey, there, short stuff," he crooned when the girl's terrified gaze flashed up to him. Her face was flushed and dappled with sweat. She was wearing a Dalmatian-print nightgown beneath the bundle of a blanket. He could see how she was struggling to suck air into an already distended chest. At the sight of him, her anxiety seemed to quiet. He smiled wide and reassuringly. "We're going to take a little ride. I want you to just sit still and not worry. Can you do that for me?"

The curly crop of red bobbed slightly. He put his hand atop it, rumpling the silken riot of color. Then he stepped back and looked at Mercy. She was breathing almost as raggedly as the child, as she stood there hugging her long canvas trench coat over a hastily donned sweat suit.

She was shaking. He was hoping he wouldn't have to perform CPR on both of them at the same time.

"Is Casey prone to asthma attacks?"

Mercy blinked at him and shook her head. He wasn't sure whether that meant no or that she didn't know. There was no more time to wonder. He took charge because it was his job and because she looked as though she was ready to come apart right there in the driveway.

"Climb on in with her and keep her as calm as possible. That means you'll have to be calm, too. Can you do that?"

A jerky nod. Not too convincing, but the best she could do.

"I'll drive." He didn't expect an argument and he didn't get one.

Wordlessly, Mercy lifted Casey and slid into the seat, cradling the gasping child in her lap. Spencer hurried around to the driver's side and slipped behind the wheel. It was then he noticed he was barefoot and without so much as his wallet. Who the hell was going to give him a ticket? They'd have to catch him first. He slammed the gearshift into Reverse and spun gravel on his way out of the driveway.

It was the longest five-mile drive he could remember. He'd been on many emergency calls but none had struck so close as this one. The sound of the little girl's distress filled the interior of the car, adding to the edge of anxiousness and urgency. He could feel Mercy quaking beside him, yet was unable to offer any comfort while driving at such a break-neck speed. Then, just as they crested the last hill before the clinic, Casey's wheezy spasms evolved into a rib-rattling cough. If he hadn't been scared nearly mindless before, he was a basket case of concern now. Each cough seemed to vibrate with enough violence to crush the fragile body gathered close to the woman at his side. Thankfully, Mercy was keeping it together, speaking quietly, soothing the ter-rified child. Hanging by her fingernails, but together and surprisingly tough. He hoped this was the worst she'd have to go through tonight. He'd seen how quickly a young life could slip away. Not this one, he prayed fervently as he squealed into the parking lot. Not Mercy's little girl.

Not his Casey.

He raced right up over the curb in front of the emer-gency entrance, jamming the vehicle into a gear-grinding Park and throwing open the door as a couple of staff mem-bers rushed out to meet them. As he rounded the back of the car, he was shouting out the child's symptoms while Casey was lifted out of Mercy's grasping arms and laid flat upon a gurney. He was just in time to grab on to Mercy as she leaped from the car, determined to hang on to her little girl. Spencer intercepted her outflung arms and wrapped her up in his own. She was too dazed to protest as the two of them hurried through the shush of automatic doors into the cool clinically scented hall.

An emergency measures technician asked her name. "Casey? Casey, honey, you're going to be just fine. I'm going to put this over your mouth and nose so you can breathe better, okay? I don't want you to be frightened. Just try to relax and breathe normally. Have you had asthma before?"

The bright head nodded as he affixed an oxygen mask over her face.

"Then you know you've got nothing to be afraid of." He looked up at Mercy. "Does she have any hypersensitivity to drugs? Any allergies?"

"I-I don't—"

Casey tugged on the white sleeve and the doctor bent down to hear her rasping claim of a penicillin reaction. He smiled and repositioned the mask with a proud, "Good girl." Then, to Mercy he said, "We'll get her on an isoproterenol inhalant. That should cut down on her distress. Is that what she's used before?"

Mercy had her hands over her mouth. Her wide eyes dropped to the slight figure on the gurney, catching the nod of a curly-topped head. "Yes," she whispered, and the gurney and Casey were whisked away. Almost at once, the strength seemed to desert her legs. She was vaguely aware of the supportive curve of Spencer's arm as he guided her toward a row of chairs. She collapsed into one, a mass of quivering apprehension.

Asthma. She hadn't known. Nor had she been aware of the drug allergy. If Casey hadn't had the presence of mind to speak up, what awful consequences could have resulted? Could she have killed the child through her own ignorance? That idea was too devastating. This child she'd sworn to protect, endangered by her care. A soft sob escaped her as she imagined the worst.

Spencer lifted one of her trembling hands and slipped it over his opposite shoulder, where she immediately clung for purchase to a handful of soft leather. His other palm opened wide between her shoulder blades and a little nudge was all it took to bring her up against his chest. Mercy burrowed there, clutching him, shaking until she was sure her few fillings had rattled loose. She was aware of him, of the fact that he had nothing but skin beneath the jacket, of the strangely comforting scent of warm man and leather enticing her senses each time she inhaled. It was a hot, heady aroma, like none she could recall.

Nor could she remember anything that felt quite as good as the band of his arm about her, the way it anchored her, the way all of him swallowed her with his heat and strength and stability. She needed it. God knows, she did. Stresses that had torn through her for the last few months finally threatened to knock down her neatly built house of straw. Spencer Halloway was stronger than straw. He was warm, hard brick; solid and at the same time, curiously yielding. She hadn't known a man could be like that; tough and soft all at once. All she knew was she couldn't let go, absolutely could not let go.

She'd almost lost Casey. The truth of that was more than she could stand. Terror and guilt beat inside her like a wild thing. The security of Spencer's arms was the only thing holding her together.

"She'll be all right." His voice was a hot caress against her hair, soothing her in all the right places. "They do good work here. You can trust them to take care of her."

Like Casey had trusted her? The shivering got a hold of her again and Spencer's embrace tightened incrementally to absorb it. Her nose was squashed flat against the firm wall of his chest. Her tears were making narrow runnels all the way down to the waistband of his jeans. His hand came up to mesh in her hair, pressing her closer, melding them into one. For the first time in her life, she didn't protest. She needed the feel of him because she was cold as death inside.

They sat like that for a long time. Neither was as aware of the other in actuality as they were of the feelings of the other. Basic feelings like need and loss and sharing. Desperate, intense emotions that slowly expanded beyond the sterile clime and worry over one little girl.

"She's going to be all right," he repeated, this time as a firm Sheriff Halloway order.

Who'd dared disagree?

Then Mercy felt his hand move upon her hair; a slow, gentle stroking that should have calmed but instead sparked alarm. It was then her panic over Casey subsided to the point where other factors came into focus. Like the fact that he was wearing next to nothing. And the way she was draped upon him, her defenses stripped naked. His proximity wasn't what woke an anxious skittering in her breast. It was her failure to protect herself.

What was she thinking? Or rather, why wasn't she thinking?

This man wasn't her comforter, her friend. He was an enemy. Not a conscious enemy, but an enemy nonetheless, who would pounce upon any mistake she might make when her resistance was low. And it couldn't get any lower than it was right now. But she'd be a fool if she didn't believe things could get worse. She knew they could. Firsthand. She had to think of Casey. She had to be alert against any danger. Spencer Halloway, though briefly a savior, was still a threat she couldn't afford to dismiss.

"I'm all right now, Sheriff. I'm sorry to be so useless. I'm usually very good in a crisis. This one just took me by surprise."

"No apologies necessary."

Whether he'd sensed her discomfort or was stirred by his own, Spencer slowly relaxed his grip on her, letting his arms loosen and ease away, the very pretense of nonchalance making the movement that much more abnormal. He straightened and sat back in his chair, giving her adequate space in which to recover.

Reflexively upon seeing her ravaged face, he reached for his handkerchief, then was momentarily bewildered by his flat back pockets. He'd been in too much of a hurry to pack the usual. He couldn't remember if he'd locked his door or taken his key. He didn't think so. He couldn't recall shutting the door behind him, that's what a scramble his mind had been in. The thought of Mercy and her child in trouble had unstrung his careful, instinctive behavior. He didn't like being careless. Being careless meant getting hurt. There was no more room on his heart for scars of carelessness. No more willingness within his soul to risk the kind of emotional tug-of-war he'd just gone through.

He'd told himself it was the mystery that drew him, and now he found himself hip-deep in involvement with the woman and her child. A few more inches and the ability to retreat would be gone. From there, it was a quick, painful slide to over his head. Time to paddle fast for shore and the safety that came with being high and dry.

"I'll go check and see what's going on."

Mercy didn't object but as he stood, her big eyes followed him, their dark centers spooky with dependence as well as denial. Trouble he didn't need.

"Do you want me to get some coffee while I'm up?"

She shook her head. "I'm too keyed up already."

He nodded at that wisdom, then disappeared into the back of the clinic where only staff and pushy sheriffs were allowed.

Mercy let her breath out in a strained sigh. Alone, she could force coherent thought back into her terror-stricken brain. Casey was going to be all right. Despite her initial ignorance, she'd done all the right things to make sure of it. She had Spencer to thank, and she would as soon as she was in better control of her emotions. Distance. Distance and detachment were what she needed. Spencer was way too close for comfort.

For a moment, while he'd held her tight, she'd had the ungovernable feeling that he was different, that he had the kind of compassion it would take to be accepting of her past. But now she could see how foolish those thoughts had been. It was worry and exhaustion that lulled her into passive hope. With reality came the same truth that had destroyed all earlier relationships. No man was interested in a woman who came carrying so much emotional baggage. Spencer would be no exception.

"Mrs. Royce?"

Her head jerked up and she focused in on an efficient-looking female in sanitized whites. "Yes?"

A clipboard was extended. "I need you to fill out this insurance form and Casey's medical history."

Mercy took the board automatically with a vaguely mumbled, "Yes, of course." Then, more strongly, "How is she?"

The nurse smiled. "The bronchodilator seems to be doing the trick. There's no sign of any infection. She's such a brave little girl. You must be very proud of her for holding up so well."

Much better than she had, so far. Mercy closed her eyes to offer up a quick prayer of thanks. Wonderful. So far, so good. "When can I take her home?"

"As soon as the doctor's satisfied that her condition is stabilized. He'll be out to talk to you in just a minute. Go ahead and fill out that questionnaire. I'll be back to get it from you in a few minutes."

Mercy's smile thinned. "Thank you."

The woman walked away leaving Mercy with an impossibly long list of questions involving a childhood she was unfamiliar with. What could she put down that they couldn't trace when something as seemingly harmless as the name of her own health carrier could betray them both?

She was still staring at the mostly blank sheet when Spencer returned through the swing doors with two plastic cups.

"It's decaf," he explained, looking for a spot to set hers. "They didn't have any bourbon to put in it. Too bad. Pretty shabby medical aid, if you ask me."

Mercy laid aside the clipboard and relieved him of one of the cups. Her hand was still unsteady. Was it Spencer that made it that way? "Did you talk to the doctor?"

"Yeah. He said everything's looking good. He was surprised you didn't have an inhaler handy. From what Casey told him, this isn't her first attack."

"No, but it's been a long time since she's had one. I'd hoped she'd grown out of them. It was careless of me not to have brought her medication. Something in the woods must have triggered an allergy."

Spencer smiled faintly as if he thought her answer plausible. His shrewd gray eyes said something altogether different. They were asking why a mother wouldn't recognize the signs of a daughter's recurring illness.

Mercy took a nervous sip of her coffee and then glanced up in relief to see Casey approaching at a shuffling walk, her small hand tucked into that of her doctor. The child looked fragile and weary, but her smile would have lit up an auditorium. Mercy quickly set the cup down and opened her arms to embrace the precious figure.

"How are you feeling, sweetheart? I was so worried."

"Fine, now." Her voice still sounded weak and thready from the abuse it had taken. "I'm sorry I scared you. Can we go home now?"

Mercy looked up in question.

"I don't see why not," the doctor told her. "Keep her quiet tomorrow and watch for any signs of bronchial distress. I'll give you a prescription for an inhaler, just in case this trouble crops up again. I don't think it should. If you'll give me her pediatrician's name, I'll forward my report to him."

Mercy stared up at him for a moment as if he'd suddenly started speaking Japanese. But she was quick to recover and offer a chagrined smile. "I've got all that information at home. I'm sorry I'm so unprepared. I was so upset, I forgot to pick up my purse. It's got my card and my group number on it."

The doctor glanced up at Spencer and seemed to be making some sort of decision. His reply was kind and forgiving. "That's all right. You can phone it in." He gestured to the clipboard. "Are you about done with that?"

"Oh, yes." Mercy hesitated, then reached for the form. And with a feigned clumsiness, managed to spill her coffee all over it. "Oh, dear! What a mess!"

The nurse bustled over with a handful of paper toweling and Mercy began blotting up the puddle of staining liquid. The few words Mercy had put to paper were soon hopelessly smeared. She handed it to the nurse with another feeble shrug.

"I can't believe I'm so clumsy. Just the stress of all this, I guess. I'd like to get Casey home. Can I stop in tomorrow and fill out another one? I'll have the rest of the information then, too.''

Casey was yawning widely and the doctor smiled. ''I don't see why not. Get this little one right to bed. The prescription can wait until tomorrow to be filled. And remember, no excitement for a while.''

''You've got my promise on that,'' Mercy vowed.

The doctor glanced at Spencer, then at the mother and child and back again. ''Kind of out of uniform, aren't you, Sheriff?''

Spencer put an hand to his bare chest as if suddenly recalled to his state of dress. Or rather his lack of it. ''Duty knows no days or nights, Doc. You should know that better than anyone.''

The doctor grinned, refusing to be fooled by what he believed to be a sham of innocence. He knew the sheriff's reputation with the ladies. And then he sighed in envy. ''Take care of these two.''

''Oh, don't worry,'' Spencer promised, adding an intimate aside. ''I fully intend to.''

Mercy found that vow more than a little disturbing.

Chapter 6

Casey could talk of nothing but the heroic Spencer Halloway.

It was Spencer this, over breakfast. Spencer that, over lunch. Mercy tried to be patient with the girl's glowing tribute but it was wearing on her hard. Because hearing about Spencer made her think about Spencer, and she was uncomfortable with the direction her thoughts were taking.

He'd been wonderful. The child was right about that. He'd stepped in with a professional cool when she'd been teetering on full-blown hysteria. He'd quieted Casey's fears. He'd calmed her own. He'd been a rock in a hard place and she'd clung like moss; she who never clung, who never lost control that way. She'd been willing to surrender the situation into his capable hands. She had been as malleable as a baby in his arms. A very trusting baby. And that scared her plenty.

Her defensive radar should have been up and quivering wildly. She should have been out digging trenches, laying mines, stringing barbed wire to protect their privacy. She should have held Spencer Halloway at arm's length in both fact and active fancy. But the fact was, she couldn't.

She kept seeing the way he was with Casey, hearing the way his low drawl rolled thick and sweet like honey. Just like an unsuspecting butterfly, she didn't see the danger until she was stuck fast. Struggling seemed to only embroil her more.

The hardest part to resist was seeing how good he was in handling Casey; like a natural parent, instinctively knowing just the right thing to do, to say. He'd been great. The stuff of preadolescent adoration and damned tough to discredit, especially when she'd come apart like a pair of imported sandals, breaking under the first sign of hard wear.

Then, more disturbing than her lack of judgment in placing all in his hands, was her willingness to linger in them, herself.

His touch had woken none of the expected terror. Her skin hadn't turned to frosted glass. Her heart hadn't started hammering out a frantic S.O.S. She hadn't been torn between the urge to scream and the impulse to be physically ill. His touch had her languishing and tame to the sensation of comfort. The feel of him had been unexpectedly, incomprehensibly, unequivocally good. Like flannel sheets. Like a borrowed sweater still holding another's body heat. Like hot cocoa laced with something stronger... wooingly, wonderfully warm.

For years she'd tried to feel those kinds of things with a man and had failed. Maybe they'd been the wrong men. She'd begun to fear she would never have those feelings at all. Until Spencer. He'd started a trickle of emotion that threatened to become a landslide. Why him? Why the one most inappropriate man in the whole world? The one who could shake her careful plan to pieces and ruin not just one life, but two. It was those darned cut-off jeans. His lazy smile. Even the sharp intelligence in eyes that saw far too much. It was the way he'd held her as if she was something that would break. As if she was something valuable.

She liked him.

He was pushy. He was nosy. He was aggravating. And dangerous. She couldn't forget dangerous. But she couldn't dismiss the way he made Casey laugh. And she couldn't refute the way her gaze anticipated the sight of him each morning. As if he was an irritating, inevitable fact of life. And she just plain liked him.

He'd let her get a glimpse of his own vulnerability. It hadn't been calculated. Oh, she knew him for a crafty manipulator, but this had been real. When he spoke of his work in Detroit, of his failed marriage, the frustration, the regret, the blame had been genuine. He'd been hurt. He was still hurting. And she felt an inexplicable pool of sympathy inside her. She'd thought only the small, the helpless, the weak could know that kind of anguish. She'd been wrong, and recognizing torment in someone as strong and capable as the sheriff of Pine Creek skewed all her reasoning. It was that shared sense of sorrow that bound them, wisely or not, one to the other.

Perhaps if they'd met under different circumstances, she might have explored the stir of attraction she felt when she was with him. But not now. Now she couldn't afford to let herself be sidetracked by her own desires. She was involved in serious business, and Spencer Halloway was the last person in the world she could risk discovering what it was. He was a threat to more than her untapped emotions. Because of who he was, what he was, he was about as welcome as the plague.

Except to Casey.

Casey, who bubbled up excitedly to find him at their back door as the afternoon wound down toward evening. He'd brought flowers. And Casey went round-eyed with her first childish crush to learn that they were for her.

Mercy could feel all her cautions slide like a pat of butter on a hot skillet. How could she be frightened of a man who thought to bring flowers to a little girl? How could she throw him out in the wake of such a tender gesture? He glanced at her over the tousle of Casey's bright hair and he smiled—a slow, knowing grin. And not even the knowledge that he

knew exactly what he was doing could dim her fondness for
him at that moment.

"Go put your flowers in some water before they wilt,
Casey."

"I'm going to keep them pretty forever."

Mercy smiled after her somewhat sadly. How like a child
to believe such a thing was possible. But she knew the flowers wouldn't last, and Casey would be disappointed. Nothing stayed fresh forever. Beauty wasn't something you could
cling to for long. It was fleeting and fragile, like trust and
hope. But she said nothing, not wanting to spoil the little
girl's innocent happiness. Lessons like that were learned too
soon. She would let the child hold on to her illusions a while
longer.

Mercy looked up at Spencer, who'd made no attempt to
enter the cabin. He filled the doorway in a way that was all
male but not quite as intimidating as it once might have
been. He was wearing suggestively snug jeans and the
leather jacket that made her immediately recall the scent of
it mingling with the sultry essence of warm skin. This time,
he had shoes on. He lounged comfortably against the doorframe, apparently unconcerned about being chased away,
but he wasn't prepared for Mercy's small smile.

"Thank you, Spencer. You've no idea what that meant to
her."

"I think I do."

Maybe he did. Maybe it was more than just a masculine
ploy to melt the unsuspecting female heart. She wasn't sure
she was comfortable with the thought of his sensitivity. It
did traitorous things to her resolve.

"Aren't they pretty?" Casey gushed as she carried the
bouquet from the kitchen. She'd dropped them haphaz-
ardly into a mayonnaise jar and was nose-deep in the blos-
soms, inhaling the springtime fragrance. "Can I keep them
in my room?"

"Sure, honey."

When Casey trotted back to the bedroom, Mercy gave their guest a shrewd look. "Was there something else you wanted, Sheriff?"

His lids lowered slightly, intimating there was much more, but he settled for a casual, "I just wanted to see how she was doing."

"Much better, thank you."

"And I wanted to ask the two of you out to dinner."

He slipped that in so nonchalantly, she almost forgot to be alarmed. "Dinner? You mean tonight?"

"Nothing fancy. No strings. You can pay your own way, if you'd feel more comfortable. I just thought the two of you might be going slightly stir-crazy about now, and I know a place down the highway that has great food."

"That's very thoughtful of you but—"

"You've already eaten?"

"No..."

"Then...?"

"We'll get our jackets."

The words just came out. It was hard to say which one of them was more surprised. They stood, staring at one another for the longest moment, then, before she caught up with the total insanity of actually going through with it, Mercy called, "Casey, get your jacket. Spencer's taking us out to eat."

All the way to the restaurant, Mercy told herself lies. She was doing it for Casey, because the little girl deserved an outing. She'd accepted so as not to make Pine Creek's sheriff suspicious—after all, he had come to their rescue the night before. She'd said yes because she was hungry and bored and restless and scared. And all those things were true, but it still all came down to one deciding factor.

She'd said yes because she wanted to spend time with Spencer.

Nothing like courting disaster, but Mercy couldn't help herself. Maybe it wasn't a bad move getting on the good side of the local law. The more she lulled his natural suspicions, the less likely he'd be watching for some sign that she was

other than who she said she was. There was nothing wrong
with a friendly dinner out. Polite conversation over a good
meal. A chance to be out among other people, to feel alive—
normal. One couldn't hide in a hole for long without looking hunted. What better way to stave off questions than to
confront them directly. This was her chance. All she had to
do was keep control of the table talk and smile. Nothing too
difficult after all she'd gone through already. What were a
few more lies?

She determinedly ignored a sudden twist of conscience.

The restaurant was perfect. It was bright and noisy, a
family spot with a side room filled with video games and
youthful music hammering out over the electronic ping-
pings. Not the kind of place to inspire soul-searching conversations or romance. Mercy gave a gust of relief and a
genuine smile up at Spencer.

"Great place."

"You can say that again!" Casey got one look at the ar-
cade and began pleading for quarters. Spencer fished out a
handful and said he'd come get her when their order was up.
He made a point of assuring Mercy that the game room was
well supervised and no place a little girl could come to harm.
She was momentarily surprised that being single he would
think of such things usually associated with parental para-
noia. But then she couldn't forget he was a lawman, used to
anticipating situations for their potential danger. It was so
easy to trust his judgment as sound. He said it was all right
and she never once thought to question it. Then, as he led
her to a corner booth, she began to wonder if she was the
one in danger.

"Mercy, do you and Casey like pizza?"

"Sure."

"Everything on it?"

"No onions."

"Beer?" he asked cautiously.

"Dark."

"A woman after my own heart." He grinned wide. "Are
you trying to seduce me, Mrs. Royce?" He let her flounder

for a moment, all blushes and wordless gaspings, then he waved down a waitress to relay their order.

"Hiya, Sheriff," the young woman in a scandalously short skirt purred as she wiggled her fanny in close and stretched her forearm out along the back of Spencer's booth. He smiled up at her with a roguish charm and she simpered prettily. "What can I get you?"

From her side of the table, Mercy held to a careful neutrality as Spencer plied his killer smile and relayed their order. She watched the way they interacted, with teasing glances and phrases laced with double meaning—the way two adults conversed when they were sure of their sexuality. It was a ritual Mercy had never mastered. She couldn't feel comfortable bandying innuendo. When she tried, her words were stilted, her body posture a torture of reluctance. She'd never been what a man would call a good date. She couldn't relax; she couldn't flirt. And she could never get any man to ask her out again. Any man except Spencer, who seemed to have no common sense when it came to her shortcomings. Couldn't he see the difference between her and their vivacious waitress? She sat like frozen rock while the other exuded primal heat. Why would he choose her over the other when he seemed so interested in the blatant invitations simmering in the woman's eyes? Or was he coming to that conclusion himself as he glanced at Mercy, then back up at the temptress jotting down their preferred toppings?

Afraid she was failing in a contest she had no intention of entering, Mercy nonetheless was seething with bruised pride. What did it matter if Pine Creek's sheriff had an active libido? So what if he liked skimpy skirts and vacuous co-eds? Her stare intensified until the flirtatious young thing glanced up and abruptly straightened, called to mind her manners.

"I'll be right back with your drinks."

Spencer watched her saunter off, then grinned back at a stoical Mercy. "I used to help her tie her shoes."

"Now I'm sure she'd love to have you untying them."

His smile widened with delight. "Why, Mercy Royce, if you don't sound a bit jealous."

"Don't be ridiculous." But even she could hear the strident snap in her tone. Jealous? Impossible. She was just annoyed. Annoyed because...because... Well, because he was her date—sort of—and it was damned insulting to sit by while someone else flirted with him. Even if she didn't want to, herself.

Then her gaze canted up for a covert study of her escort. After a critical summation, she could see why the other woman would coo over him. He was tall, lean and golden, the perfect idea of a romantic dream, a rugged hero with a uniform to boot. The ideal of strong, safe and secure. Until he let loose one of those lazy, come-and-get-it grins. Then all the courtly charm went out the window in lieu of pure devil sass. A catch, to be sure. If one was in the market. Which she was not. Depending upon whether the good sheriff wanted to be caught, which she suspected he didn't.

So all in all, the logic of the two of them being out together was inescapable. They were both single, lonely, and not looking for involvement. It should have been uncomplicated. But it wasn't.

"I was kind of surprised when you said you'd come here with me."

Mercy smiled faintly and tried a touch of teasing. "Why, Sheriff, I thought you took your sterling charm for granted."

"Everyone has their limitations."

"If you didn't think I'd go, why did you ask?"

"There was always that chance that I'd be wrong." He grinned widely and she felt herself responding.

"You admit to being wrong?"

"On occasion, and very happy to be on this one. So, why yes?"

"Woman's got to eat."

He clutched his chest dramatically. "Oh, please, don't bolster my ego. I don't think I could stand any more flattery."

She laughed. It had been so long since she'd made that sound, she was surprised it wasn't rusty. "And how could I say no after you've been so...nice to us?"

He was still smiling but his stare was dangerously serious. Like the smoky gray of dawn. Like a cool blanket of misty fog rising against a gaining warmth. "I'm a nice guy. One who knows when to behave himself." Then, with a sudden shift of his position in the booth from lounging back to leaning intently forward, he startled her with his intensity. And with his sudden claim. "You don't have to be afraid of me, Mercy. I know you're on the rebound. So am I. I don't want either of us to get hurt."

She was so flabbergasted by his directness, she could only stare.

"But I want to get to know you and I don't want you to jump every time I move."

"I—I don't do that."

"Yes, you do. Like yesterday on the boat. I don't know what you were thinking but, Mercy, you were wrong."

She continued to stare in a defensive silence, daring him with a piercing look to prove it to her satisfaction. "You know kids are a great judge of character. And Casey—"

"Casey's crazy about you. Even before the flowers."

"There you go." He leaned back again, apparently well pleased with his argument. And Mercy felt the pressure ease. "Trust her instincts and don't look so worried. I'm not going to rush you into anything you're not ready for. If all you want is a friend, I can be a darn good friend. It looks like you could use one."

Was it that obvious that her emotions were all frayed and dangling? It must have been true. Why else would her throat feel like she'd swallowed a bee's nest and her eyes be all wobbly with tears? She needed to talk. She needed a friend. But not one who was the sheriff of Pine Creek. She couldn't confide in a man sworn to uphold an entirely different set of rules. He would never understand—not as a man, not as an officer of the law. So what could she do about his sweet and totally impossible offer except smile and say nothing?

Then desperation prompted a response.

"Would you excuse me a moment?" She slid out of the booth and as he politely stood in deference to her, she went to check on Casey.

When she returned, their pitcher of beer had arrived and Mercy was of a mind to forgive their bouncy waitress her earlier indiscretions for having such good timing now. The dark amber brew provided a good break in conversation as she sat nursing her mug and looking about the restaurant with a pretended interest. She didn't want to talk about building a relationship with Spencer Halloway. In two months' time, her whole life would be changed for better or worse, and Pine Creek and its sheriff would be left far behind her. It couldn't be any other way. Not for her. Not for them. And she found it ridiculously hard to swallow past the wad of regret.

Spencer had been watching her carefully since he'd spoken his impulsive words. The last thing he'd planned to do was open the channels for commitment between them. He hadn't done that—not directly—but his overture was far and away beyond the fun in the sun he'd vowed to stick to. He watched her fiddling with her draft, avoiding eye contact with a nervous determination, as if afraid he was going to start talking to her again. What was it about this woman's wounded aura that got to him so savagely? It was more than the stray-cat-in-the-rain kind of sympathy, though he was a sucker for strays every time. Something in Mercy's wild-eyed panic and protective bravado struck a harmonizing chord in him, and the music it made was definitely, maddeningly, a love song. He could argue, he could smoke cigarette after cigarette right down to scorched fingers, and damned if he could talk himself out of his irrational attachment to this woman and her child.

He watched Mercy as she smiled at the waitress, a smile that never quite warmed her features the way that earlier glimmer had. He always got the feeling that the majority of her expressions had nothing to do with what went on inside. Just the way much of what she'd told him had nothing to do with the facts.

Spencer, you are crazy.

Crazy about the quixotic woman sitting opposite him.

He knew less than nothing about her except that possibly everything she'd told him was a lie. She was a walking anxiety-attack and as gun-shy as he was when it came to entanglements. So why couldn't he get her out of his thoughts? She could be bad news to someone in his position if she was on the run from something shady. With that meltingly soft mouth and the sudden, startling glimpses of humor and stubbornness, she could add up to more than bad news in the heart department. He didn't know what to make of her. He didn't know what to do with her. He just knew he couldn't do without her.

The pizza came and Casey returned to the table all bubbling with the news of her latest video conquest and of a friend she'd made while working her way through the second level's dungeon. Her nonstop chatter filled in the awkward void of conversation and by the time they were ready to leave, the tension index was at a manageable degree.

Until Spencer pulled up in their drive and came around to swing Casey down. Until he followed them like a mannerly escort to the door and held it open for them. Casey bounded inside, leaving the two of them on the porch. Spencer knew better than to push his luck by asking if he could come in. He'd done well in getting his wary princess out of her fortress with the lure of pizza and suds. To expect more would be asking for a prompt letdown. He understood that. And he wasn't expecting more than a chaste good-night at the door and just maybe, one of her heart-snagging smiles.

Those were his intentions.

However, when she turned to him with "thank you" on her sweet lips and gratitude warming her doelike eyes, all sensibilities scattered.

He moved slowly, giving her plenty of time to rebuff him. He could see her stiffen as his hand rose up to curl gently behind her upper arm. He could hear her frantic swallow-

ing when his other hand lifted so his fingertips could skim
the velvety curve of one creamy-soft cheek. It wasn't his
imagination. She leaned toward him. It wasn't an aggres-
sive move or even a conscious ploy. She was drawn by the
longing in his expression and by his promise not to hurt her.
And he fully meant to honor that claim.

Unless she asked him to break it.

It was little more than a feather-light touch, that first
brush of their lips. He could feel her breath shivering as she
drew back a scant inch. Her eyes were open, uplifted,
searching his as if seeking his true motives; afraid of recognizing her own. She looked so uncertain, so vulnerable,
he almost withdrew. But then her dark lashes fluttered and
lowered and her petal-smooth mouth tipped up in offering.
What kind of man could have turned it down? Not him.

She tasted like long-ago dreams and whispered secrets.
Sweet as wildflowers, as chaste as raindrops. She made him
feel like he was the first man to ever drink from the purity
of her lips. The sensation was awe inspiring. He'd kissed
women with unbridled lust, with passion, with hunger, with
selfish pleasure and conquering confidence. But this was the
first time he kissed one with reverence, with a tenderness
coaxed up from the soul. It was the first time he had the
patience to learn every soft contour, every unintentionally
sexy swell. And it was worth it. To hear her quiet, almost-
puzzled sigh, it was worth the wait.

When he touched the seal of her lips with the tip of his
tongue, she trembled. She opened for him, just a crack, just
a tease of space, and he made the most of it, sliding, stroking along that tentative crevice until, with a moan, she gave
him more. Inside, she was all sultry mystery; hot, moist,
strangely untried, for within seconds, his exploration had
her quaking. Her fingertips fluttered as her lashes had done
as they grazed his features and followed the line of his jaw.
Touching him with blind fingers, learning, memorizing, as
if she had no experiences to guide her. But that was impossible, wasn't it? As impossible as the surge of want searing

through his loins, pushing him to make a claim upon this oddly virgin ground.

It wasn't any big thing. He didn't grab her or hurt her or anything like it. In a natural progression, his arms had gone about her trim middle and as desire peaked, they constricted, pulling her gently, firmly up against him. There was nothing in his embrace to scare her, no crushing intensity, no mauling, no rough handling. Just a slow, enveloping closeness. But suddenly, she was no longer enjoying the contact. The fluid lines of her body went rigid as dry ice. Inquiring hands became actively resistant, pushing at his chest, curling into fists of objection. He was too surprised to let go immediately. He'd never in his life forced himself upon a woman. He didn't think that was what he was doing now. Yet she acted as if he were taking the cruelest kind of advantage. Worse, when she stumbled back, her parchment-pale features were stark with horror.

As if he'd attempted something awful. Something loathsome.

It was just a kiss. And she'd liked it.

Why the sudden dramatic overreaction to something she'd wanted from him in the first place?

In the back of his analytical policeman's mind came a suspicious whisper. Was her initially submissive pose just to draw him off from probing into her past? Had he, the devote doubter, been suckered in by a lying smile and the deceiving promise of what was never intended?

His voice was gruff-edged when he murmured, "Sorry. We must have gotten our signals crossed somewhere along the line. I could have sworn that was what you had in mind. My mistake."

She was scrubbing at her lips with quivering hands. Not a very flattering reception to his kisses. She was wiping them away. Her eyes were dark-centered and wide, fixed upon his with a wild beseechment. "I'm sorry. It's not you. I wanted—that is, I needed to—" She broke off with a jagged sigh.

He could see shame and guilt and grief and fright building, churning, stirring up into some terrible concoction of
apology. He didn't want to hear that she was sorry. He
wasn't sorry. He'd enjoyed kissing her. He'd wanted her to
return the feeling. Apparently, she didn't. He should have
checked the water more carefully before plunging in, even
after her assurance that it was fine.

If there was a graceful way to escape the situation, he
couldn't seem to find it. But he couldn't go on standing
there with a proverbial foot in his mouth.

"Mercy—"

"Spencer, I'm sorry. I didn't mean to lead you on. I
thought— I hoped— Oh, never mind. I'm sorry."

And with that perfectly wretched explanation, she turned
into the cabin and closed the door between them.

Spencer's phone was ringing when he opened the door.
He snatched it up with a distracted growl of his name.

"Halloway."

"If this is a bad time, Sheriff, I can call you back."

Spencer relaxed, recognizing the dry tones of Larry Wells.
Before he'd become a doctor, the youthful Larry had been
quite the hell-raiser and had spent his summers talking
Spencer into one foolish escapade after another. They'd
been friends since midnight frog-sticking expeditions and
continued to be even after they'd both gone respectable.

"No, that's okay, Larry. Just caught me on my way in."

"You sound kind of breathless. Sure I'm not interrupt-
ing something?"

"Don't I wish," Spencer muttered. "What's on your
mind?"

"You know that woman and her little girl with asthma
that you brought into the clinic last night?"

"The Royces. What about them?"

"She was supposed to stop in with her insurance information so we could get our billing process started. She never
showed. We don't usually let patients wander in and out

without making some kind of payment arrangement, but since she was with you . . ."

"It's all right, Larry. I'll see the clinic doesn't get stiffed on this one. I'll talk to Mrs. Royce and have her get in touch with you."

"That's all I'm asking, big guy. I'd appreciate the favor. She's awfully nice looking, by the way."

"Really? I hadn't noticed."

Larry Wells gave a hearty laugh. "Right. If that was the case, I'd be sending an ambulance over to pick you up. Make that a hearse." Then his tone sobered. "How's the little girl?"

"She's doing just fine. Must be your bedside manner."

"Must be. Thanks for reminding me. I'll add that into the bill. Talk to you later, Spence."

Spencer hung up and stood for a long moment, frowning pensively.

Was he imagining it or had he, in a moment of madness, just made himself officially responsible for Mercy Royce?

Chapter 7

While the cigarette he'd desperately needed but now didn't seem to want smoldered between his fingers, Spencer stood in the enveloping darkness on his back porch, his gaze drawn across the black waters of the cove.

What was it about Mercy? Her toughness or her vulnerability? Something had gotten under his skin and it itched something fierce—something that was not basic chemistry that could be safely neutralized with one quick sampling. He didn't want to be involved with her or her sweetheart of a little girl. They were a temporary situation in his life and, emotionally, he couldn't afford to make them anything more. His edges were still too ragged, his center too raw to support the weight of responsibility.

So why couldn't he just leave it alone?

The policeman in him knew something was fishy. He was beginning to suspect they were not mother and daughter as they pretended to be. Though Mercy obviously loved the child, and the feeling was returned, she showed none of the preparedness of a parent. A parent would have known about the asthma and what to do for it. A parent would have spoken right up about a penicillin allergy. A parent would never, ever have gone anywhere without a possibly lifesaving inhaler. Then there was the way she'd cleverly hedged about filling out the health and insurance forms and hadn't been back in as promised with the necessary information. Because she didn't have it to give?

Then there was the way that Casey had slipped and called Mercy by her given name, leading him to believe that she was someone else's child.

Crazy suspicions, yet he couldn't seem to dismiss them.

Why? Why all the pretense? An assumed name. A false relationship. The terror simmering behind each glance.

The professional in him urged him to launch a full-scale investigation, while the man in him wanted to wait, hoping Mercy would feel safe in coming to him with her troubles. And she was in trouble. No doubt about it. Maybe it was the unfulfilled hero in him that made him long to be the anchor in the life of someone he loved, but it couldn't be love he was feeling for her. That wasn't what was behind his irrational behavior.

He lifted the cigarette up to take a frustrated drag and was surprised to find one long cylindrical ash. He was supposed to have quit anyway, he told himself as he crushed it out and resisted the habitual pull to light another while he brooded over what to do. No answers were going to come over a filter tip and a soft evening breeze. He knew where the answers were. He'd been trained in how to get them. But something in him rejected the clinical use of his criminology skills—something dangerously weak when it came to one determined woman and her fiery-topped mini-companion.

He was about to call it a night and go back inside when he caught a furtive movement in the trees by Mercy's back porch. His heart gave a youthfully inspired leap at the thought of Mercy enjoying the same night air. Perhaps he'd just take a little stroll around the cove and coincidentally bump into her. He was supposed to remind her of her promise to bring in Casey's medical records. She didn't have to know he already suspected she had no intention of doing so. He didn't think she had them. But he wasn't about to let the opportunity of a silvery moon and a passionate breeze go to waste while he played detective; not when there were other roles he preferred to play.

He was too far away to see any distinguishing features but the moon was full and the glare of a neighboring mercury light was intense enough to bring highlight to shadows. He might not have been able to discern a face but there was no mistaking the silhouetted proportions.

It wasn't Mercy slinking through the trees.

It was the figure of a man.

Mercy didn't know why she'd thought she could sleep, but she went through the motions anyway. With Casey tucked in the next room, Mercy pantomimed her usual nighttime regime, hoping the late hour and her own exhaustion would catch up with her. But once she slid beneath the covers, she realized the futility of such hopes.

How could she rest when the remembrance of Spencer's kiss had her all wide-awake and restless inside?

I won't hurt you. I won't rush you. Wasn't that what he'd told her?

She was still surprised at herself for allowing it— No, it was more than that. She'd asked for his kiss. She'd known what he had in mind and she'd been willing—actually anxious—to comply.

Spencer had probably wooed and won hundreds of women. They probably fell over each other just to get his attention, if Miss Can't Tie Her Own Shoes at the restaurant was any indication. So with so many eyelashes batting in his direction, he couldn't have understood the magnitude of her submission.

He was her first taste of passion.

Oh, she'd been kissed before. She'd been held in intimate embraces and had stood stock-still with jaw clenched, allowing a man's mouth to claim hers. On the surface. But tonight was the first time she had opened for a man's possession.

And she'd liked it. Nothing could have prepared her for that.

All evening she'd wondered what it would be like. She'd wondered what he'd be like with a little encouragement on her part. His big hands had been so gentle in their handling of Casey, in their soothing of her own fears. Would they be less so when moved by desire? He did desire her. She could feel it emitting from him in hot waves, like heat rising off sun-scorched pavement with a rippling intensity. He'd promised he wouldn't rush her, wouldn't push her, wouldn't hurt her. Did he have any idea how hungry she was to believe those words? How she longed to slip into a natural intimacy with a man? How she'd hoped he might be different from those before him, those who'd mouthed those calming words only to betray them with their unrestrained demands? A man sensitive enough to bring flowers to a child, vulnerable enough to share past pains and strong enough not to apologize for it, might be a man with enough character and compassion to actually mean what he said.

And for all intents and purposes, he hadn't let her down. She was the one who had failed under pressure.

But his kiss had been marvelous, like warm honey and smooth bourbon; sweet, soothing, yet packing one hell of a punch. He'd stolen her breath away. Instinctively, she knew in her mind that was how it was supposed to be—what she'd been missing all these years. And her body had picked up on the rest, absorbing the sensations of excitement, of urgency, of need humming through his. And it had seemed so good, so right, those stirring forays of passion; enough to overcome her initial caution but not powerful enough to take on the darkness of her past. She'd known it wouldn't last, but it had been good right up until the final moment— the moment when rational thought was severed by ungovernable fear.

It was done. She couldn't change it. She couldn't take it back. She'd seen the confusion and frustration in Spencer's face, and she knew she'd managed, by succumbing, to do what she'd never been able to accomplish by resisting: she'd scared him away. He would see her as those before him had—as a tease and a disappointment.

However, instead of the relief she should have been feeling as the I-told-you-so whisper seeped through her soul, there was a sense of emptiness, of loss, almost as if she wished he hadn't given up so easily.

That was pure craziness, of course. Spencer was nothing but trouble, and his loss of interest was the best thing that could have happened. Sighing into her pillow, she couldn't quite make herself believe that.

She couldn't convince herself that losing this one very special man was going to be a good thing.

Resolutely, Mercy closed her eyes and tried to summon slumber. One of her past counselors had taught her relaxation techniques involving slow, deep breathing to calm anxiety. Anxiety was one thing. What shifted through her now was arousal. Regular breathing was no antidote for a heart gone flutteringly mad and skin that was hot and sensitive. The sheriff of Pine Creek was like the chafe of sunburn. Would the emotions he inspired peel off and fade just as quickly?

A sudden rattling of sound distracted her from her contemplations. At first, she thought Casey had gotten up to go to the bathroom, then, just as Mercy was settling down with that security, the noise came again. Definitely from outside. It wasn't Casey.

There was someone prowling around outside the cabin.

"Oh, my God."

Clutching the covers up to her chin, Mercy huddled back into the bed. Had she locked both doors? Could she afford to stay where she was, dismissing the sound as that made by some nighttime predator hoping to find something tasty in the garbage can? These were the north woods, after all. There were all sorts of raccoons and possums and such wandering about in the wild.

But there were also two-legged predators that might come sniffing around her foundation, and that was a danger that wouldn't go away if she rolled over and tried to ignore it. She had Casey to consider; that would not allow for cowardice now.

Slipping her long canvas coat over her nightshirt, Mercy crept through the dark interior, listening for a betraying sound. It was too quiet. She stood in the black void of the living room, bare feet freezing on the cold linoleum while a deeper chill shook through her. Then her eyes caught movement, a gliding shadow against the pulled draperies. Too big for any trash-can-raiding varmint—this varmint walked upright.

Someone was stalking about in the darkness and suddenly that invasion of her peace woke a fierce if unwise anger. The need to protect Casey rose foremost and it was startling in its intensity. What if Casey had been the one to awaken and she had seen the stealthy shadows? The imagined fright the child would incur was enough to starch Mercy's spine. No one was ever, ever going to scare that little child again if she had anything to do with it!

Her first thought jumped to Spencer Halloway and his unconditional offer of aid. But Spencer was on the other side of the cove and she was without a telephone. And besides, to draw him into this possible intrigue could arouse more difficulties than she had already—the need to invent more answers to his shrewd questions. No, it was something she had to handle herself. And she began to look about for the right method.

A flashlight in one hand and a length of firewood in the other, she unlatched the back door and slipped out onto the porch. The night draft sucked up under her coat and stroked icy shivers along her bare legs. Her toes curled rebelliously at their first contact with cold cement. With the weighty staff of wood to give her confidence, she continued forward, unwilling to use the flashlight yet for fear that the bright beam would give her away. She planned to use it to momentarily blind her enemy and gain the upper hand, hopefully scaring whoever it was away in the process.

At least that was the plan. It sounded good in her mind and she had personal outrage to fuel her courage as she tiptoed silently over the springy-moss ground cover. She was defending her home and her loved one. Whoever it was would think twice before underestimating her again.

She heard a faint rustling, the stirring of dry leaves around the corner of the cabin. A crunch made by big feet and a heavy man. She was stricken by a second of reservation. What on earth was she thinking? She was a woman with a small child inside, armed with a stick and a four-week class in self-defense. What if her prowler was armed with more than that? Then who would protect Casey?

The footsteps came closer, nearing the corner. In an instant, she would be in full view. There was no time to retreat without being seen, so she did the only thing she could and advanced in an offensive haste. A large shadow loomed out of the darkness, momentarily engulfing her and paralyzing her intentions. Then, with a battle cry that was more squeak than roar, she swung the piece of firewood with all her might and was rewarded by a muffled grunt and the thump of something long and solid measuring its full length on the ground. Then it was quiet again.

Mercy stood there trembling for a long beat, her heart ricocheting about her ribs. Then a wonderful rush of victory came, the kind early settlers must have shared when vanquishing deadly odds. She'd done it! She'd protected them.

And now was the time to identify the danger.

The beam of her flashlight cut a yellow swath through the night, bobbing between oak trees and small woody pines. She held her breath when that small spot illuminated the tread on a pair of running shoes. Whoever she'd struck down was laid out like a felled tree. She played the light up along a long stretch of denim-clad legs to the edge of a waist-length leather jacket. Even before she coaxed the beam higher, she had a particularly bad feeling growing in the pit of her belly. Then she came to a muss of tawny hair. "Oh, no!"

The intruder she'd coldcocked was none other than the sheriff of Pine Creek, Spencer Halloway.

Shock gave way to a deep abiding anger. What was Spencer doing sneaking around her cabin in the middle of the night? What secrets had he hoped to find skulking about in the darkness? A sense of private violation stabbed through her fury. She'd trusted him. She'd let him close enough to kiss her. And this was how she was repaid!

He gave a low groan as the toes of his jogging shoes tunneled sandy ground. Mercy was abruptly aware of how things stood; the sheriff knocked unconscious, she with the assault weapon clutched in hand, ready to bash him again if she was threatened. It served him right, slinking around in the dark. She didn't owe him any sympathy. She was of a mind to go back inside, latch the door and leave him where he lay. Let him drag himself off like the wounded dog he was.

He gave a deeper moan and her self-vindicating stand was shaken by the notion that she might have done him serious harm. She'd hit him pretty hard. She'd been the women's softball team's home-run hitter all through her academic career. What if he needed medical care? Could she in all good conscience leave him lying on the ground?

Mercy gave the offending piece of firewood a toss, thinking of it now as Exhibit A in the attack on Sheriff Halloway. She ran inside, cursing briefly as a brittle twig crunched under the bare arch of her foot. She returned to the scene of the crime, limping slightly, a wet dishcloth in hand.

"Oh, let him be all right," she whispered as she bent down to place the towel upon his brow.

The shock of wetness was enough to bring Spencer back to a groggy consciousness. He could feel cold, damp earth under his cheek and palms, and an ache pulsing red-hot through his temples like a tooth gone bad. His head felt like a New Year's Eve hangover. Then everything got worse in a hurry when he remembered the situation. Mercy!

His attempt to sit up was met with a dart of mind-numbing hurt and the pressure of hands upon his shoulders, holding him down.

"Stay still. You've got a good-sized lump growing there."

A woman's voice. Spencer blinked and saw only blackness. But it was night, so maybe he wasn't fading out of it again. He tried moving, this time with a cautious expectation of the pain. Palms cupped under his elbows, lifting, easing him into a sitting position. His head thundered. His mind buzzed. For a moment it was all he could do to hang on to a swimming awareness as he pillowed his throbbing head upon upraised knees. Someone had leveled him with a surprise blow to the head. The prowler he'd seen was his immediate suspect. And if the prowler had dropped him ... there could still be danger. They were outside and vulnerable.

"Help me up. Let's get inside." He didn't want to alarm her, but he didn't want to place her at any greater risk, either. Now, if he could just get up off the ground.

He was totally dependent upon Mercy to drag him to his feet. The dark columns of oak swayed and Mercy was no more than an indistinguishable face, bobbing like a pale moon before him. He managed to walk on his own with her to guide him and the relief of sinking down on the soggy sofa was quickly curtailed by a sear of brightness as Mercy switched on the lights. He squeezed his eyes shut and kept them closed.

"Oh dear," came her anxious observation. "I never meant to hit you so hard."

"You?" It came out in an incredulous stammer. "You hit me?" His dazed mind couldn't hold on to the concept of the frail Mrs. Royce taking out a twelve-year law-enforcement veteran.

"I'm sorry. I heard a noise and went to investigate."

"With what?" he moaned. "A sledgehammer?"

"A stick of firewood." She sounded almost embarrassed. Hers couldn't be anything compared to his. "I couldn't see who it was in the darkness. You came up on me so suddenly, I didn't have any choice but to let you have it."

She'd let him have it, all right. His head was echoing like a twenty-one-gun salute. A salute to his stupidity. And hers.

"Let me get this straight. You heard a noise outside, in the dark, picked up a log and went out alone to confront whoever was out there?"

"Y-yes."

"Without ever giving the slightest thought to what you might have been getting yourself into?"

His accusatory tone brought a bristle to her own. "I gave it a lot of thought. And I got you, didn't I?"

He squinted a look up at her. She was an enticing vision of just-out-of-bed rumpledness with dark eyes big as coat buttons. She looked scared to death despite the tough bravado of her words. To think she'd taken matters into her own hands and risked... He didn't want to think about what she'd risked.

Slowly, he lifted a hand to the bump she was coddling with the damp dish-towel. It was an impressive swelling. The lady had quite a swing. "So tell me, Babe Ruth, what did you plan on doing with whomever you caught out there?"

"You tell me, Sheriff. What am I supposed to do with you now?"

"Me?"

His act of surprised innocence was like kerosene on her smoldering blaze. Did he expect to talk his way out of it? After she'd caught him red-handed?

"How stupid do you think I am?" The indignant boom of her voice had him grabbing at the sides of his head. "You come sneaking over here in the dead of night, nearly give me a coronary, then have the nerve to pretend you're innocent? You owe me one big explanation unless you want to spend a few nights in your own jail slapped with invasion of privacy and trespassing."

He would have smiled if it hadn't been so painful to consider. She looked like a feisty Rhode Island Red all fluffed up in defense of its barnyard. He managed a wry crook to one side of his mouth that didn't hurt too much. "Quite a speech, Mrs. Royce. You might want to save it for the man I was after."

She looked completely, disarmingly blank.

"I was investigating a possible prowler. I saw someone moving around over here, someone too big to be you or Casey." He moved on swiftly, not wanting to give her time to question what he was doing watching her cabin. That would be something to try and explain. "I didn't want to alarm you in case it was nothing. I was looking around, or at least I was trying to, when you stepped up to the plate and drove what little's left of my common sense over the fence in center field."

"Then someone might still be out there." Fear shimmied through the hush of that statement. Then, before he could assure her that whoever it was was probably long gone by now, Mercy leaped up and ran for the hall. At first, he thought she was heading for the bathroom to give way to a bout of nerves. But it was the bedroom she ducked into, to check on Casey. She returned a moment later, as blanched as plain yogurt.

"Everything all right?"

"She's still sleeping." Her hand was shaking as she speared fingers back through her hair. Her stare looked bruised by fright as the first shivers of consequence overcame her. "I did a real dumb thing, didn't I?"

"It was very brave," he remarked gently, then tried for another smile. It was more a grimace. "But dumb."

The haunted look was back in her eyes—all dark, liquid desperation; the spooky glaze that yanked his heart up by the bootstraps. What was she involved in? Who had she thought was out there?

He could have pushed the issue just then—should have pushed it—but she was hanging on by the fingernails and he knew it. It seemed too cruel to tear away her last hold on composure. So he sought to soothe her instead.

"I wouldn't worry about it, Mercy. We get a lot of break-ins when cabins are empty for a long time. You're the first to open this one up in a while. Probably just some kids looking for mischief who didn't know you were even here."

"You think so?"

No, he didn't. But it was obvious she needed him to convince her that he did. "If it'll make you feel better, I'll go out and take a couple of turns around to make sure everything's okay."

She was smiling thinly with relief but was all concern the minute he wobbled to his feet. "Are you sure you're up to it, Sheriff?"

"Part of the job, ma'am." This time his smile was pure insincerity. He wasn't sure he could walk as far as the porch. But he managed, with her hovering behind him, just in case she had to provide a safety net. "You lock this behind me. I'll be back in a minute."

She nodded, her gaze a hollow terror out of a milk-pale sea. With her flashlight in hand, he stepped out and heard the bolt shoot home in his wake. Whatever foolish bravery she'd found before was firmly replaced by wariness now. That was good.

It took him only a moment to discover that whoever had been there was no more and that it was too dark to discover any clues as to that person's identity. Deep down, he felt Mercy already knew that. But she was fearful enough to make him want to discover it for himself. How else was he going to help her if she refused to let him?

The snap of a twig cracked like a shot in the darkness. Spencer's hand lunged for his holster as he aimed the flashlight like a gun sight. It reflected gold and red from two tiny orbs and he caught a glimpse of a fat, fur-covered body waddling out of the circle of light. A raccoon or maybe a woodchuck, made curious by all the commotion.

Jeez, Louise! He'd almost had stew meat for tomorrow's supper.

He let out his breath; then, harder to accomplish, relaxed his arm. His palm was wet where it gripped the snapped-down flap of his holster. His hand came away shaking. He scrubbed it against the other, then up and down on his jeans, but the damp feel wouldn't be rubbed away.

And as he stood alone in the blackness, he let the knee-weakening postreaction overcome him. He'd been out here stalking about in the night, ready to face danger at any instant. Part of his training stated that being ready meant being prepared to protect and defend to the limit of his life. That meant being willing to pull his gun, should the situation warrant it. He'd crept around in the shadows, searching blind for the figure he'd seen, worry for Mercy and Casey circumventing his recent reluctance to face conflict head-on. He'd had his holster unsnapped, had his hand on his revolver. Adrenaline had been surging through him like rocket fuel. He'd been primed and pumped and ready to draw in the face of the slightest threat.

If the circumstances had been a shade different... If he'd reached the corner of the cabin a second sooner... If he'd come around that blind turn and had seen a log lifted for the attack...

There was no doubt in his mind he would have pulled his gun. And he would have shot Mercy.

Spencer found his way back to the porch but instead of going inside, he dropped down onto the porch swing. The last thing he wanted to do was face the dark, raw emotions he'd hoped were dead and buried. No such luck.

It had taken him years and the calming bliss of Pine Creek to overcome the gnawing, deep-in-his-gut sickness that had swamped him and nearly pulled him under, back in Detroit. Yet here it was again, rising up from his past, a recurring nightmare of sweats and pinched-nerve anxiety, when he thought of what might have happened. And he couldn't stop it from playing out all over again in his mind.

He'd been an idealist when he joined the force, raised with a do-some-good, John Wayne mentality that had tarnished as quickly as his badge out on the streets of the Motor City.

For every wrong he righted there were dozens he could do nothing about. He could blame the system, he could fault the lack of manpower, he could rationalize about having only so many hours a day. He could tell himself that he couldn't do it all; but that didn't stop each failure from hitting him personally.

He cared too much, his superiors told him. His partners, too. He wondered how a man could be a cop if he didn't care enough.

There had been a kid on his beat, a twelve-year-old named Toby. He was just like hundreds of kids he saw every day, a product of a broken home and the hope-sapping welfare system. He'd gotten into some petty trouble and was remanded into a youth program Spencer was working with in his off-hours. The kid had been smart, too smart to think he could pull himself out of the street's vicious cycle on his own. Spencer had advised him on using the help the system offered to get back in school and back on track. And he'd thought Toby had been listening and was so proud of his success. Until Toby and his neighborhood friends were picked up for breaking into parked cars. He'd asked Spencer for a second chance but, disillusioned and disappointed, Spencer had denied it. Toby was processed through the legal system and it had eaten him alive.

Spencer let his head fall back against the cabin's faded siding. His eyes closed tightly but he couldn't shut out that final image.

The next time—the last time—he saw Toby, it was lying facedown in an alley with a chalk line drawn around him. The bullet that had snuffed out his young life had come from Spencer's own gun. He'd responded to a call for assistance; a convenience store being held up by two armed intruders. The first one out of the store had obeyed the command to throw down his gun and hit the pavement. The second had run. Spencer gave chase, following the shadowy figure down a series of dark back streets. He'd had his revolver drawn, readying to fire a warning shot. Then he'd come careening around a corner into a dead-end alleyway.

Coming up against a no-way-out situation, the kid had turned to meet him head-on with the intention of shooting it out. The only problem was, the kid had never fired a gun before and Spencer was an expert marksman. The conclusion was brief and after a departmental hearing, Spencer was cleared of any wrongdoing.

But how could he convince himself of that?

What good had he done for Toby? Where was the right in what went down in that dark alley?

He'd wanted to quit the force. He couldn't imagine ever pulling his gun again. Every day that he went out to meet the criminal element swarming over the city streets was a day spent inside a pressure cooker of emotion. Only a matter of time before he steamed down to the consistency of mush. He didn't want that to happen. Knowing it could, made him worry about those depending on him: his partner, the men in his division, those innocents out on the mean streets. He couldn't hold up to their expectations. He'd promised Toby a better life was waiting for him if only he'd trust him. So much for his promises. He'd been responsible and he hadn't followed through. No more taking on responsibilities for this Lone Ranger. He no longer had the confidence to boldly wear the white hat. It was time to get the hell out of Dodge before he made any more unforgivable mistakes.

That's when he'd thought of Pine Creek, the paradise of his childhood summers. A place where crime took a holiday, too. A place where he could still feel the good he did for the community. And where the likelihood of making those snap decisions of life and death was practically nil. What kind of lawman did that make him?

He rocked in the porch swing, listening to it creak and groan, unable to answer that single, most important question.

When he'd investigated Mercy's prowler, he'd gone into it wondering if he could draw his piece with the intention of pulling the trigger. Or would he freeze and expose himself as the sham he felt himself to be? He didn't know until a second ago when the twig had snapped and instinct had taken over. He could have drawn. He could have fired. Because that's what he had sworn to do. And Mercy was the one he was here to protect. That came from more than the badge he carried. It came from the man inside.

The one who'd fallen in love with Mercy Royce and the little girl who was supposed to be her daughter.

Chapter 8

Mercy answered his first knock. She'd changed from the long coat and slip of a nightshirt into a bulky, hide-all sweat suit. She must have been standing on the other side of the door, worrying, if her pinched expression was any indication. The sight of his own features didn't seem to relieve her.

"Whoever it was is gone now and I don't think he'll be back tonight."

"You're sure?"

He wasn't sure about anything except that he had a headache the size of the state of New Mexico. The last thing he wanted was to make any more for himself. No more making promises he couldn't keep. But Mercy was looking up at him through wide eyes that just begged for reassurance. His self-protecting intentions fell by the wayside.

"Tell you what. If it'll make you feel better, I'll bunk down on the couch for the night, just in case."

Mercy gave him a long, scrutinizing stare as if measuring the worse of two evils. As if he could manage to make any kind of trouble for her when he was practically seeing things in triplicate.

She must have come to the same conclusion, for she said, "Sit down before you fall down, Sheriff. I'll get you something for your head. I've got an extra pillow and some blankets in the closet."

He sat, listening to the sound of her bare feet plopping on linoleum, and even that sounded enticing. What was he getting into? Why had he made this woman any of his business when he'd spent the last few years turning uninvolvement into an art form? He'd thought selfless heroics were behind him, a lesson beaten into a soul too bruised to recover. Why pick now to crawl out from under that protective covering just when there was so much at risk?

He was kidding himself, of course. Involvement was no longer a decision he had the luxury of making. He'd made it, conscious or no, the day he chose not to actively pursue a search for her real identity. He'd appointed himself this woman's guardian, wise or no, and he was committed. He'd made himself responsible for Mercy and the kid.

And he'd be damned if he was going to fail them.

Mercy came out of the back rooms clutching the blanket and pillow defensively. What had she been thinking, agreeing to let Spencer stay here, under her roof?

Overnight.

On the surface, it was an easy answer: Casey. She would endure anything to keep the little girl safe, and what could be more safe than her own armed guard. But beneath the obvious excuse were others of a more subtle nature, ones she didn't want to explore; at least that's what she told herself. What harm would it do to have him close, to experience the attraction if not the actual fact of intimacy with him? None, if she could hold her ground and he, stick to his promises.

He was sprawled back on the couch, his feet up on one ratty arm, his head cushioned on the other and the long, strong length of him bowed in-between. His eyes were closed under the brace of his forearm, giving her the courage to look her fill without getting caught in her blatant ogling.

Oh, he was gorgeous, even sporting a huge ugly bruise on his temple and with leaves and dried grasses clinging in a reminder of how she'd laid him out on the ground.

And now she'd laid him out on her sofa.

Swallowing hard, she advanced into the room, trying not to look as if she were on her first trip to the dentist. Just the same, her molars were aching with tension. She managed a tortured smile and ordered, "Lean up a second."

When he did, she shoved the pillow under his head and broad shoulders. He settled back on them with a gut-twisting sigh.

"How's your head feeling?"

"I'll let you know when the demolition experts are done setting off this latest round of explosives."

She grimaced at his dry humor, too aware that she was the cause of his distress. "I got you a couple of painkillers."

"How about the whole bottle?" He sat up again and took the pills from her palm and washed them down with the water she supplied. Then he eased back onto the pillow with a guilt-inspiring groan.

"I'm sorry—"

"You said that already. It's okay. Really. Lucky I've got an incredibly thick skull." He risked a grin. "But then I bet you noticed that, huh?"

Mercy relaxed enough to return a wan smile. Then, it was back to business. "I've got some antiseptic and a bandage."

"Ouch!"

"I haven't done anything yet."

"Just warming up. Be warned. I'm a big baby when it comes to pain at the hands of a pretty woman."

He was smiling but his eyes were gunmetal direct. *He* was warning *her* to treat him with care. Oddly, that cagey attitude calmed her even more. If he was nervous, maybe it was all right for her to be nervous, too. And she was when she was around him, not so much because she was afraid but because she wasn't and she thought she should be.

She settled on the edge of the couch but the sagging cushions conspired to topple her closer to him, nestling her hip against the taut angle of his waist. He didn't move but his eyes were watchful. She unscrewed the antiseptic and its harsh odor filled the space around them yet couldn't quite conquer the scent of excitement and anticipation rising up between them. With a cotton ball stained an angry crimson, she dabbed at the split in his brow, wincing at the sound of him sucking air hurriedly through clenched teeth. She bent to blow on the liquid, aiming to ease the sting as it dried.

Only then was she aware of how she was leaning over him, her breasts brushing his chest, their faces tantalizing inches apart. That scant distance was suddenly charged with silence.

The color of his eyes seemed to change, going dark and smoky. Slowly, his gaze shifted down a degree to focus on her mouth. Unbidden, the tip of her tongue crept out to moisten her lips.

She knew what he was thinking. She knew what he was about to do. And all she had to do to stop him from accomplishing his goal was sit back. Yet she stayed quietly, expectantly still. Waiting for his kiss.

His hand came up slowly to fit against the curve of her jaw, coaxing but not commanding her response. She followed the guide of his palm across those separating inches to a contact that was close to cataclysmic. She could swear there was an audible sizzle. His mouth moved under the pressure of hers, intuitively tender, with an unthreatening leisure, sending signals of delight and desire zipping through her like a sensual information highway. A lifetime of panic lay unchallenged, given no reason to protest his unhurried overtures. So she let herself enjoy them, even encouraged them, hoping that this time she'd prove ready in mind and body for what her heart had already caved in to.

Her acceptance of his kiss led to other liberties, cautiously advanced and carefully allowed. His fingers combed back through her thick russet hair, once, twice, a third time until she groaned at the hedonistic luxury of being petted like a sleek cat. His other hand came up into play, beginning with an easy curve at the dip of her waist, then gliding upward to fill with the underswell of her breast. She reacted with an instant of tension so he halted his advance, letting his hand remain where it was without apology. He was still kissing her, more deeply, more demandingly, distracting conscious thought from what he was doing with his hands until all that existed were sensations. New, sparkling, irresistible feelings. Until there was no sense of uneasiness, just a slowly unfolding pleasure, lapping at the edges of her passion in warm, insistent waves.

Her first touch was tentative, a brush of fingertips along his hard jaw. The heat and roughness of a man's skin always surprised her. And his hair was soft. Drawing her hand through it was like threading silk; silk entwined with the occasional oak leaf. Then her hand stilled as awareness of what he was inspiring inside her peaked.

She wanted him.

She wanted him the way a woman wanted a man; naked and close, wooing and warm. As a lover. She had no time to feel the shock of that discovery because he was gently palming her breast, shaping it with the ply of his hand, bringing an ache of excitement to throb all the way to her toes. The stroke of his thumb over fleece and lace quickened a tight point of need; a need to feel him more personally, skin on skin.

As if reading her mind, he nudged his hand up under the band of her sweatshirt, the initial contact of his fingertips on her abdomen inciting a startled quiver of response. Instinct had her steeling her stomach muscles. Tension radiated outward, slowly reclaiming limbs gone lax with longing.

"Mercy, I won't hurt you," he whispered into the sudden hurry of her breathing.

And he might have been able to convince her of that. Lord knows, she wanted him to try. But just then, a frail, moaning cry sounded from the back bedroom.

"Mommy? Mommy!"

Mercy was up and off him in a flash, leaving a raw wake of emotions unresolved. Emotions that trembled through her as she went to check on Casey. What should have been a wash of relief was framed with a bittersweet regret. Now she would never know what concluding argument he could have come up with.

At least, not until she had Casey settled and sound asleep once more.

The hour wasn't all that late and Spencer was hers for the night.

Casey was having a nightmare and was thrashing about in a twist of covers, whimpering softly in her sleep. She jerked into a partial wakefulness when Mercy settled on the edge of the bed and flew instantly into the woman's arms.

"Mommy! I want my mommy!"

"Shh, honey. Quiet," Mercy urged, all too aware of Spencer in the other room. "I know you do, honey. I know." Mercy kissed the tousle of bright hair, hugging the trembling little body close to the ache in her own heart. "It's all right, Casey. I'm here now."

"Don't go!"

"I won't. I promise I'll sit right here with you if you'll try to go back to sleep." There was a moment of silence, then a brave sniffling. Mercy felt a nod against her shoulder and she smiled. "That's my girl." And very gently, she eased the warm, slack figure back under the covers, tucking them in around her in a secure cocoon. She was rumpling the penny-brilliant curls when the child's next words stilled her.

"I love you, Mercy."

Too choked to respond right away, Mercy swallowed a football-size lump and managed a hoarse-sounding, "I love you, too."

This was what it felt like to have family. This tight-chested, thick-throated sensation of caring. The wild devotion that would drive a woman out into the night to face down unknown danger with only a stick of firewood and a maternal rage to protect her. This was what she'd been missing in her own life. How could she bear to give it up now if things went against her bold plans? How could she risk losing this precious child and the swell of fulfillment Casey brought into her heart?

She was still young enough to have children of her own, but she'd shied away from the mechanics involved in their creation. The thought of sharing herself, trustingly, openly, with a man inside the boundaries of marriage brought more terror than temptation. She was wedging Mr. Stubbs back into the curl of Casey's arms when her glance strayed toward the hall and her thoughts leaped beyond to the man on her living room sofa. She was surprised by the whisper of amending hope. *Until Spencer Halloway.*

Having Casey with her made her think more and more of family. The child would need a secure future and a normal household to grow up in. That was the promise she'd made to the little girl. A family didn't have to mean a mother and a father. She'd seen many successful single-parent homes. She knew she had enough love inside her to fill both slots. Casey would feel safe and lack for nothing. But what of her own needs? A child's love was not a man's love.

There was a sudden void in her that Casey couldn't fill. Spencer made her look beyond that determined vow for Casey, to wish for someone she could love who would love her in return. Somehow, the inquisitive sheriff with his lazy grin and provoking stare, had managed to broach the best of her barriers. He'd made a place for himself in their lives. He'd carved out a niche for himself within her mind. He made her question her fears and consider what it might mean to share all that she was with another, flaws and all. Wasn't love supposed to overlook past blemishes?

But hers were more than slight imperfections. Hers were huge, insurmountable scars. How could she expect any man, even a man like Spencer, to forgive and forget a past like her own, especially when she couldn't seem to put it behind her?

Casey had drifted back into the undisturbed slumber of youth, leaving Mercy free to return to the unfinished business in the other room. Now that the heat of the moment had cooled, her reservations rose up to present a formidable problem. She'd let Spencer believe she was prepared to see their passions through to their conclusion. But was she? Did an invitation to spend the night under circumstances such as these automatically imply a shared bed? No, but perhaps her eagerness to accept his kisses had. She stood in the darkened doorway, fretting over how to proceed.

Did she waltz back in pretending nothing had flared between them? Would he expect her to sink right back into his arms and onto his lips without a moment of hesitation? A tremor of indecision possessed her. What did she truly want? To let this opportunity pass, her chance to know, to really know, what it could be like with a man as sensitive and relentlessly sexy as Spencer? A man who seemed to have sealed the psychological wall holding all others at bay? What if she couldn't let go again? What if she froze up at his touch in a knot of unresolved terror? How could she explain in a way that he would understand? In a way that wouldn't compromise a truth she couldn't tell? She didn't have that much faith in anyone except Amy. Amy who had known her and befriended her when she was still a fragile shell, who'd helped to draw her back into the world of the living. Or at least, up to its periphery where she could watch if not partake.

But talking to Amy was different. Amy was a woman. Because of her gender, there was an implicit empathy. Because of her profession, Mercy's story didn't shock her. It outraged her. She was taking no risks in divulging all. But with Spencer, she hadn't the slightest shred of security. He was a man. He was a *law*man. She had no way of guessing what he would see through that contrasting point of view. She was deathly afraid to find out.

Coffee. She would walk in casually and put a pot on to boil. Maybe that would give other things a chance to simmer and steep. Perhaps something natural, something wonderful would evolve from that point on. But she would never know until she forced two leadened feet to move forward, one reluctant step at a time.

It was quiet, so quiet she could hear the ragged sound of her own breathing. Spencer had taken off his leather coat. It was draped over the back of the couch and he was nowhere in sight. She approached with caution, seeing his grass-stained running shoes standing negligently at the corner of the sofa with white athletic socks puddled inside them.

What else had he discarded in her absence?

A purely wicked speculation got a hold of her then. She was imagining with a mouth-drying clarity, that expanse of furred midriff rising up to an exquisitely proportioned chest. He would be tanned and toned and...so very, very male. Her palms itched in anticipation of that tough and tempting terrain.

She took a bracing breath and rounded the couch. Glancing down, she realized a plummeting disappointment.

Spencer Halloway was not lounging back on her cushions, chafing for the chance to get her back in his arms.

He was sound asleep.

"Mercy?"

The piercing whisper cut through her determined slumber. Blinking groggily, she looked up into Casey's perplexed features. "What is it, pumpkin?"

"Did you know Sheriff Halloway is on our couch?"

Now she was wide-awake. She'd curled up under her covers what seemed like only minutes ago, never expecting to fall asleep, and here it was morning. And she had their overnight guest to explain away to a very curious child. She did the first thing that came to mind.

She stalled.

"Shh. Be very quiet. Don't wake him up."

"I don't know how he could hear me over all his snoring." She giggled, then was serious once more. Mercy read no avoiding the issue upon the somber frown lines puckering Casey's sunburned brow. "He's got an awful big bump on his head. What's he doing here?" And she plopped down on the edge of the mattress with no intention of moving until she heard the entire truth.

"The sheriff thought he saw a stranger outside the cabin and came over to make sure we were all right. I heard him moving around in the dark and thought he was a prowler. I—I sort of hit him with a piece of firewood."

"You did? Wow!" Dark eyes rounded with admiration. Mercy got the feeling that she'd just taken a giant leap upward in the child's estimation.

"He wasn't feeling very good and was worried about leaving us alone so I let him sleep on the couch."

The connotations of a man staying overnight zipped right over six-year-old Casey's head. But no such luck when it came to the possible prowler. Her puckish face pinched up with uncertainty. "Was there someone sneaking around outside?"

"I don't know," Mercy answered truthfully, wishing she could do otherwise. "Spencer couldn't find any signs of anyone in the dark last night. Maybe he can round up some clues this morning."

"Was it them?" That came out in a hushed whisper of dread.

"Spencer thinks it was probably kids looking to get into trouble."

But Casey's fears weren't so easily stilled. Her freckles stood out starkly against milk-pale skin. "You won't let them take me back, will you?"

The quiver in her tone set Mercy's determination in stone. "No, sweetheart, I won't. C'mere."

She opened her arms and Casey was quick to fill them. The rightness of the two of them together overwhelmed all else. They belonged to each other; family. And no one was going to separate them. Not the law, not the courts, not the faceless phantom creeping about their cabin in the dark. She would make certain of it in August, but until then, she had to be more careful than ever.

Last night's fright inspired a whole new level of danger. Now was the time to dig in deep and wait it out. She couldn't afford to be found before Amy got back and helped her put things to right.

And that meant keeping one very noisy sheriff from discovering anything potentially harmful.

He smelled coffee and bacon. The aroma tickled under his nose like a seductive perfume, waking his olfactory nerves to the promise of breakfast.

Who was making him breakfast?

Spencer gave a restless toss from stomach to back, meaning to discover his whereabouts, then lost all sense of place as he misjudged the width of his sleeping quarters. Sliding, shouting with surprise, he found himself deposited abruptly upon his back pockets on unyielding linoleum.

"Good morning."

There was no mistaking the hint of amusement in Mercy's voice.

It took only an instant for everything to rush back then; the whens, the wheres, and the whys...a little too late to keep his dignity from bruising. This was not exactly the impression he'd hoped to make on his first overnight at Mercy Royce's. Not waking up alone, on the couch. Or rather, on the floor.

What had happened? He had the distinct recall of her feasting off his kisses on this very couch. Then...Casey had cried out in her sleep and Mercy had gone in to check on her. While he waited for her return, he'd made himself more comfortable on the couch. He'd leaned back into the cushions, his mind a sensual swirl of possibilities, his eyes closing to capture them in graphic three-dimensional imagination and... He'd fallen asleep.

Was there no end to this humiliation?

He'd worked so diligently to impress the cool Ms. Royce with his charm and his vitality. To get so far, then to lose it all to a snoring oblivion. Life was cruel. But she was making him breakfast.

"How do you like your eggs?"

"Definitely not sunny-side up this morning," he grumbled, dragging himself back onto the saggy cushions to scrub the sleep off his face with his palms. The brusque movement aggravated the soft calypso beat between his ears into a full-scale symphonic percussion section. His ravaged moan won a far-from-gratifying concern.

"How's your head? I was beginning to think you'd lapsed into a concussion coma. Except that you were snoring too loud."

Terrific. What a great first impression to make upon a lady; that his sinuses were more active than his libido. "You would have done well to let me expire in peace."

She gave a soft chuckle and he began to hope all wasn't lost.

"Hi, Spencer."

"Hey, kiddo."

Casey's bouncing on the cushion beside him had him gritting his teeth but he smiled through it. There was something about waking to the smell of breakfast cooking, to the sight of a beautiful woman and the animation of a child. Maybe Mercy had hit him harder than he'd thought. Or maybe he was just a little bit covetous of the glimpse of life he was getting. Even a hardened bachelor could get sentimental over a good hot meal he didn't have to scrounge from the cupboards himself.

"Boy, you sure do snore. You had the windows rattling."

Spencer grimaced. So much for a romantic view of family life.

"That's some knot on your head," Casey went on enthusiastically. "You must have gotten whooped a good one."

"A home run in any ballpark."

"Can I help you look around outside for clues?"

"Casey." Mercy's tone was deep with warning. "Let Spencer alone until after he has his breakfast. You do want breakfast, don't you?'' She suddenly sounded flustered. "Or were you planning to jog first?"

"A man doesn't jog to the beat of the *1812* Overture. Right now, a nice, quiet, nonmoving breakfast sounds great."

He glanced over to catch Mercy watching him from the breakfast bar. She quickly averted her eyes but not before he saw a glimmer of something subtle in her gaze. Longing. Could it be he wasn't the only one with a soft spot for shared breakfasts? That idea gave him enough encouragement to risk the misery of hauling himself to the table. She met him there with a cup of black coffee. The gesture seemed so routine, so natural and intimate, they were both startled into silence. Again, their gazes mingled until Mercy grew uncomfortable and turned back to the stove.

"Everything's almost ready. Hope you're good and hungry." Her spatula paused in midair.

"Starved," came his husky reply.

She began shoveling food onto his plate with a burst of restless energy.

She had just settled down to enjoy the bounty she'd prepared after bringing Casey juice and Spencer catsup for his eggs.

"So what do you want to do about last night?"

Her fork hung in midair. Her gaze darted up as fast as the color in her cheeks. "Wh-what?"

He smiled lazily at her misunderstanding and was none too quick to clarify it. "About the prowler."

"Oh." The forkful of hash browns disappeared, followed in rapid, conversation-staving succession by several more. Spencer wondered if she meant to clean her plate before answering, so he gave a gentle prompt.

"You could ride into the station with me this morning and fill out a full report. That'd get things in motion."

"What things?" He was not imagining her apprehension.

"An investigation. Strictly routine in these matters. But unless we can get a hold of some real physical evidence or an eyewitness, there's not much chance of coming up with a suspect.

"Then it seems kind of silly to go to all the trouble of filing a report. I mean, why waste the manhours when there's nothing you can do, anyway? You said yourself it was probably just kids."

"Probably. But not positively."

Mercy was very pale and her silverware clattered with agitation as she continued to eat with all the enthusiasm of someone stuffing in sawdust. "What else could it be? I certainly don't have anything worth stealing. Not even a TV set."

Spencer didn't answer her. If she didn't know what she possessed of immeasurable value, he didn't want to frighten her by bringing it up. A good-looking woman like her living alone on a lake with a little girl. No phone. No close neighbors. The possibilities had his stomach in square knots. He put down his fork, finding he no longer had an appetite for her home-cooked meal.

But she had one hell of a line-drive swing.

"It's a good idea to have something on record. In case other incidents start occurring around the lake. If it's a Peeping Tom, someone's bound to spot him, then we can link together a solid history of criminal behavior." He made it sound reasonable, like the right thing to do. But still Mercy hedged. And he had to wonder why.

"I'd rather not get involved. Chances are, we'll be gone before you have any more trouble. I'm out of time off at work and couldn't afford to come back up here to testify about something I didn't see. The only person I can identify is you. So, unless you're the Peeping Tom, I'd just as soon forget anything happened."

Her words made sense but her reactions didn't. She was buttering her toast like she was leveling cement, with firm, hard strokes and far too much intensity.

She wasn't worried about troublesome kids or aberrant window-peekers. So then what did that leave? Who was she afraid was prowling around her cabin? And why?

He couldn't force her to file a report. The added paperwork was never encouraged by his small office staff. Lots of people didn't want to get involved. This wasn't her property, after all. That didn't make them suspicious people, it just made them indifferent citizens. But it wasn't her reasonings that chafed him, it was her downright refusal to do so. Was it because she was leery of filling out one of the forms, of giving answers to pertinent questions like where she lived and what she did for a living? And who she was if not Mercy Royce?

If she didn't want to file a report, he should have let it go at that. He'd done all that was required of him by suggesting it. Speeders and weekend drunks were the worst he wanted to involve himself with. He'd come to Pine Creek to avoid tensions and complications that could get sticky—and get him hurt. And this one had the feel of something very sticky. She was afraid, yet unwilling to do anything to gain protection.

In his book, that meant only one thing: that the secret she was protecting was worse than the threat she was ignoring.

It was time for him to face the very real possibility that she was involved in something contrary to the law. And that made her his problem with a capital *P* whether he wanted it to be or not.

And the hard part was in finding a way to pursue the professional without ruining his chances with the personal.

Chapter 9

Chet Allen jerked awake behind the wheel of his old Bonneville sedan and straightened with a yawn. A quick glance around told him that all was quiet on the lakefront. Mercy Royce's cabin was dark and as still as a weekday-morning church. He glanced at the lighted dial of his watch. Five. Time to pull the plug on this exciting stakeout detail. He gave a wry smile as he turned over the ignition and backed his big bomb of a car out onto the lake road.

So much for Spencer's suspicions.

With his oldies rock station pulsing against the window glass, Chet ignored the speed limit on his way into town. He was chilled to the socks and irritated by the dead-end assignment. Not so much as a ground squirrel had stirred all night long.

Prowler? He snorted.

Sure, he could use the extra overtime, but the next time Spencer Halloway wanted to know who was sneaking over to his girlfriend's house for a little after-hours hanky-panky, he could freeze his own butt off spying on her.

His mood hadn't improved by the time he shoved his way into the quiet, night-shift station house. His response to Judy's cheerful good-morning was a guttural growl on his way to the coffee pot.

"Spence checked in yet?"

"Not yet. How did it go out at the Cheswicks'?"

"Not a creature was stirring. Waste of time. Can't see what the sheriff's interest is in this one. A single sighting of someone walking around at night is hardly cause for a commotion. Waste of time and money, if you ask me. But then no one asked me." He dumped three packs of sweetener into his coffee with a heaping scoop of creamer for a chaser and gave it a vigorous stirring. After a sip, he added another pack.

"The sheriff has his reasons," Judy corrected with a cool clip of loyalty, turning to ignore him.

Chet lingered to put in a purposeful dig. "Yeah? Like that Royce woman looking pretty hot in short shorts?"

Judy sniffed. "I won't dignify that with an answer, Chet Allen." She shoved a sheet of paper into her typewriter and began hammering away, angry at the idea of Spencer ogling another woman. Chet stayed by her desk, his expression suddenly pensive, his coffee stirrer making slow, thoughtful circles.

"What reasons?"

Judy spared him a haughty glance, then continued with her pounding.

"Come on, Judy. What's the deal with her? If it's official business, I've got a right to know what it is."

Judy leaned on her typewriter to confide the baffling replies to May's identity trace. There was no Mercy Royce—at least, officially.

"So what does Spence think? He got any theories on why she's hiding out under an assumed name?"

"He's following up on a couple of things himself, strictly off the record," Judy answered.

"What kind of things?" Chet posed that casually but inside, his mind was whirling. If something was going on and

Spencer wasn't seeing to it as duty demanded because of a personal involvement with the woman in the Cheswicks' cabin, Chet could well be sporting that sheriff's badge himself sooner than anticipated.

Judy's gaze sharpened with suspicion. "You can ask him yourself."

Chet shrugged as if it really didn't matter. "Maybe I will, maybe I won't. Don't think it's going to amount to anything anyway."

"I wouldn't be too sure."

"Why do you say that?" He didn't dare look up from his cup. He could feel a fever-bright flush of excitement heat his face and if Judy guessed at his interest, she would clam up tight. He'd made the mistake of coming on to her too strong when she'd started working in the office, and she'd been prickly around him ever since. She'd set her sights higher. Like behind the sheriff's badge.

"Are you seeing Spencer this morning?" Her words were almost a coo. Chet wanted to gag.

"Was supposed to have breakfast with him. Why?"

Judy hesitated, then pulled a telex sheet out of her In basket and studied it. "The sheriff asked me to keep an eye open for anything coming across the wire that might even vaguely connect to the Royce woman and her little girl."

"And?" Chet's eyes fixed on the paper she was studying until he was close to salivating with impatience.

"And this came in last night. I don't know if it's anything important. It might be nothing, but—"

Chet snatched it deftly from Judy's fingers. "Well, then, Spence won't mind me looking at it." He read the message and held to an impartial expression. His heart started pounding like a jackhammer and sweat broke on his brow. It took him a minute to control his breathing so his voice would give nothing away. "Could mean something or nothing." He was folding the sheet into a pocket-size square. "I'll pass it on to Spence and see if it's anything he thinks we should act on."

Judy looked ready to protest his high-handedness when the phone buzzed on her desk. "Pine Creek Sheriff's Department." Her shoulders shot back a notch. "Oh, hi, Sheriff Halloway. He's right here, Sheriff. Chet, Spencer wants to talk to you."

"I'll take it in his office," he rumbled, hurrying in that direction. "There's something in there I need to read off for him."

"Line two."

"Thanks."

Chet slid into the glass-partitioned room and snatched up the receiver before Judy could do any more gabbing. "I got it, Judy. You can hang up now." He waited for the click, then began, "Hey, Sheriff. What can I do for you?" He listened for a moment, then said truthfully, "Nothing in the least bit suspicious. Even the crickets were drifting off. Anything else you want me to follow up on? Okay. No, nothing's new here so you might as well take your time getting in. Okay, I'll tell her. Will do. See you later."

He let the receiver settle and risked a sly smile before going out into the main reception area. His voice shifted into a cool drawl, his posture subconsciously mimicking the sheriff's. "Judy, Spence is taking the morning off. Said he'd be in about one if May needs him for anything."

"What did he think about the telex?"

Chet waved a dismissing hand. "I read it to him, and he seems to think it's nothing," he lied. "Guess he'd be a better judge of that than you and me, wouldn't he?"

Judy agreed that was so. She never thought Spencer was wrong about anything. Stupid girl.

"Well," Chet went on casually, "I'm going to run home and grab a couple of hours of sleep, a shower and a change of clothes. If anything comes up that you can't handle, just ring me there."

But Judy was already distracted by the ringing on another line and Chet was able to duck out without offering any other explanations.

Out in the parking lot, he drew the single page from his pocket and gave it a scrutinizing look through cold, scheming eyes. It was the description of a missing child, a possible runaway. A child by the name of Cassandra Pomeroy.

And the description fit the Royce girl right down to the last freckle.

Spencer hung up the phone and allowed himself a moment of frustration. He was spinning his wheels. Mercy's comment the other morning had made an impression upon him; one about as deep as the Grand Canyon. The summer was almost half over and when it was gone, Mercy would be, too.

He'd asked Chet to keep an eye on the cabin, afraid that Mercy would recognize his own four-wheel drive and get all bent out of shape about him being overly protective. So much for his hope that whoever was sneaking around the night before would come back for another shot at whatever he'd missed. Spencer wasn't sure he could justify asking Chet to pull another shift, not without a report on file. And Mercy had made that very clear—no report. So that left him in the uncomfortable position of trying to help her when she was determined to push him away. It was irrational, unprofessional behavior on his part, but he'd resigned himself to it. Mercy upset the balance between head and heart. He'd given up trying to make any sense of it. All he knew was there was precious little time to get to the bottom of the mystery surrounding her.

It was more than his attraction to her. He'd made himself responsible, like it or not, for her and Casey the minute he'd pulled over on that rain-slicked shoulder. His insides congealed into an aching mass of anger and fear when he thought of someone deliberately stalking them.

He'd followed the footprints around their cabin. They weren't made by any mischievous kids. Whoever had an interest in the redheaded pair was very methodical and very professional.

Their so-called prowler had watched them long enough to go through three cigarettes while waiting out of sight in a stand of trees. The idea of someone patiently biding his time, spying upon woman and child without their knowledge, had him clenching his teeth. Then, when this stranger was certain that the coast was clear, he'd circled the cabin, pausing at every window. Just trying to look in or trying to find a way in? Spencer went nearly crazy over that one.

Gut instinct demanded that he shove aside Mercy's prudish reservations and set up camp in her living room. They were in possible danger and there was damned little he could do about it a world away on the other side of the cove. But unfortunately, the self-sufficient Ms. Royce wasn't about to let him take up housekeeping. She was batting a thousand in the self-preservation department and he had the throbbing head to prove it. He hadn't wanted to scare her out of that smug security with the facts he collected outside her house. Maybe he should have, just to shake her out of her complacency. She needed to know who her enemy was, and he got the feeling that she, mistakenly, was more afraid of him being on the inside than of the prowler creeping around outside.

Because he was a sheriff or because he was a man? He'd picked up on an unnatural fear of both things from her. The lawman in him wanted to protect her. The man in him wanted her. And she was making it impossible to achieve either goal. He was the right man for both jobs—the hard part was making her believe it, too.

There was something out there that scared her enough to send her into hiding under an assumed name with a child who was not her own. There was something inside her, too, that frightened her just as badly. He'd tasted her terror in their first kiss, he'd seen it swimming through dark waters of desperation in her glassy stare. And it was hard for him to know that she categorized him with both those fears; as a danger and a threat. If she would let him, if she would trust him, he could show her how wrong she was about him. He knew she was interested. That sharp tingle of sexual awareness went both ways. If he could get beyond the barriers she threw up every time he invaded her personal space, he could move her to feel the same fierce sense of longing that chafed him through his days and made his nights a restless misery.

He could make her forget everything she'd been through and every bad thing that had been done to her. He could make her soft pale skin flush hot with yearning, could make her burn with impatience and soar with satisfaction. For a moment, he was lost to the imagining—the spill of her pouty breasts in his palms, the silken stroke of her legs moving next to his, the ragged caution in her eyes melting beneath a blaze of passion. He could do those things for her. And in doing so, would relieve some of his own demons, too. Mercy Royce made him want to trust again; made him think about picking up the ties of commitment to see if he could make a knot that would hold forever, this time around.

But she had to want him to.

Spencer wandered out onto the porch to stare across the glassy waters of the cove. He couldn't force her to trust him. He had to earn that, and the lady was not making it easy. If he could find some way to put her external fears to rest, that would be the cornerstone of his campaign upon her heart. Mercy wasn't going to give a damned thing away. She'd huddle up inside that little cabin and let her worries devour her alive before she'd speak a word to ask for aid. He knew it as surely as he knew his own middle name.

What he didn't know was why.

So, if she wasn't going to crack and spill her secrets, where else could he go to learn them?

And it was then, as if in answer, he saw a flame-topped moppet bounding down toward the beach with bucket in hand.

Taking advantage of a child was a loathsome ploy. Something a worm would do. Someone lower than a worm.

Or someone desperate to get close enough to do some good.

"Hi, Spencer!"

How was he ever going to get over the way his chest seized up at her exuberant cry of welcome?

"Hey yourself, kiddo. Any luck this morning?"

"See for yourself." Casey extended her bucket proudly and Spencer dutifully examined the collection of wet rocks lining the bottom.

"You've got some real beauties there." He grinned up at her. "Almost as pretty as you and your mom."

Casey's smile of pleasure faltered slightly. She wasn't as good at role-playing as Mercy. He could see she was uncomfortable with the lie, but she was a smart kid; the best way to get out of telling lies was to change the subject.

"How's your head?"

"Booming about as loud as the fireworks they'll be shooting off over the lake in a couple of days to celebrate the Fourth of July. Your mom sure has a mean swing."

Again, the subtle downward cant of her eyes.

"Think you might like to watch the fireworks from my boat? That way the trees don't get in the way."

Casey's features lit like a sparkler, then immediately dimmed. Spencer knew the reason without asking.

"Of course, we'd have to ask your mom first. Do you think it would be all right with her?"

A shy hopeful smile. "I could ask."

"You do that and let me know. Maybe we could have our cookout then, too. Hot dogs and fireworks. Holidays don't get any better than that."

And Casey was nodding in full agreement.

"You haven't seen any other strangers creeping around since the other night; have you? Or heard any noises you couldn't identify?"

Casey shook her head. "I'm sure your deputy would have scared him off."

"My—"

"He had his car parked off the side of the road all night." Her tone lowered conspiratorially. "I don't think we were supposed to see him."

Spencer nearly groaned aloud. So much for being clever. He'd have to take some time out to teach Chet the fine points of stealth.

"Mer—Mom acted real mad about it at first but I think she was glad he was watching out for us. I know I slept better knowing he was there."

With that result, maybe it was better that Chet had bungled the undercover work. He hated to think of the two of them crouched in their beds, fearful of every sound. It was time to take a stronger stance.

"Casey, you know I'd never let anything happen to hurt you or Mercy, don't you? You know you can come to me for any reason."

She nodded without hesitation. "You came to the rescue when I couldn't breathe." And her eyes glimmered with hero worship.

"And I'd come to the rescue anytime you needed me. For anything. You and Mercy mean a lot to me."

Her gaze lowered shyly. "We like you, too."

Spencer smiled slightly, wondering about that "We." "I could keep you a lot safer if I knew what was wrong."

Her eyes darted up, round as shiny pebbles. "Nothing's wrong."

Then why was her tiny voice quivering like a hummingbird's wing?

"Casey, I know Mercy told you not to trust strangers. She's right in doing that because she loves you and wants to keep you safe. I'm not a stranger anymore. Do you think I'd try to hurt you?"

She smiled at that. "No, of course not, silly." She bumped her pail into his kneecaps playfully. "You're our friend."

"And friends help each other when they're in trouble, don't they? I'd like to help you, Casey. Mercy's done a great job of keeping you safe but there are some things she can't handle by herself, as much as she'd like to think she can."

"Like the man peeking in our windows."

"Yeah, like that man. Do you know who he is, Casey?"

She shook her head somberly. He didn't think she was lying this time because she was looking him right in the eye without so much as a flicker. So much for that idea. On to the next one.

"Do you know what he wants?"

That fidgety nervousness of guilt was back. She wouldn't meet his eyes. Her fingers knotted together in a tangled pattern. "No." It was a quiet whisper.

"Is he going to try to hurt you?"

She swallowed hard. "I don't think so."

"I can't do anything to protect you unless I know the truth."

Her lips thinned into a surprisingly stubborn line. The resemblance to Mercy intensified with her mounting mistrust.

"Casey, you said I was your friend."

She wouldn't be baited by that. She crossed her arms over her spindly chest and stayed mute.

"I want to help. Talk to me."

"I can't."

"Why, honey? Can you tell me why?"

She shook her head. The sudden glimmer of anxious tears gave his conscience a brutal wringing but there was more at stake than this moment of hurtful confrontation. Much more if he read his instincts right. No six-year-old was going to be this close-lipped about any secrets unless the situation was dire. Unless the consequences had been drummed into her. He couldn't see Mercy purposely terrorizing a child unless the reason behind it was more than monumental.

What the hell were they hiding?

"Are you mad at me, Spencer?"

He erased the pensive scowl from his face that so alarmed her and smiled tightly. "No, of course I'm not."

"Are you still going to be my friend?"

"You bet. We still have a lot of fishing holes we haven't tried. And don't forget our date to watch the fireworks."

She took a grateful little breath and he felt like the worst kind of dog for baiting for her trust, then misusing it.

"Casey, where are your mother and father?"

"Wh-what?"

"I know Mercy isn't your mom, that it's all been pretend." He let that sink in for a fragile moment before adding softly, "And I know how much she loves you and you love her. I don't want to make any trouble for you. All I want to do is help you."

Big glittering crystals wobbled on the pale fringe of her lower lashes. Her thin little chest was heaving almost as if the terrible asthma attack had returned to torment her. "I can't tell you." It was a raw sob of anguish, pleading with him to let it go.

But he couldn't.

"Casey, why aren't you with your parents?"

"They're gone."

"Gone where? Like on a vacation?" he prompted gently, sitting down on the dock so they were at eye level and taking up one of her suddenly cold hands in his for a warm chafing.

"Gone to Heaven."

The shell around his heart cracked wide open. He didn't know what to say, how to express the awful feelings of regret and shame welling up inside him. So he said nothing and merely opened his arms to her. She filled them in an instant and was clinging, crying softly within the secure wrap of his embrace.

She'd lost her parents. He couldn't imagine a more horrible pain or anyone being low enough to force that kind of grief upon a child again. It explained some of what he'd wondered. But not all. Not the big things.

So after her sobs had worn down to weary sniffles, Spencer held her away and supplied a large linen square. She blew her nose with loud gusto.

"I miss them," she mumbled thickly, lifting red-rimmed eyes in a plea for his understanding.

"I know, kiddo. I lost both my parents, too. It's a hard thing to get over, but someday the hurt of it will go away and the remembering will put a warm spot in your heart, just like they're inside with you, living there always.''

"Really?"

"Yeah, really."

Her smile was soul-piercingly brave. The wanting to believe blossomed in her eyes after the generous watering of her tears. Then the all-too-adult look of distress was pinching at her features.

"Am I in trouble, Spencer?"

"Why would you be in trouble, sweetheart?"

She glanced around nervously and confided, "Mercy told me not to tell anyone that she wasn't my mom. She said there'd be trouble."

Spencer cupped her heated cheek in his palm. "I'm not going to let that happen, sweetheart."

"You won't tell her I told you?"

"Not if you don't want me to. But you know what? It would be a lot easier for all of us if we didn't have to pretend anything anymore. Mercy's taken real good care of you but she's afraid of something. If I knew what that something was, if you could tell me about it, I can make that fear go away."

"You can?"

"I sure can. We both can if we work together. Because we both love her, and we don't like to see her so unhappy all the time." It was surprisingly easy for him to speak of love, not because it was a lie but because it was the truth. Children understood truth a lot better than most adults gave them credit for. That simple admission made him a powerful ally in Casey's mind, and that was exactly the break Spencer had been hoping for.

She looked up at him as if he were a superhero from one of her cartoons. "You can keep that man from coming back?"

"I think I probably could if I knew what he was after. Do you know what that is, sweetheart?"

Brought back to that again, Casey hesitated, clearly struggling between her newfound trust in Spencer and her love for Mercy.

"Let me help you, Casey."

His gentle coaxing, combined with the heroic image she carried of him, was just too much. She exhaled sharply and confessed, "I think he's come to take me back."

"Back where?"

Just then, Casey's gaze lifted to a spot beyond his shoulder and her features tensed and trembled. Spencer followed her stare and saw Mercy bearing down upon them. She was close enough to have heard their last exchange.

And she was furious.

Chapter 10

"Casey, go on inside."

Mercy's voice cracked like brittle ice over a February puddle. She angled up between the anguished child and the threat of Spencer Halloway, becoming a human barrier.

Casey hesitated in the face of her tirade, then looked up at Spencer, her gaze full of regret and a hint of reproach. "You said she wouldn't be mad."

Spencer leaned back, bracing himself on his palms in his most nonchalant manner. Busted. "She's not, sweetie. Not at you. Go on up like a good girl."

Casey lingered, looking between the two of them, her expression growing dark with confusion as she picked up on their complex adult signals. She was clearly reluctant to leave Spencer to a seething Mercy.

"Casey, go now!"

Casey flinched at the unfamiliar snap of the command. With a soft cry, she bolted up the slight slope, coltish legs carrying her in an awkward dash while her bucket swung wildly in her hand. Spencer could tell by the way her shoulders were hitching that she was crying again. He hadn't thought he could feel any worse. Surprise. He would stand on his head for the upset little girl to make amends for this later, but right now, there was other, much more serious business at hand.

And that hand was whipping toward his face at lightning speed.

"You son of a—!"

Spencer caught her wrist, intercepting it scant inches from his cheek. Mercy's whole arm was shaking with a violence that seemed to both shock and gratify her. Spencer got the feeling that she was striking back at something much bigger than him and his heavy handling of a child's emotions. And he wished at the same time, that he'd let her make contact. Maybe the feel of a good sting of retribution upon her palm would flush out some of the repressed tension eating through her.

And maybe it would make him feel better about what he'd done.

"Mercy—"

"Of all the low-down, sneaky, dirty things— How could you?"

Opting for the best defense being a good offense, he said calmly, "You wouldn't tell me what I needed to know." As if that excused him.

"You? You don't need to know anything! We are none of your business. Do you hear me?"

Half the lake probably heard her. But she wasn't through. A volcano didn't simmer for as long as this one had without spewing some incredibly forceful steam.

"I don't know who you are to think you can just come poking around in what doesn't concern you. I tried to be polite. I tried to be not-so-polite. But you just wouldn't listen. Leave us alone! We don't need your help, Sheriff Halloway. And we don't want you making things worse."

"What could be worse than teaching a little girl how to lie, or to live hiding out like criminals and jumping at every shadow?"

Mercy huffed for a moment, unable to grab on to an answer, then furious because she had none. She knew he was right but she was so—so angry! At him for his relentless interference. At the situation for being so unfair. At life and fate for being so cruel, not once but twice. And all that anger she'd held to for the better part of her life came spilling forth in a dramatic eruption.

"We're doing just fine! At least we were until you came around with all your questions, raking up the past, getting Casey all upset, pushing your way in where you're not wanted. Who asked you, Spencer Halloway?"

He could reasonably have pointed out that she had on several occasions; with her signal lights flashing for aid, with her midnight knock on his door while Casey wheezed in the car, when she made up the couch for him and laid out breakfast the next morning. She had asked him in lots of little ways but never in the one he wanted—the way that would invite him inside where the real trouble lay; where the shadows lay dark and desperate and were even now growing in her haunted eyes. That frantic look compelled him to push just a little bit harder, when a decent man, a kinder man would have backed off. Maybe he wasn't all that decent or as nice a guy as he told her he was. But damn it, he was tired of her excluding secrets!

She wasn't finished, not by a long shot.

"I'm doing fine on my own, Sheriff. Or is that a crime? If you've got some reason to be snooping around, intimidating a little girl, let's hear it. Otherwise, I want you out of here right now, and I don't want you coming back."

She suddenly realized that he was still holding on to her wrist and they began a tug-of-war when he refused to release her. She was panting hard, flushed with emotion, not all of it remotely close to anger. The glacial sheen in her eyes was slowly dissolving before the heat of that desperate glimmer.

"Let me go." It was part demand, part beseechment. And Spencer knew the difference between a woman who said she wasn't interested and one who was just plain scared. This one was scared.

"There are three things I want to say and I want you to listen. Can you give me the benefit of that much?"

"It depends on what they are." She was breathing hard, not about to give an inch as her eyes narrowed suspiciously.

"First, you're right about me having no official cause to bother you. You've done nothing wrong that I'm aware of unless you consider lying a federal offense."

She took a big breath and he held up his hand so he could continue to speak his piece uninterrupted.

"Second, I didn't intimidate Casey. We were talking, like friends talk. Friends who trust each other. You might want to try that some time, Ms. Royce. And thirdly, you are very much my business, whether you like it or not."

She went still in his grasp, her gaze wary and oddly vulnerable, an explosive combination. "What makes you think that?" Her voice contained a heart-tugging tremor, as if she couldn't bear to think that was true.

"Because I care about you and Casey. Because I worry about you hiding over here behind all your secrets while who knows what is out there looking for you. Because you're in some kind of trouble and won't admit that you need help. I can help you, Mercy, if you'll let me."

"No."

That wounded cry escaped her in a close cousin to a sob, then she was again trying desperately to slip from his hold.

Spencer was frustrated by her rebellion, but trying to hold on to her called for an application of superior strength he was reluctant to use on a woman. Especially one as skittish as Mercy Royce. She wasn't a suspect. She wasn't guilty of anything that he knew of. Except of not wanting him as badly as he wanted her. And while that was demoralizing, it was hardly criminal. If he let her go now, she'd run and he'd have no excuse to go after her. She wouldn't give him one. So, if he couldn't let her go and he couldn't manage her by force, he would have to find another means of restraining her.

Mercy wasn't prepared for the sudden tug on her wrist that brought her tumbling into the hard wall of Spencer's body. His free arm was instantly molded to the curve of her waist, yanking her up between the spraddle of his legs and tight against him. She could feel the hard swell of his thighs and the bite of his belt buckle. That oval of metal would probably leave an indelible design imprinted upon her belly. The other things instantly acting upon her senses were the dusky male scent of him and the red-blooded heat of him. Both switched on a clawing panic of self-defense from within.

A wild, moaning sound tore up from her throat but he swallowed it down with the crush of his mouth. The sense of being confined, overwhelmed, had her fighting even as the softening of her lips recognized a battle lost.

He was a great kisser.

He'd kissed her before but both those times, he'd been a gentleman. Not now. This time, he was that dangerous man she'd known lurked beneath the laziness. It was a hot, wild, open kiss. His tongue dove in without a cautious test of the waters and began doing strong, rhythmic laps inside the wet well of her mouth. Those hard, compelling strokes continued until her head spun.

If she was determined to walk away from him, he seemed just as determined to leave her with a stunning memory of how good they might have been together.

Her hands flew up to push him away, only someone had forgotten to tell her fingers not to clutch at his shirt and hang on for the sweet rough thrill of her life. He took her on a breathless E-ticket ride, racing up to incredible heights, then free-falling into the next upward swell. She'd never experienced anything like it. She was frightened but at the same time was sucked in by the pull of momentum. Her heart was knocking like the clickety-clack of a roller-coaster car racing along the dangerous twists and turns of the rail. Out of control.

Then he was moving her, hitching her up even closer, making her ride the surging labor of his chest, fitting her intimately to the jut of his arousal. And somewhere deep inside her, an anxious beat of resistance strengthened, growing louder, faster, bigger until its pounding overwhelmed the pleasure. Until she tore her mouth away to gasp, "No, please!"

Spencer released her this time and Mercy lunged backward, tripping, nearly falling in her frantic scramble for space and breath and saving sanity. She was trembling, gulping, her jaw quivering. She made a sound, a soft bleating sound like that of a wounded animal when hurt and dazed and desperate to escape pain. And Spencer was so shaken by it, he couldn't react. This was no coy protest, no angry refusal. It was a gut-deep, soul-dark cry of fear and it echoed through him until his every sense was shivering.

Good God! What had happened to her?

Her eyes held a fever-bright glaze, seeing him and more than just him. That spooky stare scared him plenty.

"Mercy—"

"Leave us alone. Please! Just leave us alone!"

And there was nothing he could do to halt her mad rush toward the safety of the cabin. Nothing but regret his impulsive actions.

The tears didn't start until she'd closed the door and leaned back upon it. Then they were a flood, pouring from a broken dam of emotion no amount of will could repair. Mercy sagged against that door, that symbolic barrier between herself and all she wanted, all she feared. And she sobbed until her chest hurt, until she became aware of Casey's bright, frightened stare. It was care for Casey that brought her back from the edge of complete collapse.

"What did you tell him, Casey?" Her tone was uncustomarily gruff from the tears and the rasp of fear. Casey's sensitive soul was aquiver.

"Nothing. I didn't tell him anything." Then she hesitated and on second thought, spilled it all. "Well, just that my parents were dead."

"What?"

"He already knew you weren't my mommy. I couldn't keep lying to him, Mercy. I couldn't."

Mercy catapulted away from the door to race into the bedroom. Casey followed, alarmed by her frantic actions. She stood watching as Mercy jerked out their suitcases and began yanking open dresser drawers.

"We've got to get out of here now," she was panting to herself. "We've got to be long gone when he figures it out for himself. I knew better than to trust him."

Suddenly, Casey grabbed on to the stack of clothing in Mercy's hands, wrestling her for its possession. From someplace inside the wild vortex of fear, Mercy realized who and what she was fighting. Not just Casey for control of the clothes. Not just time before their secrets were exposed. It was Spencer. Spencer Halloway and the feelings that roared to life when she was with him. It wasn't the panic; she'd been dealing with that forever. It was the longing, the wanting what she'd never dared asked for, never dared expect.

The thought of loving him plainly terrified her.

"You can trust Spencer."

When had Casey begun to sound so old and reasonable? Probably when Mercy had started acting with the abandon of an impulsive child.

Mercy took several gulps of air and reined back on the adrenaline galloping through her at a runaway pace. She had to make the child listen. "Casey, honey, you don't understand the trouble he can cause us."

"Yes, I do. But he won't. Spencer's our friend. He would never hurt us. He told me so. He did!"

A smile trembled on Mercy's lips as she marveled at the child's naiveté. Or was it her incredible intuition? What was it Spencer had said about a child knowing whom to trust? Instinctively, she wanted to believe in Spencer, too. She wanted him to be some larger-than-life knight on a white horse, here to rescue them from the dragons of the past. But she couldn't risk it. Not with Casey in the balance.

"Casey, Spencer is a sheriff. He'd have to do his job. It wouldn't matter if he didn't want to." Because when he found out who they were and the lies they'd told, he'd be the lawman not the man. And any feeling, any hope kindled between them in this verdant paradise would end. Circumstance would stop it dead. Spencer Halloway was not a man to tolerate lies, and she hadn't told him a single truth since she'd been here. Just as she'd been hiding the truth from herself. The truth that she'd fallen in love with the sheriff of Pine Creek.

Then Casey came up with the most unexpected, most hard-to-defend-against statement that pinned all Mercy's logical arguments to the wall.

"I don't want to leave, Mercy. I want us to be a family. Here."

It wasn't a request, it was a firm declaration. Mercy stared at the determined little girl, stunned. "But Casey, we can't."

"Why not?" Her chin came out in a stubborn jut, the same way Mercy's did when she was fighting to get her own way. "I like it here. I like Spencer. And I don't want to go back. Not ever."

Mercy sat down on the edge of the bed and pulled the child into her arms. "Oh, honey, we can't stay. This isn't our home."

"It could be."

It could be.

Why not? What did she have to go back to? A moderately good-paying job that gave her no satisfaction. An apartment in a complex that demanded white-backed drapes and allowed no children. Rooms without a heart, a life without a soul. She'd found those things here, here in Pine Creek with Casey. With Spencer. And she didn't want to leave, either. But she knew they had to.

But maybe not today.

She heaved a tremendous sigh, the wall of her resistance worn away by one insistent little girl.

"Why don't you help me put this stuff back in the drawers, okay?"

Casey leaned back, beaming. "Okay!"

It made sense to stay, she told herself. She had no idea where else to run. And besides, this was where Amy would come when she got back to the States; where they would plot out their campaign to claim Casey. They were so close. Only a few more weeks.

And ironically, while Spencer posed a danger himself, she knew he would keep them safe from any other threat.

As she watched the child lining the dresser drawers with her possessions, Mercy's mind was miles away. Or at least across the cove.

What was she going to do about Spencer?

How close was he to discovering everything?

And what would he do about it when he did?

Spencer had set up camp on his back porch with the precision of a commando. His sleeping bag nicely padded the metal swing. A thermos of coffee was within his reach. He'd thought about bringing a pack of cigarettes out but decided against it. The gnawing urge to have one would help keep him awake.

From his comfortable headquarters, he panned his infrared spotting scope across the face of the Cheswicks' cabin, looking for any unusual movement within that sharp red-and-black field. He'd bought the high-powered hunting scope to follow the nighttime habits of prospective freezer food. Deer, even the wily old bucks with their trophy rack of horns, were creatures of habit. They often returned to the same spots, and while Spencer couldn't shoot them during the evening hours, he marked their established trails and waited along them in the daylight to make the inevitable kill. Criminals were like that, too. If they established a pattern, they usually stuck to it.

If Mercy's prowler escaped unharmed the first time, like as not, he'd be back to try it again.

And when he did, Spencer would be there to bag him.

Whether Mercy liked it or not.

Right now he wasn't in a great position to ask for her permission.

He didn't want to dwell on what had happened that morning. He knew that though he'd been wrong to question Casey, he'd been right in his intentions. What he'd managed to uncover had only increased the mystery. Then there was Mercy's reaction, or rather, her overreaction. To his veiled interrogation of the child. To his possessing embrace. The first, he could understand. The second left him in a spin of confusion. He'd never known a woman to run so hot and cold in the span of a second. He'd never wanted to win one over as much as he wanted to claim Mercy's trust. Once he had that, he sensed the rest would follow. And then he would make her feel safe with him if it was the last noble thing he ever did.

Only he didn't want it to be the last thing they ever did together. He was dying to make love with Mercy and to make her feel loved. His dreams were erotic enough to earn a triple-X rating. But first he'd have to find a way to get her to forgive him.

Then they could deal with her secrets.

Considering what he knew of her situation, he should have realized it would come to a conflict of interest sooner or later. Between the lawman who wanted to learn what she was hiding and the man who wanted to learn how to please her. He wanted that collision course to come later. After he'd earned her faith. If it could be earned.

All was quiet across the cove. Lights blinked out in a pattern as Mercy put Casey to bed, then retired herself. He thought of her sinking down upon her mattress, of her long legs stretching out between cool sheets. And he didn't need the lack of nicotine to keep him edgy, with that image teasing through his head.

"Sheriff, this is base, do you copy?"

The crackle of his radio knifed through his fanciful musings. With a grumble of annoyance, he set his scope aside and went inside to answer the call.

"Halloway here. What's up, Judy?"

"We've got a disturbance over on 10, some kids drag racing. There's reportedly alcohol involved."

"Where's Chet?"

"I haven't been able to raise him, Sheriff. Do you want me to try again?"

Spencer sighed savagely. Fast cars, dumb kids and drink. A deadly combination. Either he acted on it now, or he'd be bagging a couple of them by morning. "No, I'll handle it. Stay on your toes in case I need some backup."

"Will do, Sheriff. And Spencer . . . be careful."

"That's a roger."

It took only a moment to strap on his pistol and snatch up his coat, movements so routine they didn't consciously register. He locked up his house and sped out for Interstate 10 with lights flashing, praying as he negotiated the undulating hills that he wouldn't be too late to prevent the inevitable, that he wouldn't be making any midnight calls at some parents' front door with the news no one wanted to hear.

Interstate 10 had a marvelously straight quarter-mile stretch, an unbearable temptation to any kid with a hot car and revved-up hormones. Spencer knew firsthand. His sports car had been the quickest in the county. He'd been reckless then and kids were no smarter now. He just wanted to make sure they grew up to regret it.

He pulled across the blacktop right where the racing strip ended in a tight curve. Nicknamed Deadman's, of course. By the time his rollicking little friends reached it, they'd be slowed to a manageable speed and still numbed by the adrenaline high. Easy pickings. Even if he didn't catch them, he would note their cars and pay them a little visit in the morning when their heads were banging and their consciences were ripe for his lecture.

Spencer heard the unmistakable sound of engines whining at top end and a fraction later, two vehicles hurtled abreast around the corner. Rubber squealed and smoked as brakes slammed on and both cars took compliantly to the sides of the road. Several other spectators followed in their own vehicles but were going at a controlled speed. They were able to do agile 180s at the sight of his roadblock and, like the loyal friends they were, disappeared to let the speeders face the music alone. But not before Spencer identified each one.

The racers had shut down their engines and were waiting for his approach. Spencer took his time, letting them sweat off a little of the alcohol with brain-clearing panic. He stepped out of his truck and ambled leisurely up to a flashy car, leaning down to address it's pasty-faced driver. He was relieved to scent no trace of alcohol on the boy, nor did his gaze seem bleary. He looked honestly scared at being caught.

"Heya, Jason. Any idea how fast you were going?"

Anxious eyes canted up to him and the boy risked a fleeting smile of pride. "Top-ended at eight-three, Sheriff. Did I get close to your record?"

"Not even close enough to smell my fumes." Spencer flipped open his ticket book and started writing. "Think you could get this rocket ship home at a legal speed? I'd hate to impound it, because I have a feeling you're not going to be driving it anytime soon and this could be your last chance behind the wheel before you're a cautious old man like me."

"Think you're right, there, Sheriff," the boy murmured glumly. Then he sharpened defensively. "But I wasn't drinking. Honest, Sheriff Halloway. You can ask any of them. They'll tell you."

"I plan to. That'll be in your favor, Jas, if it's the truth." He tore off a citation and passed it inside. "This is for you. Better get a summer job to work it off. I'll expect a call from your dad tomorrow."

"Yes, sir."

"Go on home, now."

The engine purred to life and the car did a sedate loop on the road before heading toward Pine Creek with its tail between its legs. And that left the gleaming black convertible on the other shoulder.

There, Spencer found his worst nightmare.

The driver, the sixteen-year-old son of the town's post-master, was leaning out the passenger door. He'd been in the middle of emptying out the cans of evidence when the urge to empty out his belly overwhelmed him. Sharp odors of sickness and beer were thick and Spencer was muttering curses even as he hauled the wretched and weeping young-ster out of the vehicle on rubbery legs.

"Tommy, you know better. Your dad said he wasn't go-ing to throw your bail if I had to wake him up to come get you in the middle of the night again. My jail's good and clean, but it's not any place for a boy your age to make a second home. What's wrong with you? When are you go-ing to get smart?"

"Don't call him, Sheriff Halloway," the kid began to whine in shameless gusts. "You don't have to call him. I won't do it again. I promise!"

"I've heard that kind of promise before, just before zip-ping up one of those heavy-gauge plastic sacks. I don't want to call your daddy to the morgue to identify you there. Bet-ter he pick you up at the station."

"Better for who?" he moaned in misery.

"You know the drill, Tommy. Where did you get the il-legal liquor?"

"What liquor? We wasn't drinking, Sheriff. Honest." That was followed by a condemning hiccup.

"Yeah, right. I suppose that's a new cologne you're wearing. Tell me now or I'll find out later. I already IDed the rest you were running with. Someone's sure to talk to save their own butt. It might as well be yours, seeing as how yours is the one in the sling at the moment." His tone grew impatient just as he was growing eager to put an end to this game and get back to his night watch on the lake.

"It wasn't one of the guys, Sheriff. Really. I'm not lying. We was all hanging out in town, you know, looking under each other's hoods and B.S.-ing. Like we always do. We weren't doing nothing wrong."

"Okay. Then what?"

"Then this old guy comes up, maybe about your age." He didn't notice Spencer's grimace. "He started dissing our cars and saying how only we country boys would drive such sissy wheels."

Spencer gave an exasperated sigh. The kind of predictable earthshaking challenge that would start a war. "Ticked you off plenty, right?"

"Yeah, damned—uh, darn right. So he brings out a couple of six-packs and a fifth and asks which one of us is man enough to show him what we're made of."

Spencer was starting to get a real ugly feeling inside, gnawing away on the edge of intuition. "And I'm sure all you big men were anxious to show him."

The boy flushed and mumbled, "We knocked back a couple of drinks and he said he'd pay us each fifty dollars to put on a race for him. Fifty dollars! I can wax cars down at the 76 station for a week and not clear that."

What acne-prone kid could resist the lure of cold cash and a challenge of his manhood? It sounded pretty calculated to Spencer. He just couldn't pinpoint why some out-of-towner would go to so much trouble to put wild kids on the road to court disaster.

Unless it was to draw the sheriff's attention.

"This guy with the money and the beer, what did he look like?"

"Big fellow, almost as tall as you but wider, heavier. Dressed sharp, city boy. He had a lot of money on him."

"And where is he now?"

"Don't know. After the first race, he disappeared. He gave us a couple more six-packs and told us to have a good time on him."

Spencer didn't like what he was thinking. Not in the least. Those thoughts were heading back in one direction: toward Big Bear Lake and a certain cabin.

"Tommy, you get back in your car and don't even think of moving until your dad comes to get you." He reached in to snatch the keys out of the ignition. "Which way was this guy going when he left?"

"North."
North, toward Big Bear Lake.
And Mercy.

His tires screamed along the blacktop. The strobe of his flashers pulsed in time to his rapid heartbeat. The jolt of the big tires leaving smooth pavement for hard-packed sand and gravel had him airborne in his seat belt and slammed him down with spleen-bruising force, but he didn't back off the accelerator. He manhandled his truck around the bumpy lake road as his radio hissed to life with the message he didn't want to hear.

"Sheriff, we've got a hit-and-run victim at the Cheswicks' on Big Bear. Ambulance is at the scene. Do you copy?"

"I'm there, Judy."

And as he rounded the final bend in the road, the scene was laid out before him under the nightmare glare of emergency flashers.

Chapter 11

Mercy couldn't have been asleep for long. Casey's muffled cries reached through her weary veil of slumber like a subtle shake to the shoulder, rousing her with a mutter and getting her to her feet before her eyes were all the way open. Parenthood, she thought with a groggy sigh. The good with the bad. The bad was the plague of Casey's nightmares breaking into her fitful sleep. The good was being there to comfort her.

She didn't bother with a robe. Most of the time the child needed no more than a consoling presence and a soothing voice to send her deeper into a more pleasant dreamland. If worse came to worst, Mercy planned to climb in beside her and they could be company for each other's troubled thoughts.

She was just leaving her room when Mercy realized something wasn't right. A cool breeze brushed over her bare legs and arms, and yet she distinctly remembered shutting all the windows. It was then Casey's mumbles sounded again—not as vague restless murmurings but with sharp, purposeful intent. Anxious cries for help.

Mercy darted around the corner and switched on the light. Nothing, just an impotent clicking.

What on earth?

"Casey?"

She was answered by a frantic scuffle of sound. Sounds she couldn't identify. Big, scraping sounds, like something being dragged.

"Casey!"

Mercy raced to the bathroom across the hall and flipped that wall switch. Brightness flooded the small space and spilled over into the child's room—illuminating a pair of writhing legs as they disappeared through the open window.

Mercy stood dumbfounded, unable to grasp the sight or its meaning for a long, paralyzing moment. Then, with a cry of disbelief, she ran through the cabin, pausing long enough to grab up the iron poker from the heat stove before dashing out recklessly into the darkness.

There was a partial moon overhead, enough to thread through the leafy foliage and delineate a big shadow moving awkwardly between the trees on its way to the road. The beam of a flashlight flickered an erratic pattern up ahead, because whoever held it had a struggling little girl in his grasp.

"Casey! Let her go!"

Mercy charged after the figure, bashing into one of the hidden tree trunks with her shoulder. She staggered in a reeling circle blinking back tears of pain and panic for several precious seconds before she was able to continue.

"Mercy!" The child's voice was shrill with fright, redoubling Mercy's efforts to reach her.

She could make out the sinister shape of a waiting car parked off the side of the road up ahead. If the abductor reached it, Casey was lost to her. They were on the drive now and able to run without obstruction. Mercy was barefoot but the man was trying to subdue a wriggling child. Fearing she wouldn't be able to catch him, Mercy flung the iron with all her strength. It tangled up in his stride and he went down, cursing blackly. Fortunately, he didn't fall on the little girl and Casey was on her feet as soon as the hold on her lessened, and she came running back toward Mercy.

Seeing the big figure rise up off the ground, Mercy grabbed Casey's hand and began to run back toward the cabin. What she'd do to protect them once they were there wasn't as important as getting inside with a locked door between them. That, at least, would slow him down and give her time to think of something. There was oven cleaner in the cupboard to temporarily blind him. She didn't want to consider the kitchen knives. And there was always firewood. She could bash him senseless, tie him up and be gone before he came around.

Unless, of course, he carried a gun.

Twin stabs of light bounced over them as a car gunned into the drive. Mercy leaped to the safety of the trees, hugging Casey to her. It couldn't be their pursuer. He hadn't had time to return to his vehicle.

Spencer!

The hope flared and was as quickly gone as she caught sight of a huge, unwieldy luxury car hopping the ruts of the drive while barreling ahead at a reckless speed. Right into the man who was chasing them. There was a sickening thump and a figure flew up over the hood, skidding off it to crash into the dark bushes beyond. The car screeched to an immediate halt but didn't shut off as a man jumped out from behind the wheel. A man with a badge pinned to his shirtfront.

The next few minutes sped by in a surrealistic haze as Mercy crouched in the shadows of the surrounding oaks, clutching a trembling Casey in an unrelieved panic. She could hear Spencer's deputy's moaning apologies as he bent in the darkness where the body had been thrown. Then there was the crackle of the police radio and a frantic summons for an ambulance. Briefly, just briefly, Mercy was shamed when the hope that it would arrive too late flashed through her mind. She didn't know who the man was who lay on the ground most likely unconscious, but she knew what he was and who had sent him.

He'd come for Casey.

How? How had he found them so quickly? What had she forgotten? Where had she been careless?

Then it came to her with uncomfortable clarity. The obvious. Casey's medical history—the one she'd known nothing about. Anyone looking for the little girl would have thought to check medical facilities for any treatment given to a chronic six-year-old asthma sufferer.

A private investigator worth his salt knew how and where to ask the right questions.

And as soon as he was able to talk, she'd be faced with a whole slew of them herself.

She'd better hope she had the right answers.

Spencer angled his truck in between Chet's big Bonneville and the open-backed ambulance. He was out the door before the engine quieted and racing for the gurney two paramedics were working over the bumpy ground toward the emergency vehicle. A single glance told him the figure draped upon it was too large to belong to Mercy. Before he had a chance to react to that relief, Chet was on him.

"I never saw him, Spence. He was just there in front of me before I could stop."

"He got a name?"

"Sweeney from Detroit and he's carrying a private investigator's license in his wallet."

"What the hell happened here, Chet?" he demanded as his gaze darted about the blackness and settled upon the welcome sight of the woman and child. Safe.

They were tucked back out of the glare of strobe lights. Mercy was in her nightshirt. Her hair was loose and wild about a pale, pale face. The look in her eyes took him in the chest like a hollow-tipped slug that went in small and burst out big; a lost, sick-with-fear look. She held Casey in a straitjacketing embrace.

"I was doing some surveillance on my own time," Chet began weakly, then let his tone swell with self-importance as he continued, "and I saw this fellow's car parked alongside the road, empty. I was just fixing to investigate when I heard the commotion in the drive. My guess is he'd been trying to break into the cabin and Mrs. Royce chased him off with that fireplace iron. I heard her yelling and turned into the drive to respond when he stepped right in front of the bumper. E.M.T.'s say it's probably just a concussion but maybe internal injuries, too. I didn't see him, Spence. It wasn't my fault. There was no way I could have stopped." That was said more in sullen self-defense than with any kind of sorrow.

"It's all right, Chet." He put a hand on the deputy's shoulder. "What about them?" He nodded toward the two frightened figures.

Chet was suddenly all cool professional. "I tried to question the woman but she wasn't forthcoming with any answers. She was asking for you. Probably in shock."

Spencer was taken by the need to get all of them out of there so he could have a private word with Mercy. The past minutes had stolen years from his life and his blood pressure was still gushing like Old Faithful. The details could wait until morning. He needed to know that Mercy and Casey were all right. "Put it all in your report. You ride on to the hospital with Mr. Sweeney and I'll see to things here."

Chet hesitated, a hard stare settling on the woman and child. Then he muttered, "All right, Sheriff."

"Give me a call if Sweeney comes around and does any talking. I want to hear his story. Stay with him. I don't want him going anyplace."

Chet nodded grimly and headed for his car as the back of the ambulance was closed up tight. Both vehicles pulled out and headed for Pine Creek—leaving Spencer in the drive with two traumatized females.

"Are the two of you all right?"

The concern-warmed tone of his voice stirred an immediate reaction in Casey. With a soft cry, she pulled from

Mercy's grasp and came flying toward him. He caught her up midleap and surrendered to the rush of protective feeling swamping him as thin arms and legs tangled about him like twist-ties. If anything had happened to this precious child... To either of them...

With Casey sniffling against his shoulder, Spencer approached Mercy. She was standing so stiff with tension, each tiny tremor shook her like a leaf in a high wind. She had that bolt-and-run look about her so he moved slowly, locking in eye contact to hold her in place until he could reach her. Her eyes were all dark, liquid desperation.

And when he was close enough, he opened the way to his opposite shoulder, not knowing what she'd make of the invitation. She slammed into him with the force of a steam train, her arms whipping around his neck, her hot, damp face pressed into the open vee of his collar. As his arm curled around her, she said his name just once. It was a low moan, warbling with a panic stilled, like a prayer answered; as if no relief could be greater than what she found in his embrace. And the storm in him was uncontainable, thundering along his pulse in an unsettled beat.

"Let's get the two of you inside."

Surprisingly, it was Casey who was full of protest. "No! I don't want to go back in there!"

"Casey, it's all right," he crooned into the tousle of bright hair, but her head was shaking in an unarguable negative. "I'm here. I'm not going to let anything hurt you."

"I don't want to go back inside."

"The man who scared you is gone. He won't be back. He can't hurt you."

"I don't care!"

"Okay, sweetie. It's okay. Then how about you come home with me?"

It came out quite naturally as the obvious solution. He never in a million years expected Mercy to go for it but she was pulling back from his embrace with a murmur of, "I'll get our things." Then she padded back into the cabin without another word.

Spencer stared after her, his blood suddenly thick with trepidation. If Mercy was giving in this easily, something must have scared the hell out of her. Something a lot worse than some unknown prowler outside their door.

She returned within minutes, dressed warmly in fleece sweats, an overnight case in one hand. She didn't try to take Casey from him but instead walked in a subdued silence at his side all the way back to his still-running Blazer. That meekness was enough to kick his worry into overdrive. Curiosity and questions could wait. First, he wanted them locked up safe and secure inside his house.

Casey was nodding off by the time Spencer unlatched his door and he carried her straight to the spare bedroom. Mercy followed more slowly, stepping across the threshold as if she were crossing into dangerous territory. She wasn't sure what she'd expected from his bachelor quarters, but this was a pleasant surprise.

His wasn't a simple cabin made up of haphazard throw-togethers. It was a home, full of warmth and charm and welcome. The interior walls were exposed peeled log and the floor smooth wood. A huge stone fireplace rose up through the center, and exposed beams crisscrossed two stories above like the natural lacings of the great oaks outside. All the furnishings were glossy wood and rich earthy colors woven in vibrant Southwestern patterns. There was a sense of harmony in the whole and a feeling of serenity stole about her. It was a place where she could belong.

The large room she stood in had a vaulted ceiling. In quick acclimating glances, she could see a kitchen and an octagonal breakfast room off to one side, both with the same rustic appeal. Behind the fireplace were bedrooms and a bath, and in the rear, an entire wall of windows overlooking an enclosed porch and the lake. A wooden staircase spiraled tightly upward in one corner, linking to an open loft spread out above the sleeping areas. Starlight twinkled in through several generous skylights. It was as if nature had been invited in to share the splendor of the evening with them.

"Out for the count," Spencer announced as he gently closed one of the bedroom doors and came to join her. Noting her interest in the surroundings, he asked, "What do you think of the place?"

"It's beautiful. When you said log cabin, I was thinking Abe Lincoln rustic. This was not what I pictured."

"It was what I pictured all those years I lived in Detroit. We had a house in one of the suburbs where all the homes looked like some giant cookie cutter came down the block, stamping them all out in an identical row. The only difference was in three choices of vinyl siding and two different colors of shutters. I hated the uniformity of it."

She nodded in shared contempt. "So you bought this place." Her tone expressed approval.

"No. I built this place. Or most of it."

Mercy's brows soared. She was duly impressed.

"My folks owned the lot. We had an old trailer on it for years. When I quit the metro division, it was like a hole I could crawl into to lick my wounds. When I decided that this was the place for me, I bought out my parents and started taking out trees."

"You cut down your own trees?"

His chuckle was whiskey warm. "Not to use as walls, no. This was from a kit. Some friends and I put it together like a big box of Lincoln Logs blocks. Over the years, I just added on things I was comfortable with. I've been kicking around the idea of a hot tub for this summer's project. Great stress reliever, I hear."

What Mercy found was a stress reliever was the low drawl of his voice, all deep and rich like the wood around them when he was speaking of things he enjoyed. It was easy to share his sense of satisfaction. It was easy to fall into an appreciation of his dream.

Then Mercy's brow knit together in confusion as she tried to puzzle something out on her own.

"I was wondering—never mind. I don't want to intrude on your privacy."

He smiled slightly. "I'm the sheriff of a small town. There's very little about my life that I can consider private. Ask."

"I was wondering why your wife didn't want to make her life here with you." Then she cringed at the sound of her question. "I'm sorry. That's awfully personal."

"No. Actually it's ancient history." And he was surprised to discover that it felt that way, too; old, faded, almost forgotten since Mercy had crept in to consume his thoughts. "It wasn't this place she didn't want to make a life with, it was me."

Mercy was shocked by that blunt statement. "I find that very hard to believe."

Her amazement was a sensory stroke along his ego, sending frissons of sexual awareness through him. And because he didn't want to alarm her with the sudden rumpled-sheets turn of his thoughts, Spencer angled away from her and knelt before the hearth. "How about a fire? I enjoy them in the evenings until it gets too hot to be comfortable. Why don't you sit down and make yourself at home?" He nodded toward the Aztec-print sofa invitingly arranged near the fireplace.

Mercy sank down upon it in an odd mood of compliance. It did feel like home in his cozy log sanctuary. The peace was seductive and the fire he kindled in the grate lulled her with its hypnotic dance. She realized he was talking about himself, setting up this intimate scene to relax her. She also knew questions about this evening's events were waiting. But he'd done his job well, creating this opportunity for spiritual easing.

No protests rose. No feelings of suspicion, no anxiety about his plans. Not even a vague uneasiness about being in his home. Her ever-vigilant wariness had taken an unexpected vacation. And she found she didn't miss it. This was nicer—this warm sense of contentment, this slow building of...trust. And better was the elemental anticipation as she watched him tend his fire, stoking it with patience, arrang-

ing it with care to allow for the longest-lasting, most satis-
fying heat.

Would he treat her like that, too?

"I was different in the city," Spencer was saying to the
flames. "Like a fraying seam, pulling apart so fast you
could never quite catch the edges to keep it from raveling
any farther. I can't blame Paula, my ex. I made her a lot of
big promises and when I couldn't keep them, she felt I'd
failed her and our marriage. She had plans for my career,
and cementing me back together when I was cracking apart
like papier-mâché wasn't what she had in mind. I let her
down and I left her society world for one I felt comfortable
in. She didn't want to come with me, and I guess I really
didn't care as much as I thought I would that she stayed behind."

He made it sound simple and detached, but Mercy could
intuit the pain behind his words. He'd been betrayed by a
woman who'd sworn to love him, to stick by him and support him. Her summation was edged in protective outrage.

"I think she was the one who let you down."

Spencer glanced back at her, surprise glimmering in eyes
as dark as wet lead. He managed a one-sided smile. "Yeah?
Maybe. It doesn't matter now. We're both happier with the
choices we made. She got on with her life fast enough. She's
married to some investment broker and they have two kids.
And me, I think I'm finally ready to get on with mine, too."

Actually, he was somewhat startled by the truth of that
claim. Old baggage was gone, tossed out to make room for
this fragile woman and child. He, who had guarded his
emotions so closely he'd installed a dead bolt along with the
combination lock, was taking wild risks with his heart when
it came to this mysterious duo. They could hurt him. They
could ruin him with the secrets they concealed. But with
them, he'd discovered a fresh-air happiness, a soul-ripping
need that was worth every bit of the chance he was taking.

Now, if he could only convince her to risk a little on her
end.

"How about coffee with a little something therapeutic added to it?"

Mercy nodded. That sounded just right. Just like being here with Spencer held a deep, stirringly sweet sense of rightness. She leaned back against the cushions with eyes closed and let her wounded spirit sigh. She could almost forget the terrible sequence of events leading up to this sequestered paradise. Almost.

This feeling of peace was temporary, just like Spencer's goodwill was temporary. Both would be gone in the morning when that private eye started talking. Then it would be all over for her and Casey. All for nothing.

She couldn't let that happen.

Was she a guest in Spencer Halloway's house? Or a pampered prisoner?

"Here you go. Careful, it's hot."

Her gaze flashed up and Spencer was disappointed by the return of her edge-of-a-scream anxiousness. He'd hoped they'd gotten past that. Apparently not. She reached up for the cup, more worried about the brush of his fingers than the heat of the ceramic glaze. And because her features were shadowed once more, he didn't join her on the couch as was his original plan. Instead, he sank down upon the plush rug in front of the fire, letting its warmth make up for her sudden chill.

If she wasn't willing to move on to something more pleasant, he might as well get right to business.

"Want to tell me about tonight?"

"Should you read me my rights first, Sheriff?" As a joke, it fell flat. As a measure of her tension, it was right on the money.

"Do I need to? I was under the impression that you were the victim in all this."

"The victim is usually the one burdened with the proof of innocence."

What had given her such a jaded view? he wondered, as he sipped his coffee without giving it a chance to cool. It seared his tongue, just as her mistrust seared his heart.

"I wish I could argue that, but I've been in law enforcement long enough to know you're right."

"Is this an official inquiry, then?"

"No. You can give your statement in the morning. This is just me wanting to know what the hell happened. I get pulled away on some very suspect call, then when I get back, your front yard is all lit up with bubble lights. Was it the same guy, Mercy?"

"How would I know?"

She did know. He was sure of it. Her stare was fixed on her cup and her knuckles were white with strain. She knew and she wasn't saying.

"Just tell me what you remember."

"Casey's cry woke me up. When I turned on the light, I saw her bedroom window had been forced open. I went out to confront the man who had tried to break in. About then, your deputy pulled into the drive and knocked down that poor man with his car. He called for the paramedics and then you showed up. That's about all there was to it."

Maybe, but he didn't think so. She recited the facts too unemotionally, as if it was a story that didn't involve her. He'd seen her in that front yard, clutching Casey. She hadn't been uninvolved. She'd been terrified.

"You went out after this man, not knowing who he was or what he wanted, or whether he'd hurt you."

"We've already established that I'm not very smart when it comes to threats upon Casey." Her tone growled in a defensive register.

"But how do you know Casey was in any danger?"

"The man was trying to break into our house. That doesn't exactly take a quantum leap to figure out." She could have sounded quarrelsome, even annoyed. But she didn't. She sounded teeth-rattling scared.

"Why?"

"What?"

"Why, out of all the homes on the lake, most of them standing empty, did he choose yours? You said yourself there's nothing inside for anyone to steal.'' That said, he tightened the screws. ''What was he after, Mercy?''

She stared at him, her expression shutting down into an impassive mask. But not before he caught a glimpse of what she was trying to hide behind it. Panic. Helpless, wild, cornered-animal panic. And as much as he wanted to soothe away that raw distress, he needed to know the truth. Now.

Her reply was so disdainful, he almost smiled at its sheer bravado. ''How on earth would I know what was on a criminal's mind?''

''I'm not sure he was a criminal.''

''He was breaking into our house!'' That was angrily, defiantly thrown at him. He could hear Mercy's breathing accelerate into quick, shallow gusts. Her grip on the coffee cup was like a hold on a life ring. Her gaze was locked on his, hers wide and frightened yet still glimmering with a last-ditch resistance. She would fight him to the end. He admired that about her. And it made him mad as hell. Why couldn't she just tell him the truth? She had to know he was going to find it out sooner or later. Sooner would be better for all concerned. And the sooner he knew the facts, the sooner he could be working on how to protect her from them.

''He's a private investigator. Want to hazard a guess on who hired him? No? Or maybe about what he was hired to do? No guess at all?''

Her jaw clenched tight.

Time to stop pulling punches.

''He was there for Casey, wasn't he?''

Chapter 12

Mercy bolted off the couch.

"I don't need to listen to your badgering. I'm getting Casey, and we're going home."

"Home where?" Spencer was up, too, blocking her path to the bedroom door. "Where does Casey live, and with whom?"

"W-with me."

"Who are you, Mercy?"

Her eyes went round and glazed and he knew what she saw through them. An enemy. He knew he was fast losing her. He had to make an impression that would break through her defensive barriers once and for all.

"Damn it, Mercy, I'm trying to help you!"

"Then leave us alone! Spencer, please just leave us alone. If you care anything at all about Casey, you'll—"

"What? Let you run away from me again? I do care about Casey. And about you. Why can't you understand that? I am not your enemy."

Instead of answering, she made an abrupt move to go around him. To halt the evasive maneuver, Spencer grabbed on to her forearm, then was surprised by her sudden cry of hurt. Certain it was nothing he'd done, he immediately slackened his grip and steadied her with the curl of his hand upon her other arm. She continued to struggle, the fight costing her dearly, if her soft sobs of distress were any measure.

"Mercy, what is it?"

But she was breathing hard to overcome the well of tears in her eyes. She didn't want to be weak at this very critical moment. She didn't want his sympathy or his aid. She wanted— She wanted—

"Mercy, stop. Stop fighting me. What is it? Tell me what's wrong."

Vision blurred behind a veil of pain, she did as he ordered and the throb of discomfort eased. "I bruised my shoulder. I—I ran into a tree." She flushed hotly. It sounded so foolish now, that brave rush to Casey's defense. "It's all right. I just want to get Casey—"

"It's not all right. And you and Casey aren't going anywhere. At least, not tonight." And before she could crouch back into her defensive mode, he undercut it with a crisp, "Sit down. I want to look at that shoulder."

She held her ground for a long moment and Spencer was afraid he was going to have to apply sterner measures. Then at last she backed to the couch and settled with all the equanimity of a coiled snake.

"That's better," he growled. "Now let me take a look at your arm."

When he reached for the zippered front of her sweat jacket, Mercy flinched, that naked flare of warning back in her big dark eyes.

"Okay, you do it for me. And believe me, my motives are purely Good Samaritan." He tried to hold to a serious face but an irreverent smile slipped out. "Well, I'll try to keep them that pure, anyway."

She relaxed slightly and tugged the zipper down a few modest inches, just far enough to slip the edge open over the site of her distress. Craning her own neck, she could see an

ugly discoloration staining the area beneath her collarbone. It looked as nasty as it felt.

"Can you move your arm?"

She rotated it and winced. "Yes, but it hurts," she confessed.

"Let me see. Easy, now. I know what I'm doing. All-
varsity football in high school. I've seen my share of bruises.
This is nothing new."

Mercy held herself rigid, the breath seeming to solidify in
her lungs when he touched her. His fingertips were warm
and their warmth radiated outward like streaks of fever.
With palm resting lightly on the bruised area, he manipu-
lated her arm, his manner sombér, his hands gentle. He was
close enough for her to feel the heat of his body, and despite his tender handling, the air between them grew as
charged as the barometric pressure readings before a storm.

"Does this hurt?" His voice rumbled like fast-closing
thunder.

"Not too bad." Hers whispered like the soft ripple of a
compelling wind.

His head came up suddenly, as if he was abruptly aware
of a change in the weather. A sultry front seemed to be
massing and he was unsure whether to brave it out or retreat until it blew over. He opted for caution.

"No serious damage done from what I can tell" came his
cool, professional judgment. "I've got an ice pack that will
probably take the worst of the pain away."

"All right."

He didn't go for it right away, too absorbed in the signals
flickering between them. He recognized the snap of sexual
need, he just didn't know what to do about it.

Once he rose to his feet, the tension should have eased but
it didn't. It followed him, tight as a muscle cramp about his
heart, as he rummaged through his bathroom cupboard in
search of the sports pack he used for ankle strains. Locat-
ing it at last, he returned to the living room only to be arrested by the sight of her sprawled, all liquid invitation,
upon his sofa. Her head was back, spilling auburn hair

along the sofa cushions. The angle gave a slight arch to her torso, lifting her breasts against the hug of soft fleece as if offering them for the cup of a man's hands. His palms itched. His pulse kicked into a churning overdrive. Knowing it wasn't an intentional pose didn't make it any less provocative.

"Here you go. Hold this right over the ache and it'll be better in no time."

Kneeling down, Spencer wondered what he could apply to his own ache, for the thoughts heating up inside him hardly called for Red Cross-approved techniques. He'd given her a sanctuary for the night, had promised her safety, had vowed not to take advantage of his position. Crazy pledges to make, considering what he felt for her; had felt since the very beginning. He was nervous around her, he who was never at a loss with flirtation. But it had always been serious business with Mercy. Always, even before he was ready to believe it. He hadn't looked upon her as a passing lover. He'd seen her as a mate. He'd been bewitched by a winsome smile that stirred all the right chemistry within him. Her tenacious courage and tugging vulnerability had hooked him from their first meeting.

He'd once believed that these things were possible between a man and a woman but had given up on that ideal after Paula's abandonment. Mercy was making him a card-carrying romantic all over again. And he didn't mind it in the least, until he thought he might yet lose her.

She applied the cold pack, wincing slightly at the first contact, then gradually relaxing. He couldn't say the same about the way she watched him. Like he was both salvation and curse. She just couldn't decided which. Not the most flattering summation.

"Thank you," she said with that damned irritating air of self-sufficiency in her sultry, bedroom voice. Talk about a contradiction. "I'm sure this is all I'll need."

Spencer nearly groaned aloud. He'd never met such a needy female nor one quite so determined not to need another. What could he do to convince her his intentions were sterling if not altogether pure? The best way would be in honoring his vows not to push her, to play the friend she needed. But "friend" had never come close to filling the bill.

How to convince her to let him get close enough to become something more?

"Better?" His question was as soothing as the ice-pack application, warmer than any heat treatment.

"Hmm, much."

Mercy was stalling, running out of ways to keep him at arm's length and from pursuing his line of penetrating questions. *Who are you?* he'd demanded in a voice that said he wouldn't be put off for long. Seeing him on bended knee before her, she could almost be fooled into considering him harmless, but she knew better. She knew there was a badge pinned to his coat and the code it represented was attached just as firmly to his soul.

As tempting as it was to give in and trust the man, there was no ignoring the fact that the man and the law were one and the same. She felt safe in his home; but "safe" was a relative term. In here, he became the danger—to her mission, to her resolve. A frighteningly seductive danger. If she wasn't careful, she would be as trusting in him as Casey was. That would be folly, knowing what she did about his moral resolutions.

Her cautious gaze gave him a covert and plainly covetous once-over, charting those broad shoulders that could support so much. Oh, how enticing the idea of surrendering all into his care had come to be. If only she could yield all into his capable hands, to lean upon him with the faith of a child. But that she couldn't do.

Who are you, Mercy?

She couldn't let him find out.

Then came what she'd been dreading.

"Mercy, we've got some serious talking to do."

"I'm very tired, Sheriff. It's been a long, trying evening. Could we postpone the questioning until morning? I'm really not up to it now."

He might have been caught by the fragile tug of her voice but somehow she doubted it. Spencer Halloway was too darned smart. He read nuances of intent the way others read street maps and he knew when hers were leading off in a wandering direction out of town. Though he wasn't led astray, surprisingly, he didn't push ahead, either.

"You can take my room. It's right through there. I'll bunk on the couch. There are clean towels in the bathroom if you want to grab a shower first. That might help relax you enough to forget all this and get a good night's rest."

His no-strings offer clipped right through her ragged defenses. A shower sounded like a slice of heaven. But something in his all-too-sudden resignation had her reluctant. Was it because she didn't want him to back down from his determined sensual assault? That was a silly notion. A hot shower, undisturbed sleep. That's what she needed, not a prolonged tight-rope conversation with the all-too-intuitive sheriff who was getting uncomfortably close to discovering all.

"That sounds like just what I need. I—I'll see you in the morning."

"I'll be here." He gestured to the sofa with a disarming half smile.

And she got while the getting was good.

The bathroom was luxuriously modern after the compartmental quarters of the Cheswicks' cabin, all angled redwood wainscotting, creamy porcelain, plush forest green towels and warm brass accents, boasting a full tub as well as a standing shower. As inviting as that tub looked, she felt uncomfortable with the idea of lounging naked in the sheriff's bathroom. Shower it was. Hot steam pampered her strained senses and a fluffy towel buffed them into a cozy state of bliss. She swallowed down a couple of pain relievers for the dull throb in her shoulder and meant to head straight for the safety of her isolated bedcovers.

But somewhere along the line, those noble plans were derailed by what could have been an innocent intention. Instead of to the safe, solitary bedroom, she returned to the main room where a bed of orange embers cast all into muted shades of shadow. He'd used the time while she was in the shower to make up the sofa with a pillow and the careless toss of a quilt over one arm.

Spencer was kneeling at the grate, prodding the last of the firewood into a rekindling glow. A brief flare cast his lean features in strong angular lines and played like molten gold through his tawny hair. He'd stripped off his shirt and shoes and for a long moment, Mercy was mesmerized by the way the flickering firelight moved with flattering strokes along the powerful swells and hollows of his upper body. Though he was motionless, the shifting pattern of light created rippling highlights over well-developed arms and the broad brace of his shoulders. In his crisply creased gray uniform, he'd always appeared sleek and graceful. In the flesh, he was a muscular male animal: virile, potent, hard. A fluttery sense of exhilaration warred with her basic caution. She could have quietly slipped away to avoid the potential danger but instead, she advanced upon it.

"Spencer?"

He looked up. Without the brightness of the fire, his eyes gleamed like black diamonds. He seemed surprised, then a complex expression took command of his features. His voice was an inviting rumble. "I thought you'd turned in."

"Not yet. I—I wanted to thank you. I don't know what Casey and I would have done if you hadn't been there for us tonight."

He shrugged and the movement was strong, fluid poetry. "Just doing my job."

"It was more than that and we both know it. I wanted you to know how much we—how much I—appreciated it."

"Glad to help." And he went very still because she continued to linger, looking like there was more on her mind but she was trying to decide on how to approach it. She looked so vulnerable standing there, struggling for the right things to say, well knowing what the consequences might be for every second she remained. As impatient as he was to learn what caused her hesitation, he continued to wait, fearing a slight push on his end would lead to a retreat. Let her come to you, emotional logic whispered.

Her voice came out very small.

"I was scared."

He didn't say anything. He didn't move. Sensing there was more. Letting her get it all out.

"I was so glad to see you."

A hitch in that last word betrayed her. Spencer reached out a hand, not up to her, but down beside him to pat the rug invitingly. Making it her choice.

She sank down upon the spot he suggested, then after a moment's hesitation, did the natural thing and leaned into him to collect the comfort she knew awaited. His skin was hot beneath her cheek, soft yet tough like silk, and soon dampened by the tears she tried not to shed. His arms came up in an easy loop, surrounding but not confining. Support that didn't demand surrender. And with a shaking sob, she slipped hers about his taut middle, hugging as tight as she could, as if his very solidity would overwhelm the reality of her fear.

And it did. Slowly, soothingly, his presence calmed her spirit. But instead of a restful peace, in its wake rose an elemental agitation. It was disturbing but not distressing, and Mercy pondered the difference. The difference was trust. She was anxious but not afraid. Not of Spencer.

He would have held her for as long as she rested quietly, seeking solace. But the minute she lifted her head and they were breath-sharing close, that was the end of his chivalry.

He wrapped his hand in her hair and slid the other up to frame the side of her face with tenderness. His kiss was warm, his mouth molding to hers, tempting hers with the slow glide of his tongue. It stroked wetly along the seam of her lips before pressing insistently between them. A shiver took her. And pleasure, wild and raw, awoke inside.

His tongue touched hers in silky introduction, inviting it to join in, to sample, to share; and Mercy responded with a tentative wonder. She was drawn deeper into those velvet-dark feelings as he withdrew, coaxing her to follow across

the juncture of their kiss into an exploration of her own, as
his fingers brushed along her cheek and jaw in praising encouragement. In the hot cavern of his mouth, she tasted
danger. Pursuing it boldly, she found desire.

Mercy felt her body heat. Eddies of longing quivered
through her as he trickled a row of melting kisses down the
arch of her throat and sucked at the caroming heartbeat he
found at its hollow. Her hands fluttered upon the sleek curve
of his back, then pressed palms flat to draw him up closer.
Her spine bowed, her breasts yielded to the hard contour of
his chest. And from someplace deep within the feminine
soul of her, passion rumbled to life.

Spencer lifted up his head just then, pausing long enough
for her to stop him if she chose. When she didn't, he allowed her a brief gulp of air before taking her under again,
this time with a no-holds-barred hunger.

He hadn't meant to go so far so fast, but when an urgent
little moan sounded in the back of her throat, when her
fingers made needy indentations along his spine, he couldn't
remember caution.

His hands pushed up under the edge of her sweat jacket,
following the enticing curve of her torso until his thumbs
snagged under the swell of her breasts. He moved his hands
higher, feeling the fleshy weight and firm softness fill them.
He worked the fabric up with the hike of his forearms and
suddenly she was beautifully bared to him. Spencer was
dizzyingly aware that she didn't fight him. Her head was
thrown back, her eyes were closed, he could feel the hurried pulse of her need within his palm.

The wet heat of his mouth sent a jolt of sensation through
Mercy, followed by anticipating shudders. Her palms
pushed up over the bulge of his shoulders to cradle the back
of his head, holding him to her bosom. A sweet ache speared
all the way to her bare toes and back up, seeming to settle
with a pooling heat at the juncture of her thighs. There, a
throb of yearning began to beat like a hard little heart.

Mercy was so seduced by the unfamiliar sensations flow-
ing through her body, that her self-preserving panic failed

to surface until he eased over her, using his weight and superior size to push her back against the solid bulk of the sofa. His shadow blocked out the light from the fire and in the darkness, there was only the impression of smothering male bulk and overwhelming male heat.

An inarticulate cry escaped her, so wild and despairing, Spencer went instantly still above her. She thrashed beneath him, the movements mindless, as desperate as the sudden chug of her breathing. Elbows and knees became sharp instruments of denial, pushing, poking in protest when a simple word would have stopped him just as effectively. Then it came, breathless and shrill in objection.

"Don't!"

Spencer dropped back onto his heels. He was gasping for control, grappling for patience when confusion and full-speed-ahead passion wrestled for possession of him. Need cut through him, sharp and fierce, aching like the aftermath of an unfair blow. How long could he play this will-and-won't game with her? True, he was no inexperienced boy with hormones overriding reason, but there was only so much a man could take when it came to sexual torture of this cruel and unusual nature. If she wasn't interested in the destination, she shouldn't have set out upon the road.

"I usually don't misread signals this strong," he began in a passion-rough voice. "If you're planning to say stop, it's a good idea to do it a little earlier on." And he couldn't help the edge of annoyance that crept into that gruff sermon. "I didn't hear anything that sounded like stop. Did I miss something?"

One look at Mercy curbed the bulk of his libidinous demands. She was pressed back against the couch, her knees drawn up between them as a barrier. But what held him totally at bay was her expression. In a face that was deathly white and oddly void of emotion, her eyes were huge and just as blank, as if terror had wiped them mercilessly clean.

She was seeing something through that flat, fixed stare but it wasn't him.

"Mercy? What's wrong?"

It was finally the shock and bewilderment in his features that brought Mercy off that high ledge of fright. She edged her way down with a tense caution, as if any move on his part would send her scrambling back for that distancing safety. When the sense of time and place and partner had returned to her gaze, they regarded one another for a long, wordless moment.

He deserved an explanation but Mercy couldn't think of one that would adequately cover for the truth.

"I'm sorry, Spencer. I just can't stand feeling—"

"What?"

"Helpless."

He thought she was crazy, Mercy realized in dismay. Crazy or the meanest sort of tease. How could she make him understand how difficult it was for her to overcome her fear of intimacy? She could only venture so far before the pleasure of the moment shifted to their inevitable destination: Spencer's bed. Better he think the worst of her now than discover the truth of it there. There, where all the lovely feelings he'd stirred to life would turn into a frigid denial. Where she feared she'd find disgust in the touch she cherished.

She couldn't stand to fail him on that basic male-female ground as she'd failed others before him—others who didn't mean half as much to her as this tender lawman. Better that he look at her now with frustration than later with pity.

"What's wrong, Mercy?"

She cringed beneath that quietly asked question. What could she tell him? The truth? And have him withdraw as if she had some kind of contaminating plague? She couldn't endure that—not when her defenses were so low and her heart was stripped bare of all but guilt and shame and the helpless love she felt for him. It would kill her if he despised her.

So she held herself away from him, girded behind her silence and her secrets, that isolation pushing him away more effectively than anything she could have said.

"You know I'd never hurt you, Mercy. You know that, don't you?"

She managed a stiff nod.

He started to take a hold of her hand but she jerked it back as if the gesture contained some kind of threat. Tears of frustration and fright quickened in eyes that begged his understanding. Yet how could he come close to understanding if she withheld the reasons for her abrupt behavior?

He didn't move toward her again, nor did he withdraw. He watched her and she felt uncomfortably vulnerable beneath his steady stare. As their stalemate grew increasingly awkward, Mercy frantically sought a way to break it, a way that wouldn't hurt him or expose her for the emotional sham she was.

"Spencer—"

"When did it happen, Mercy?"

She must have misunderstood him.

"Tell me."

His tone was soft, full of gripping intensity. A man who refused to be denied his answer. Mercy started slightly and began to shake her head, not wanting to link his question to any sort of comprehension on his part.

He couldn't know. He couldn't guess. He wouldn't be regarding her with a look of pure compassion if he guessed what was hidden behind her denial of their shared desires.

But Spencer Halloway was an intuitive man. He saw more in her silences than he'd ever learned through her words. What he saw was ugly. What he recognized was a woman's worst nightmare. And it was with a determined tenderness that he brought it to light, up from the guarded and guilty shadows of her soul where she'd suppressed it in secret shame.

"When were you raped?"

Chapter 13

There was no evading his question and unexpectedly, Mercy felt relief. No more pretending she was something she was not. No more pressure to maintain a normal response when what she felt was anything but normal. That right, that ability had been torn away from her. And now Spencer would see her as she truly was. Flawed. Scarred. Scared.

She'd never been able to discuss it comfortably. A shame so indelibly ingrained didn't wear away. It was part of her emotional makeup just as her reactions were instinctive. Cover it up and try to forget it. Only it wasn't something so easily buried.

Her first attempt to expose the trauma was met with such a hard rebuff, it had taken her years to build up the bravery to try again. None of the resulting experiences had helped. She'd seen psychologists who listened with compassion and explained away the guilt she suffered. They cleansed and dressed the wounds but nothing could lift the scars. Scars that deepened every time she tried to confront a normal relationship. Failure reinforced her subconscious blame, making her feel all the more ashamed, all the more different and distant. She hadn't connected with her own emotions, not until Casey. Then all those old pains, all those repressed fears were forced to the surface. She recognized them out of necessity, but she hadn't dealt with them directly, personally, until Spencer.

And now he was waiting for her to explain.

"It was a long time ago." Her voice was soft and inflectionless. She had to stay remote if she was to speak of it at all.

"How long, Mercy?"

"When I was almost a teenager, a couple of years older than Casey is now."

She saw the shock register in his face, then more subtle emotion hardened behind his eyes. Fury. Disgust. And the small flame of hope flickering briefly around her heart extinguished in that awful moment of revelation. She'd known things would never be the same between them once he knew the truth. He would never look at her the same way again.

"Was it someone you knew?"

Her arms crossed defensively over her breasts, hugging to the feelings of helplessness, to the deep ache of betrayal. Anger trembled in her voice. Her therapists would have called that a good sign. "It was someone I trusted, someone who should have been protecting me instead of defiling the trust of a child."

"Who was it, Mercy?" His question was sharp, fired in his policeman's voice. Mercy couldn't look at him.

"It doesn't matter, Spencer."

He reached out to her, then. His hand moved to engulf hers with a slow, sliding possession, his fingers crooking, curling hers into his palm, holding them nestled there, surrounded by safety.

"If it still matters to you, it matters a lot. Talk to me, Mercy."

Because his words promised the same gentle handling that he offered with his tender grasp, she was tempted to tell him all. The truth hovered, begging to be told. But she didn't reveal it. Those secrets weren't hers alone to reveal. Instead she gave a resigned sigh designed to mask the pain.

"It didn't do any good at the time, and I can't see that it will be any different now. Telling you the ugly facts won't change them."

Because he was watching her closely, Spencer saw the brief spasm of denial cross her expression and disappear beneath her tough act of self-sufficiency. And he knew if he pressed her for more, what he'd get would be a distorted version of the truth, if it contained truth at all. What he'd touched on here was just the tip of the emotional iceberg. What lay beneath the surface were those damaging facts she wouldn't tell. To get to them and to the heart of her, there was only one path to use. And that was trust. To take it, he would have to ignore the forceful fury inside that demanded details and accountability.

Oh, how he wanted to learn that name, to get his hands on the bastard responsible for the guilty shadows in Mercy's eyes. To him, there was no crime more vile than the violation of the innocent, and no one as defenseless as a child. But the more important crime was not the one that happened years ago, it was the one still perpetuated in Mercy's mind: that she was somehow to blame for what had been done to her.

Very slowly, he lifted her hand. Her gaze flickered to him in a wary response and he could feel her fingers tense as she considered pulling away. Then they trembled beneath the warm caress of his lips. She seemed bewildered, as if she hadn't expected him to display compassion. What kind of insensitive creeps had she been involved with before?

"Mercy, the facts are ugly. The man who did this to you was ugly. But that ugliness hasn't rubbed off on you."

Surprisingly, she laughed at that; a soft, bittersweet chuckle. "So I discovered after years of counseling. And here I could have saved myself all that time and money by coming straight to you for those healing words."

He wasn't fooled by her gruff humor. She was far from healed. She wore her wounds like a protective armor against further injury, as a means of keeping the world at bay. But he wasn't satisfied to be held at arm's length.

Not any more.

"You'll find my prices are reasonable and my couch much more comfortable."

There was no disguising her stiffening as his fingers stroked hers, just as his suggestion caressed her senses. Her glance darted upward in a nervous recognition of pillow and blanket. His bed.

"Thank you for the offer, *Dr.* Halloway, but I've done my time on the couch. My problems have been sliced and diced and puréed by the best of them. I know all the proper jargon. But understanding the clinical whys and wherefores doesn't change the fact that I lost my freedom of choice, nor does it give me back the childhood that was stolen from me. Talk is just talk. It doesn't change how I feel."

"I'm sorry."

And his sympathy sparked rebellion. Temper flared at the injustice of it. "I'm sorry, too. I'm sorry that I can't be the woman you want, Spencer. I'm sorry that I can't give you what you need."

"Is that what you think is important to me? That I go away disappointed?"

Her silence was his answer.

"What about what you need, Mercy?"

She stared at him, too startled to do more than mouth an unspoken rebuttal. Unspoken because no one had ever put it quite that way before. She'd always approached her difficulties in terms of how they related to others, focusing on how she could cope with their ideals and demands, how she could fit in by ignoring her inner pain.

She'd never realized that she should be able to make those demands, too; that she should be allowed her own expectations. She'd just assumed that those reasonable rights had been stolen from her, as well. She'd assumed no man would want her, knowing the emotional baggage she came with. Spencer Halloway was telling her flat out that she was wrong in that thinking. He was telling her it wasn't her problem alone.

And she wanted desperately to believe him.

He still held her hand gently in his, a touchingly old-fashioned and somehow searingly intimate gesture that triggered a thrum of awareness. Of him as a man, of him as a potential lover.

"Mercy, healing begins in the heart, not in the mind. I ought to know. You helped me learn that particular truth when I didn't want any part of it. I'd like to try that cure on you if you're willing."

When she said nothing, he brought her hand up once again, this time pressing his kiss not to her knuckles, but to the soft skin of her inner wrist, where her pulse scurried in sudden anxious anticipation.

"You do have a choice, Mercy. You can choose to hold yourself back from those who care. No question about it, it'll keep you from getting hurt again, but it'll also keep you from some of the greatest joys life has to offer. Or you can take a risk and trust in what your heart has been trying to tell you."

She was looking at him through bruised eyes, listening through a wounded spirit. He could have pushed his case harder but just then, he realized it was time to back down and let her weigh her own decision. Too much in her life had been decided without her consent. In this one, most personal thing, the choice would be all hers.

Then he'd have to find a way to deal with it.

"I want to make love with you, Spencer."

That was voiced with flat-out honesty. It surprised both of them a little. The rest came harder.

"I want you but—but I'm afraid I'll disappoint you, that I'll disappoint us both."

"Then why don't we go into it with no expectations at all and just see what happens?"

"Can we do that?" Hope quivered like fragile crystal and made him desire to protect it that much more.

''We can do anything you like. All the hard choices are yours. I already know how much I want you. And I've already told you, I will never, ever hurt you.''

Her gaze was skeptical as she assessed the situation. Spencer had been many things to her. She'd feared him as a potential enemy. She'd shied from the intensity of his sexual appeal. He'd done his best to discover her secrets, using sweet talk, trickery and probably methods she knew nothing about. But he hadn't denied that. He'd never told her anything but the truth and she had no reason to believe he wasn't telling it now. Because even though she couldn't trust his work, she'd always been able to trust the man.

She drew away from him, rising up to sit on the edge of the sofa. She gave a slight bounce on the cushions. ''You say this couch is comfortable?''

His smile started out small and kept on coming. ''It sure is.''

Mercy hesitated but it wasn't from reluctance, it was from inexperience. She didn't know what the next move should be, even as her yearning intensified to a palpable degree. Not wanting her uncertainty to change into any excuse for shame, Spencer assumed control of the direction if not the pace of their intentions by easing up onto the couch beside her, making his movements gentlingly slow.

When she didn't try to withdraw, he took her anxious face within the big frame of his hands and brought her to him for a kiss that went a long way toward soothing the doubts of a lifetime.

He nibbled at the fullness of her lips, letting her know he found her incredibly sexy because she seemed to have big doubts in that department. Crazy to him, but very real to her. He feathered his tongue along their soft seam to express his soul-deep desire for her. She wouldn't have believed it if he told her in words, so he would show her. He wanted to fill up her senses so there could be no room for fear, no space for regret, no chance for retreat. Because she deserved to know what she'd been missing. And he wanted to be the one to fill in all the blanks.

But Mercy wasn't thinking about fear or regret or retreat. She was humming like a high-tension wire. Her body ached with an emptiness she'd never felt until Spencer pointed out the void. Knowing he could fill it had her restless. Knowing he would fill it left her impatient.

But Spencer was in no hurry. If no one had ever bothered to explain the finer nuances of love to her, she wouldn't be ignorant of them for much longer. He teased her with the scattering of his kisses, letting them sprinkle upon her face and down her neck and along her fleece-covered shoulders. A low purr of pleasure escaped her lips and sent shudders spiking through him in a fever-hot rush. His hands slipped down the sleek column of her throat and followed the flare of her collarbone before stroking downward and around, flanking the curve of her breasts, then conquering them with a light, encompassing pressure. She arched toward him, lost to the feeling. Her nipples rose, diamond-hard, against his palms and the throb of her need echoed in the moan that escaped her.

"Spencer..." A mindless request for more.

He shifted on the sofa, and seeing the way she tensed when his shadow crossed her, he redirected his seduction. The last thing he wanted her to feel was threatened. Wild. Free. Even wicked. But never intimidated.

She was bemused by his sudden change in tactics but she let him lift her up off the cushions so he, himself, could recline back upon the low, rolled arm. Then she was smiling as he draped her over him, along the intriguingly hard contours of his body within the protective cradle of one arm. She snuggled in, absorbing the enticing warmth of bare skin and basking in the sense of pampered luxury. A contented sigh escaped as she nestled her head beneath his chin.

"Your fire's going out."

She was watching the last of the embers struggle in the grate when Spencer gave a low and lusty chuckle.

"I don't think there's much chance of that happening anytime soon, sweetheart."

She blushed at his meaning and enjoyed a naughty speculation. That was a surprise in itself, because she'd never been able to take sexual matters lightly. It had always been grim business before, to be endured and quickly forgotten. Nothing to be enjoyed.

With Spencer, the whole atmosphere was different; simmering, expectant, playful and yet unbearably passionate. And she gave herself over to those sensations. It wasn't news that she found him exciting. It wasn't even a revelation that his touch could make her burn. What struck her suddenly was her desire to excite and touch in return. To make him burn for her.

Except, being the take-charge kind of man he was, Spencer wasn't about to let her give until she'd taken all he had to offer. And he planned for that to take all night.

His caresses began again—slow, sure waves that wore away the banks of her reserve, undercutting modesty, washing away thoughts of resistance. She let them build, let them lap against the foundations of fear until no hints of uneasiness remained. She'd been waiting to be swept away for a lifetime and had known this was the man almost from the beginning.

He knew what she wanted before she realized it herself. When her breasts began to swell and fill with a heavy ache, his hand was there to relieve that tension. When the weight of his palm upon the barrier of fleece grew distracting, his fingers slipped beneath the hem of her jacket to soothe bare skin. Her responses came from a well of womanly instinct because she was past coherent thought.

To feel, to absorb, to enjoy became all.

His palm rode intimately along the curve of her hip, following that contour to the seam of her thighs. A vague pulse of alarm quickened. When his attention lingered there, her restlessness increased, a confusion of heated welcome and a stir of discomfort. He was too close; too close to the source of her shame. She wanted him to return to the safer seduction of her breasts, even as a foreign heat began massing in urgent contradiction.

"Easy, sweetheart," he whispered. "You're doing fine. Just fine."

When his hand tucked beneath the band of her sweat bottoms, she found herself lifting slightly, allowing him the space to nudge them down. Though her bulky top still swaddled her hips, a feeling of helpless exposure came with the baring of her legs. He didn't hurry. His palm soothed along the long line of her thigh, stroking, gentling, taming her reluctance with the magic of his touch. She was lost to the liquid sensation of falling, sinking deeper into the drugging pleasures he was tempting to life. Then her knees parted, a subconscious invitation punctuated by her breathy moan.

The light brush of his fingertips was like the striking of a match head. The flare of heat and want was instantaneous and all consuming. His unrelenting touch commanded her fears and vulnerability, overruling the whisper of panic with a louder voice of need. And all the while as he teased and tempted and tormented her into a frenzy, he was talking, murmuring low, sweet words of praise that she failed to grasp word for word. Something about a wild sense of right, a wicked sense of need, a wonderful sense of belonging. She felt it all.

He called her beautiful. He called her hot. He called her sweetheart huskily, the sound like the tearing of raw silk. And she came apart like the rending of that exquisite fabric, with a raspy cry of discovery.

She didn't move again for the longest time. Her body melted over his like the drizzle of hot butter over popcorn. Beneath that saturating warmth, Spencer sizzled, an unpopped kernel ready to explode.

"Sweetheart, we have to move," he murmured into the tousle of her hair.

"Huh?"

"This show hasn't exactly been approved for general audiences, you know."

Thoughts of Casey woke a mutter of concern.

"Hang on. Let's relocate."

Spencer stood with Mercy bundled to his chest like a sleepy kitten. She never opened her eyes as he carried her into his bedroom. There, the dying glow of the fire couldn't reach them. In those sultry shadows, Spencer skimmed off Mercy's sweat top and eased her down upon his sheets.

The feel of her bare skin sliding on that cool surface brought Mercy's eyes open and instantly, a protesting cry escaped her. She scrambled wildly for the opposite side of the mattress, legs flailing as she wedged her knees under her, her hands yanking up the covers to cocoon her nakedness. Her breathing sounded labored in the sudden stillness.

Without hesitation, Spencer reached for the light on the bedside table. A soft illumination came to life and he almost regretted it. Darkness was better, for it hid the sight of her terror from him. She was crouched in a mindless pose of self-defense, her features ravaged with alarm, her dilated pupils glazed and unseeing. Nothing had ever acted as strongly upon him as that stark image. And it was a struggle for him to appear unaffected.

"There. Is that better? I forget how dark it gets in here. I think I'll just leave this on in case you have to get up in the night. One trip to the emergency room is enough for any one summer, thank you very much."

And the continued brightness would keep her from confusing his silhouette with a threat from her past.

His casual tone lessened the severity of her alarm but the caution was still there when he sat on the edge of the bed. He waited a few moments, then asked conversationally, "If you're tired, I can go bunk on the couch."

She started to relax. "Are you tired?"

"No. I'm pretty sure I'll be up for a while."

His grin spread slowly, inviting a gleam of seductive devilry to creep into his gaze. Mercy couldn't resist.

"In that case..."

She scooted across the bed to where he waited. Spencer, her sensitive, unbearably sexy lover and friend. That deep, delicious want to return the favor was back and she intended to act upon it. She may not have known much about the mechanics of making love but she knew what she liked when it was done to her. And she was pretty sure he'd like it, too.

She took his lean face between her palms and took his mouth. Hard. She wasn't half as gentle as he had been. She caressed the warm cords of his throat with her hands, with her lips, letting them trail from shoulder to shoulder around the prominent ring of his collarbone. He made no move to touch her, did nothing to interrupt the bold flow of her curiosity as her kisses eased down to taunt a tightly beaded nipple, while her fingers worked dexterously at the button of his jeans. With a groan, he dropped back upon the bed to make it less complicated for her.

But suddenly, she was in no hurry.

She touched him through the taut hug of denim, surprised and bemused by the way he pulsed to life beneath her palm. She waited for the intimacy of the act to arouse her inner panic, but those feelings lay dormant within her. She grasped the top of his zipper and slowly drew it down, daring the smothering sense of helplessness to stop her. Her awareness of him, her desire for him increased to spite the provocation. Surely the fear would reassert itself as she wrestled his jeans down over his hips and skinned them from his long legs. Nothing but the mounting throb of excitement rose in response.

She'd waited years to learn what love could be like when unencumbered by the past. Her chance was here at last. No way was she going to let it pass her by.

Mercy slid up alongside Spencer, seeking out his mouth and the hot tangle of his tongue, her desperation fueled by the intrinsic trust his patience with her had nurtured. Her patience was gone, devastated by the silky way he explored the inside of her mouth. They were side by side, touching each other, discovering each other with restless strokes and urgent kisses. The pressure massed to the brink of nuclear meltdown. Something had to give.

With a careless groan, Mercy abandoned all to thrust her leg up, letting it ride Spencer's hip. It was an unmistakable request that he return to show her more of the shattering ways her body could respond to him. She gasped as he cupped her with his palm, sighed as he sought and found the sensitive nub hidden for far too long in the protective custody of her fear. He freed her with the sensual insistence of his touch, making her shake, making her moan. Making her ache to discover what had been held unfairly from her. Making her burn to find a woman's fulfillment in his arms.

When he left her briefly, she followed him with the clutch of her hands, begging softly, shamelessly, "Spencer, don't stop now."

"Don't think of it as stopping," he panted. "Think of it as proceeding with care."

He was fumbling in the drawer of his nightstand, cursing, sending the lamp teetering. Shadows careened off the walls and Mercy, amazingly, found a smile quivering upon her lips as she observed his frustrated efforts—because it was his urgent need of her that had him so uncustomarily clumsy.

After all his fishing he landed a foil packet, but for the life of him, he couldn't rip it open. The fact that his hands were suffering from an earthquake of anticipation didn't help matters.

He cursed again, more fluidly and descriptively this time. "I hate these things. I can never seem to manage—"

"Let me."

He was so stunned, he never thought to react as Mercy lifted the packet from his sweaty palm. She peeled it open neatly and he waited for its return. Only to have her astonish him a second time.

"This can't be much different than putting on a pair of panty hose, right?"

There was a hell of a lot of difference! But somehow he couldn't form the words as she eased the snug latex on and followed it with a maddening rub of her fingertips. He wanted to praise her for taking this unexpected initiative but his mind was blanked by sensory overload.

The sound of his ragged breathing and the scrape of her nails running up from hips to shoulders were the only sounds; an erotic prelude. Their eyes met, his a glimmer of quicksilver, hers a deep well of uncovered passion. The boundaries were gone. Expectation hung hot and heavy between them.

Spencer took her down to the mattress with a deep, soul-possessing kiss. In that prone position with his size and strength looming over her, Mercy felt a flicker of distress. He distracted her from it by pouring lavish attention upon her mouth, then her breasts. When he moved up from that maddening concentration, she was too dazed by desire to assemble a single protesting thought.

He lowered himself against her, letting her sample his weight, letting her get accustomed to the feel of his hard arousal pushing along the groove of her thighs, waiting for her to open the way to the deepest level of intimacy a man and woman could share.

She tensed beneath him briefly, her knees gripping together as if to hold cruel memories at bay.

"Easy, sweetheart," he crooned in a voice as passion rough as a cat's tongue. "I won't hurt you, Mercy. Whenever you're ready."

Slowly, her legs relaxed and eased apart, allowing him to settle between them. She was still breathing in quick, anxious snatches but she wasn't trying to fight him. He was braced on his forearms to keep the crush of his body from pinning her. He was tickling wet kisses along the tense line of her jaw, teasing hard points of pleasure with the scrub of his thumbs over her suddenly all-too-sensitive nipples. He was waking her to the rich textures of delight and when she had taken all she could stand without buckling beneath the intensifying wonder of it, she gripped his flanks with the flat of her palms and tugged him toward her, rough in her demand.

She was so ready for him there was no question of going slow. He sank without resistance into a welcoming well of moist heat. She took all of him in with a reverent cry of his name then held him there with the twining of her long, long legs about his. He gave her all the time she wanted, letting her soak up the sensations of fullness, of completion. And when her hips gave an encouraging arch, he began to move, stroking her with fire and the fever of longing, replacing every bad remembrance with galvanizing pleasure. Making her moan, making her writhe, making her claw at him in a blind need for release.

Tremors shook along her limbs. Her breath gave in a huge sob of satisfaction as the contracting walls of her body sucked him down with her into an inferno of relief.

For what seemed an eternity, neither of them found the strength to move. Then, with the utmost reluctance, Spencer eased over onto his side, keeping her cuddled close against him. With the utterance of a well-contented sigh, he reached for the top of his nightstand, rummaging until his fingers closed over a fresh pack of cigarettes. A few soothing draws were just what he needed to celebrate the splendor of their union.

Then Mercy leaned over him, her breasts grazing his chest as her hand slipped on top of his.

"You don't need those, do you? I thought you were trying to quit."

His heart stumbled into an immediate sprint. And he found plenty of things with which to occupy his mouth and hands as the desire for a smoke was quickly forgotten.

Spencer slept like the dead. He was sprawled across the bed with the careless abandon of one unused to sharing his sheets and finding himself alone in them was no surprise until his foggy mind was seduced by images of Mercy. He wasn't supposed to be alone this morning. And a lazy smile of pure male satisfaction crossed his face. This morning he was entertaining a guest. But where was she?

He glanced at his clock. It was minutes before five. Early. Still plenty of time to...indulge a little. He shut his eyes and waited in a drifting luxury for the alarm to call an end to his lethargy.

And for Mercy to rejoin him.

As his senses sharpened by degrees, he listened for the sound of her moving about somewhere in his house. There was only silence. Too much silence.

He was alone.

Frowning slightly, he tugged on his jeans and a faded T-shirt. Maybe she'd decided to slip in with Casey so the child wouldn't be scared upon waking in a strange room. That made sense. He tiptoed to the second bedroom and peeked inside. The bed was neatly made, its quilt as smooth as the surface of the lake. Not a ripple of disturbance. But plenty of disturbance was rippling through him.

Mercy and Casey were gone. No note. No goodbye. They'd even locked his front door behind them. He stood there for a moment, too stunned to react. He couldn't believe she would leave without—something. Somehow this stealthy desertion lessened what he'd felt with her as they'd made love. He thought they'd found trust in those tangled sheets, a sense of kinship in their soulful kisses.

He didn't like thinking he could be wrong.

After hurriedly slipping on shoes, he climbed into his Blazer. It probably wasn't the smartest thing to do, charging after her at the break of day to demand her intentions, but he was feeling scared.

That feeling dug in deep when he turned into their empty drive. The car was gone.

Leaving his motor running, Spencer jogged up to the door. He banged until the wood vibrated and his hand ached, even after he knew he'd get no answer. Because he couldn't face the fact that he'd so misread the situation. He couldn't believe what the silence told him.

He circled the cabin, unconsciously following in the prowler's footsteps as he stretched up to peer in each window. The cabin was all tidily arranged, the beds made, the counter cleared. There were no toiletry items in the bathroom. No wisps of unmentionables in the bedroom. No sign of a child in residence.

The stick was in the refrigerator door to aid in its defrosting.

Then it hit him hard. That truth he'd been trying his best to ignore.

They were gone.

Chapter 14

Two things hammered in Spencer's head as he drove into Pine Creek. The first was his foolishness in letting emotions override instinct. He'd known Mercy was not what she seemed, yet he'd purposefully ignored the signals of mind to placate the longings of heart and body. The second was deeper than the ache of self-doubt. He was wondering if she'd used their night of passion as a ruse to stall his professional investigation long enough for her to make plans to flee.

Were his feelings for her based upon a lie he'd wanted desperately to believe?

It was a little late to rely on standard procedure, but that's what he would do. If he'd stuck with the guidelines of his office rather than detoured by way of his own desires, he wouldn't be racing frantically into work with a bruised and broken heart and a battered ego. He couldn't afford to get sidetracked again.

He told himself his professional pride was in the balance. A lie, of course, because it was his emotions that were careening wildly since he'd discovered she was gone. Angry chagrin was easier to handle than the sense of wounded disappointment. He couldn't afford to focus on how much her abandonment had hurt him.

He'd been on that roller coaster of blame before and it was a ride he'd sworn not to take again. To cover up the burn of betrayal, he would concentrate on the reasons and leave the results alone. He had questions to be answered, questions a smart man would have prioritized over the search for emotional fulfillment. A little late but better late than never.

How could he have been so blind as to trust her with his own track record of heartbreak to go by? He should have known she was going to run rather than face the surfacing truth; yet he'd foolishly hoped she would turn to him for help once he proved himself reliable. He'd laid down his cautions, even his career before her needs, and she'd burned skid marks over them in her hurry to escape. He had every reason to be furious with himself and with her.

So if that was the case, why was it worry rather than wrath provoking him now?

Answers. He needed answers. The logical place to start was at the Pine Creek clinic with their would-be prowler.

Except there he discovered that P.I. Sweeney was floating on an oblivious painkiller high and being prepped for a trip to the closest hospital for exploratory surgery. Nothing major for the poor detective; he was going to recover just fine. But it was a serious dead end to Spencer for the moment.

"Sorry, Spence, no way could you get a coherent word out of him now," Larry Wells told him regretfully. "I understand your deputy made a nuisance of himself at the hospital and for some of it, Sweeney was conscious and able to talk. I don't know what was said, though. And speaking of things being said, whatever it was you told Mrs. Royce, thank you. She stopped in yesterday to pay her bill, in full. In cash."

But Spencer wasn't listening. He was on his way through the mechanical doors. On his way to find Chet Allen.

He was working on a major headache by the time he stepped into the station, and his gut was grinding glass-tight when he considered what he had to go on: a woman with no traceable identity with a child who was not her own, a mystery prowler close to comatose carrying a private investigator's badge, and a deputy bucking for vehicular manslaughter. The woman, he was crazy in love with. The P.I., he couldn't interrogate. And the deputy was wearing a chip of arrogance on his shoulder the size of a telephone pole and was being unprofessionally close-lipped about his business.

That was more stress than a morning cup of coffee could deal with. Hell, he'd even forgotten his cigarettes in his hurry. He had to find something to chew on to relieve the tension massing inside him and it looked like it was going to be Chet Allen's butt.

"Chet's in your office, Sheriff. He says he wants to talk to you."

Spencer nodded and glared through the wall of glass to where he could see his deputy sitting behind his desk with his feet up on the heat register. The knot in his belly started throwing acid. "Good. I want to talk to him, too. May, I want you to find Amy Cheswick for me. She's a lawyer and just recently married. I want a current location. She's supposed to be somewhere in the Caribbean, and I need her voice on the phone before the day's over."

"Yes, sir, Sheriff."

"And I want an APB on the wire for the Cheswicks' Pontiac. It's a 1993 Grand Am, blue in color." He rattled off the plate number from memory.

A pause, then a somber, "Right away, Spencer."

Spencer stepped into his office and closed the door softly behind him.

"Something on your mind, Chet?"

The low drawl of his voice startled the daydreaming deputy. His feet dropped back to the floor with a clunk and he swiveled somewhat guiltily to face his senior officer. As an afterthought, he leaped up out of the desk chair and let Spencer calmly assume it.

From that position of authority and power, Spencer regarded his nervous underling, keeping his expression stoic and letting the silence draw out until it became intimidating.

Spencer knew all about cops like Chet. They were bullies who liked to abuse their badge to make up for flaws in self-esteem. They were long on aggression and short on compassion, which in his thinking should be reversed in a good officer. He knew Chet had been trying out his chair, not because it was comfortable, but because he wanted to be sitting in it himself. And for the sake of Pine Creek, Spencer hoped that would never happen.

In the years Spencer had been sheriff, he'd developed a paternal fondness for the community. And despite all his reservations, yes, they were his responsibility. It was time he stopped shying away from that idea. He was as committed to them as he had been to his misplaced ideals while serving in Detroit. Only here, good things could grow and he could watch it happen. He could make it happen. If he could keep Chet on a short leash and choke chain.

If he could unravel the mystery of Mercy Royce.

"What did you find out from the P.I.?"

Chet hauled back his shoulders into a strutty posture but his eyes narrowed at Spencer's crisp tone. "I rode with him to the hospital and he did manage to come around for a bit before they got him admitted and shoved me out. Doctors don't understand about police procedures and priorities." He sneered that in contempt.

"No, they don't. Guess they somehow got the mistaken idea that saving lives was more important."

Chet's jaw stuck out belligerently.

"So, what did he tell you? Besides threats to sue for wrongful injury."

Chet paled slightly at that reminder, then his features grew furtive and sly. "Could be you'll want it kept just between the two of us, Spence."

Spencer stiffened at that implication. "What did he say, Deputy? Tell me, then put it—every word of it—into your report."

Chet made a sullen face, then growled, "He couldn't give me all the details—client confidentiality, you know—but from what he would say, after a lot of heavy convincing on my part, was that he's working on a possible nonstranger abduction case involving a little girl. Look familiar?"

Chet produced a color photo with a flourish, his features a study in smugness as he watched Spencer's face for a reaction. He was disappointed if he expected much.

"Looks like the Royce girl," Spencer commented with a detachment that clearly puzzled his deputy.

"Yeah, damn straight it does. And that means your pretty little girlfriend is up to her hip pockets in a possible kidnapping. Want me to pick her up?" The gloating gleam in his eyes was impossible to miss. His smirk said he thought the sheriff's libido had gotten in the way of his duty to the law and he was anticipating the humbling to come.

Spencer wasn't about to oblige him. "I've got the situation well in hand, Deputy. What I do want you to do, is follow that P.I. to the hospital in Ludington and see if he comes around long enough to make any further statements on who might have hired him."

Chet's features fell with disappointment. "Aren't you going to call in the feds?"

"For what? They don't have the time or patience to involve themselves in our suspicions. Do you have a definite ID on the girl? An official report of a kidnapping on file?"

"Well . . . no."

"Then there's no way to run a check to see if any federal warrants have been issued. If you want to call them and tell them that you have no problem wasting their time with your groundless allegations, feel free, but I plan to wait until I've done everything I can do on this end before I hand over my case to the Bureau. That's my job as the sheriff here. Now, go do yours."

Chet lingered, chafing with a frustrated sense of failure on the cusp of what should have been victory and again, Spencer Halloway was to blame. If Pine Creek's sheriff wanted to play fast and loose with his career over some fugitive with great legs, he didn't want to miss his opportunity to step in and fill the void. The information he hadn't shared was the ticket to undermine Spencer's protection of his lady love. And now was the time to make it pay off—with a long-distance phone call, not by wasting his time escorting a vegetating accomplice to Ludington. Getting ahead was all in knowing when to make a move.

It was time for his move.

The sheriff's chair was plenty comfortable and he couldn't wait to make it his own.

Spencer didn't trust his deputy's slick smile nor his, "Whatever you say, Spence," promise. But he didn't have time to keep his eye on Chet Allen. He had other pressing priorities.

He looked down at the photo clutched in both his hands. There was no doubt it was Casey Royce. And Spencer had no doubt that Mercy was her nonstranger abductor. He hadn't betrayed how that news devastated him. Mercy, a kidnapper. It didn't make sense, yet it did. He knew Casey wasn't her child and that they'd come to Pine Creek to hide from something. The fact that Mercy had stolen the child?

But what he'd learned in his time spent with the two of them didn't support the kidnap profile. Casey was happy and well adjusted. She obviously adored Mercy and made no attempt to convey in the times they'd been alone together that she was with Mercy other than by her own free will. Of course, the courts didn't recognize the wishes of a six-year-old. And if Casey's parents were dead and Mercy had taken her from her legal guardians...

Why hadn't Mercy come to him with the truth?

He could understand her wariness at first, him being an officer of the law, but later, when they'd grown close, closer than close, why hadn't she confided in him then? She'd trusted him enough to let him breach her fears of personal intimacy but not enough to ask his professional assistance.

Why had she run? Why couldn't she have waited to speak to him?

She wouldn't have run if she didn't fear the law more than she trusted in love. The thought of the two of them fleeing blindly from dangers they couldn't share with him was more than he could stand. Part of him wanted to find them and protect them. The other part was hurt enough to only want to track them down for an explanation. That was the prideful part and it was easily ignored in favor of his attraction to the woman.

Attraction? It had been more than that even from the beginning. It was love he felt for Mercy, and he was afraid it was too late to do anything about it. If he'd been less worried about putting his own emotions at risk and had spoken those words to her the night before, would she have run from him?

Or wasn't she in the least bit interested in his heart? Had she been taking advantage of his emotions all along?

Was he out to rescue a victim of unfair circumstances or on his way to play out the pain of betrayal one more time? The chafe of wondering steeled him for what he had to do.

"I'm heading out for a while, May," he called as he strode by her desk without a sideward glance. "Patch through on my truck's radio if you get any of that information I asked you for."

"Will do, Sheriff."

And as he drove north—he'd figured they would head north—Spencer wondered what he was going to do when he caught up to them.

Mercy blinked back the buildup of moisture in her eyes to focus on the barren blacktop ahead. She was driving fast for nowhere in particular. All she knew was she had to get away.

They were running low on cash after paying off Casey's medical treatment so they would have to find someplace cheap to put them up. She couldn't risk using her credit cards. Too easily traced. Just because one investigator was out of the picture didn't mean more wouldn't follow.

And she had to get a hold of Amy. Things were getting out of hand, first with Spencer, now with that hospital-bound P.I. She needed more than a friend's support. She was in dire need of legal direction.

Mercy cast a look at Casey. The child was still pouting within the wrap of her seat belt. She hadn't liked the idea of leaving Big Bear Lake or Spencer Halloway. Neither had Mercy, but she was the more realistic of the two of them. Spencer was an officer of the law and she was breaking it. No matter what had passed between them, no matter what he felt for them, he would have to do his job. And forcing the man she'd come to love to take that kind of tortuous middle-ground stance was too cruel. Better she leave than make him choose.

It was without a doubt the hardest thing she'd ever done. When she'd awakened in his big bed, curled in the comfort of his covers and content with the knowledge of what had transpired hours earlier, the last thought on her mind was escape. He'd been stretched out on his back, a long lean length of gorgeous man, concentrating on slumber. His face was turned toward her. The tousle of his tawny hair and the shadow of his morning beard woke wonderfully warm sentiments and a melting need within her. She'd never shared the early-morning hours in intimate companionship and she marveled at the way the sheets held his scent.

The woman in her rumbled with desire.

Her first impulse was to wake him with a kiss, to taste his quickening passions. With a purely female smile of confidence, she bet she could make him forget his morning jog while working his heart rate up to a healthy number of megabeats per minute. And she found she wanted to, on this morning and all those that followed.

Heat rose as she considered what had gone on in those same sheets. It wasn't a blush of shame. It was a scorch of sheer pleasure. Spencer had shown her the difference willing participation could make when a man and woman came together. He'd made her burn. He'd made her twist and pant for relief. He'd made her ask for what she wanted, made her realize her own desires had importance. He'd made her explode into so many beautiful pieces that what reassembled in his arms wasn't the same frightened, guarded soul. He'd made sweet, wild, freeing love with her. And she'd allowed it because she loved him. Because she trusted him the way she'd never allowed herself to trust in any other.

But then the remembrances of the previous night expanded beyond what they'd discovered in each other's arms. To the reason for her being in Spencer Halloway's home. A reason that had nothing to do with the satisfaction she was feeling now and everything to do with why she shouldn't be lingering in bed, considering the impossible.

And with a prompting panic, she slipped from the bed to pad into the next room. There, she leaned against the doorframe to watch Casey sleep, deeply, safely. But for how long? How was Mercy ever going to forget the sound of the child's terrified cries? Or the sight of her being borne away in a stranger's grasp?

Savoring the memory of Spencer's bed and a shared future with him was a delicious fantasy, but keeping Casey safe was her one priority of the moment. The one she couldn't fail in at any cost.

So she'd suppressed all thoughts of potential romance and had spirited a groggy Casey away from Spencer's home. She hadn't looked back, afraid that if she did, the knowledge of what she was walking away from would overcome her resolution.

As she'd stuffed all their meager belongings into their suitcases, Casey had sniffled and sobbed.

"I don't want to go, Mercy. I want to stay here with Spencer."

So did she. But there was no use them both crying about it. "We can't," she said with the necessary sternness while hustling her to the car. That argument was to herself as well as the child and it had to be a tough one.

"Why? He'll take care of us. He'll make sure we can stay together with him."

Too close for comfort sharing the child's tears, Mercy had been cruel with both their dreams. "No, Casey. When he finds out the truth, he may not want us with him at all. Honey, we can't afford to trust anyone but each other. Not now. Not yet."

"But Spencer promised! He promised he would take care of us!"

"And I'm sure he meant it at the time. But he didn't know who we were when he made that promise and we can't expect him to hold to it now. It's time to go, Casey. If they catch up to us, not even Spencer and Amy can help us."

So the child had allowed Mercy to bundle her up in the car and hadn't said a word as they headed north, but Mercy didn't kid herself for a moment that all was well with Casey. Pulling her away from Pine Creek was yanking her from a place of security, the first place she'd found peace and happiness for a long time. That's all anyone had done lately, uprooted her from where she felt comfortable. No wonder she resented it this time, too. Maybe more so, because she'd trusted Mercy to take care of her fragile needs.

Mercy could tell herself she'd make things right, could promise it to Casey, but for now, she was damaging the child's delicate spirit as harshly as those before her. It couldn't be helped. Casey would understand—if not today, then when she was older. But today, Mercy had to listen to her small hitching breaths; and no matter how convinced she was of doing the right thing, those tiny sounds cut right to the quick of her. It was the sound of betrayal.

"We should be in Traverse City in about twenty minutes. We can stop for some breakfast there. What are you hungry for?" Mercy glanced at the averted face. "Pancakes, eggs or fast food?"

No answer.

"Casey?" she prompted gently.

"I don't care."

"Pancakes, then," she decided for them, trying to sound cheerful when her heart was aching. "Or maybe some of those blueberry waffles you like so much."

No response. The child wasn't going to make it easy. But then, none of it was easy.

Just then, the car gave a suspicious lurch and without a hint of trouble brewing, the power began to ebb even as she pressed the accelerator to the floor.

"Oh, no! Not again! Not now!"

But the vehicle had no sympathy for her moaning plea. With a few coughing sputters, the engine went dead and the dash was a glare of warning lights; all just a little too late. She fought the sluggish wheel and managed to get them off to the side of the road. Desperately, she tried the key again and again, pumping the peddle in defiance of common sense until the vehicle wouldn't so much as groan when she tried to crank the engine over. It answered with an impotent click.

Finally, Mercy abandoned the effort and dropped her forehead against the wheel, ready to wail and admit defeat.

"What now?" Casey asked after a long minute passed. "Do we walk?"

Mercy sighed miserably and straightened. "We wait, honey. Someone's bound to pass by, then maybe we can get a lift or at least, arrange for a tow."

But minutes slipped by into anxious quarters of the hour. After three vehicles whipped by without even slowing, Casey whined, "Mercy, I'm getting hungry. It's hot in here. Can we go back?"

"Someone's bound to stop any minute," she said with more confidence than she was feeling. The child's restlessness echoed her own. The longer they stayed crippled on the side of the road, exposed and vulnerable, the more they were in danger of discovery.

Despite Casey's wishes—and her own—they couldn't go back, not knowing what waited there.

Another car crested the far hill and Mercy was motivated to step out of their Pontiac and onto the edge of the pavement. She started to wave her arms. There was the blare of a horn and she jumped back to flatten against the Pontiac's quarter panel as the vacuum of the vehicle speeding by sucked at her clothes. Muttering a few choice curses under her breath, she squinted down the highway again.

The sun glared off chrome and glass as the next vehicle topped the hill. With a sigh, Mercy garnered her courage and stepped out onto the hot blacktop. She started flagging her hands over head, frantically at first, then slowing, finally stopping. She heard the hum of four-wheel-drive tires and the whine of downshifting as the truck began to slow. Her face grew impassive as she watched the vehicle edge off onto the shoulder and pull to a stop behind her.

The door opened and a tall figure in a Stetson hat and dark glasses stepped down.

"Having some engine trouble?" came the low, all-too-familiar drawl.

"Spencer!"

Casey came hurtling out of the car to leap into the lawman's arms. While Mercy told herself Spencer Halloway was the last person in the world she wanted to see, she couldn't help the way her heart leaped in similar abandon. Nor could she ignore the foolish hope that now Spencer was here, he could somehow take care of everything.

But that time was long since gone, and she knew it just by looking at him.

Spencer smiled down at the child who'd tangled arms and legs about him, then he looked to Mercy. His eyes were hidden behind the tinted lenses but there was no mistaking the no-nonsense thinning of his mouth.

Her time had just run out.

Chapter 15

"Are you going to take us back home, Spencer?"

The question gushed out of Casey in obvious relief as she beamed up at him.

Home, she'd said. Mercy felt a bittersweet tug of longing. To her, home had become that small vacation cabin with Casey wading in the water and the enticing threat of Spencer Halloway's insistent company. No other place had ever held her with that kind of emotional tie. Nor had any other man.

Spencer set the child down and instructed gently, "Get Mr. Stubbs and climb on into the truck."

Smiling, Casey scurried to obey.

Spencer extended his hand toward Mercy, palm up to demand, "Keys."

She placed them in his hand. What else could she do? They were as useless as her attempted flight.

Spencer popped the trunk and unloaded their bags. After stowing them in the back of the four-by-four, he locked up the car, then looked at last to the woman standing on the edge of the highway.

"Get into the truck."

A flat, emotionless order.

"Spencer—"

He jerked the door open for her with a short, violent pull. It was the only betrayal of his temperament. He was furious. Without a word, Mercy climbed in. He slammed the door and she gave a little jump. It felt for all the world like he was shutting her inside an animal's cage. He stalked around the rear of the vehicle and hopped up behind the wheel. Then, with gravel-flinging brevity, he made a U-turn on the two-lane and headed back toward Pine Creek.

"Can I sit back here, Spence?" Casey and her stuffed pet were crouched at the rear window watching the ribbon of roadway unfurl behind them.

"If you promise to stay sitting down and don't fiddle with anything."

"I do and I won't."

Silence settled in the front seat. Mercy stared straight ahead. Her heart was banging in her chest. At last, she risked a sidelong glance at Spencer. He gave her his crisp profile. His jawline looked like it had been broken out of granite with one clean stroke and was just as likely to soften. It would have been easier to believe he was angry because she'd tricked him, but she knew that wasn't even close to all of it. She'd hurt him with her abrupt disappearance and her unwillingness to confide in him. No apology could soothe away those jagged edges. But maybe an explanation would.

It was hard, though, so hard to think of what she could tell him. Even after the intimacy they'd shared, some of the words just wouldn't come. Her first instinct was still to protect herself and Casey; no matter how deeply she cared for Pine Creek's lawman, he hadn't managed to gain that level of security clearance.

But it was obvious, she was going to have to tell him something.

"Who are you?" Spencer began so brusquely, Mercy gave a nervous start. "Don't bother telling me any more lies. It's too late for that. What are you to Casey?"

"I'm her aunt," she told him softly. "Her father was my brother."

"Was?"

"He and his wife were both killed in a car accident a couple of months ago. It's been very hard on Casey. She's just started to come out of her shell."

"So you decided to take her on a little vacation, changing both your names," Spencer observed dryly. When Mercy had no reply, he shot a piercing glance at her. "You don't have legal custody of her, do you?"

"I'm working on it, Sheriff" was her polished-as-steel reply.

"And in the meantime, you have private investigators after you. Who else, Mercy? The police? The feds? Anyone else I should know about?"

"Not that I know of." She looked straight ahead, her own jaw going tight as she summed up her reasoning. "That would be too...messy."

Her sear of sarcasm set Spencer back a bit but it didn't sidetrack him from his questions. "So who is she supposed to be with?"

"Someone who doesn't deserve her." Again, the cold, harsh summation that was totally out of character with the compassionate woman he'd come to know. She hadn't given away much about herself, but that he was sure of.

"I don't believe that's your decision to make, Mercy. Usually the courts have something to say about it."

"Yes, it is my decision. I'm the only one with her interests at heart. They don't know Casey. They don't love her like I do." Then she gripped her jaw shut and glared out the front window. End of discussion.

Spencer sighed in frustration and concentrated on the road ahead. They passed the sign to Big Bear Lake.

Mercy swiveled to watch it whiz by. "Where are we going?" Her voice quavered.

"I told you. Into Pine Creek."

"To your office," she concluded grimly.

He didn't answer, which was, of course, her answer.

"What for?"

He canted an incredulous look her way. "What for? You were witness to an attempted B and E and the vehicular injury of a pedestrian. My deputy could face suspension. I need your report on file."

"That's it?"

"For starters."

Mercy wasn't naive. That "for starters" would end with all her secrets spilled and Casey taken from her. If she allowed Spencer to take her into his station, if she had a police report on file—and she wasn't such a fool as to make up information for that legal form—everything would be over.

"Can't you just take a statement from me right here?"

"No."

"And if I refuse to say anything?" She wasn't really thinking of withholding the truth—like Spencer said, it was a little late for that—but she wanted to test the waters, just to see what might be waiting.

"I can get your mail redirected to my jail for failure to cooperate in an official police investigation." Let her think on that one awhile.

She was thinking, hard and fast and frantically. And it all narrowed down to her handsome captor. "You said I could trust you, Spencer."

He stiffened warily at the slight accusation in her tone. What was she up to? "You can."

"Then just pull over and let us out. Pretend you never found us. We'll be long gone and no one will think to question your part in it." The desperation came spilling out, snagging on her words, bringing a shimmering dampness to the corners of her wide eyes.

"I can't do that, Mercy."

"Because you're the sheriff of Pine Creek." She spat that at him as if the words had a bitter taste.

"No," he countered softly. "Because I care about you and Casey, and I think you're in way over your heads in something that's going to get you hurt."

"You don't know anything about it!"

"No, I don't, so why don't you tell me?"

"I trusted you," she lamented in a wringing anguish, keeping her voice quiet so Casey wouldn't overhear the fright in her tone. "I believed you when you said you'd never hurt us. I let you get close to us. I let you into my heart. I let you—" She broke off hoarsely, then finished with a faint, "I let you close to me."

He cut that argument right off at the knees with a gruff, "If you trusted me so much, why were you running in the other direction? Why didn't you come to me when there was still a chance that I could do something to help you?"

"If I'd told you everything, I wasn't sure if I'd be dealing with the man or the law." Her probing glance said she still wasn't sure. And that uncertainty stabbed right to the heart of him. Because he didn't know, either. So he changed the subject.

"Was everything you said and everything we did together part of your charade?"

Mercy twisted on the seat, staring at him with tears of hurt standing in her eyes. "No. How could you ask that? No. That was real. All of it."

When he didn't respond with a word or a sign of belief, Mercy's chin quivered, then firmed determinedly. Why should he believe her? She'd done everything in her power to keep him at arm's length. She'd done nothing but lie to him. She'd lain in his arms and then disappeared without a word the next morning, escaping like a thief of hearts. Why should he believe that if it was possible to put the past behind her, there was no place she'd rather go than back to his cabin to explore a solid relationship with him? That the term *home* applied to a house of logs and a man of tender passions? But as he'd said, it was too late to go back, too late to make any of her choices over again in his favor.

They both sat in silence as the truck neared the small community of Pine Creek, the tender trust of the night before failing fast under the tension of the moment.

"How come we're stopping here?" Casey wanted to know as she hopped down into Spencer's arms. When he settled her on her feet in the station's parking lot, she tucked one of her small hands into his much bigger one. The gesture had his heart wiggling like a salmon on a snagging hook.

"Mercy has some forms to fill out."

"What kind of forms?" She readjusted Mr. Stubbs under her other arm and looked up at Spencer through guileless, soul-snatching eyes.

"About the other night," he told her gently, as if his tone could lessen the reminder. It did. And it didn't. Her dark eyes grew shadowed.

"That man's not in there, is he?" she whispered, hanging back against his hand.

"No, sweetheart. He's in the hospital. You don't have to worry about him. He can't hurt you. And I'll make sure he never scares you again."

Then, over Casey's mop of bright hair, he caught Mercy's chiding stare, reprimanding him for making that empty promise. But Casey believed him and that was half the battle as the child towed him toward the entry doors.

"C'mon, Spence. Let's get these forms filled out and go get some breakfast. Do you like pancakes?" she gabbed as they passed through the front and into the waiting area. "My favorite is blueberry waffles. Can we get some around here?"

Then her happy chatter ended so abruptly, Spencer stopped and looked down at her in question. Her eyes had gone wide and staring. The color had drained from her face, leaving her freckles to stand out like splatters from a paintbrush.

"Casey? What's wrong, sweetheart?"

And he followed her stricken gaze to an older couple seated in the waiting room.

"Oh, my God!" That moaned from Mercy as she came in behind them and saw who was waiting. She snatched Casey's hand from Spencer's and glared up at him as she swung the child protectively behind her. Her expression was mottled with rage and a terrible confusion. "How could you? How could you do this?"

"But I—"

"How could you talk about trust while leading us here—to them!"

Spencer was at a loss over her distress. Especially when the fashionably dressed woman hurried from her chair to throw her arms around the child with a cry of, "Oh, Casey, here you are! We were so worried!"

"I'm fine, Grandma. I've been with Aunt Mercy."

The woman looked up through eyes glistening with tears. Mother and daughter, no mistaking that. "I'm sure she's been taking good care of you, pumpkin. But now it's time to go home where you belong."

"No!"

That burst emotionally from both Casey and Mercy. Mercy pulled the little girl out of her grandmother's embrace and it didn't escape Spencer that Casey went willingly into Mercy's care.

"You're not going to take her," Mercy stated with a purpose of pure steel.

"Now, Mercy, please don't make this difficult," her mother began to plead.

"Difficult? For whom? Casey's staying with me until the hearing and you know why, Mom. Don't pretend you don't. It's time you faced the truth."

The older woman's features contorted with grief and upset. "Oh, Mercy, please don't start with that again."

"Start? I never should have stopped!"

Then a smooth male voice intruded. "I think the courts will be the ones to put a stop to it. You've put everyone through a considerable amount of worry and expense, Mercy. For heaven's sake, don't make things worse for yourself."

Spencer was totally lost. He watched the man approach. He, like the woman, was impeccably dressed and his gold wristwatch and Italian shoes insinuated a casually toted wealth. His smile was broad and easy, showing a lot of white teeth. A slick society package.

Spencer was familiar with the type.

"I'm Jeffrey Cooper, Cassandra's grandfather. And you must be Sheriff Halloway. You don't know how glad we were to get a call from your office."

A big hand thrust forward and Spencer was distracted by Mercy's subtle reaction. She flinched back, hugging Casey to her, pushing against his side in a nonverbal request for protection. From her father? Spencer puzzled over that as he took the proffered hand in a brief, politically correct press of the palm.

"I'm afraid you have the advantage over me," Spencer began carefully.

"These are the Coopers," Chet interjected as he came into the waiting room wearing his best "I've got your butt now" smile. "I did a little poking around with what I learned from the P.I. and linked it to a missing-child report. These are Cassandra's legal guardians."

"What missing-child report?"

Chet produced it with a razzle-dazzle flick of the wrist. "This one. Came in a couple of days ago. Didn't you see it? Or were you too busy playing house with Ms. Pomeroy?" And he was secure enough with his underhandedness not to cringe beneath Spencer's spine-dissolving stare.

"Pomeroy?" Spencer looked at Mercy, feeling as though he'd dropped into the middle of an episode of "Twilight Zone." "That's your name?"

"Yes."

How nice of her to be so forthcoming with it now!

"Now that everyone's been introduced," Chet began with a syrupy smile.

"Shut up, Chet. We'll discuss your failure to observe the correct lines of departmental communications later. In my office." That lingered with enough inherent threat to leave the deputy pasty-faced and sullen. "Until then, file your report and make sure it's in triplicate . . . just in case."

Then, while his deputy sulked, Spencer continued smoothly. "I'm sorry for the inept handling of this matter, Mr. and Mrs. Cooper. You shouldn't have been called in until I was advised of the situation and had a chance to get things smoothed over for everyone. I'm not usually kept in the dark about my staff's investigations. There's no reason for this to be awkward. Why don't the two of you step into my office for a moment and we can get things straightened out."

It wasn't a request, and though Jeffrey Cooper leveled a narrowed glare upon Mercy and measured the distance between her and the front door, he escorted his wife into the glass-walled room Spencer indicated with the sweep of his hand.

Unable to offer any personal reassurances from the awkward position he was in, Spencer rumpled Casey's hair and provided a comforting smile. To Mercy, he gave a cautioning look, a "Don't you dare run" warning, followed by a fleeting smile he hoped she'd find heartening. She didn't return it. She had to know where his loyalties lay but still, she looked petrified. They both did.

"May, could you fix Ms. Pomeroy a cup of coffee and see if you could rustle up some milk and a doughnut for Casey?"

"I sure can, Sheriff. Come on over here, sweetie, and pick one. We've got chocolate sprinkles and glazed—"

But Casey hung back, adhering to Mercy's pant leg like tree moss until Spencer tipped up her chin with his fingertips and supplied his most melting smile. "It's okay, Casey. I recommend the jelly-filled, myself. More of your major food groups that way."

The child didn't surrender to his charm. She was frightened beyond the thaw of an easy smile. And Spencer would know why before any of them left the station.

As he started toward his office, Casey's fragile call caught him by the heartstrings.

"You're not going to let them take me away, are you, Spencer?"

He didn't know what to tell her. But Mercy's features stiffened; she noticed he made no promises. She let go of the child and gave her a slight push.

"Go ahead and get a doughnut, honey. The sheriff will do the best he can."

Coolly delivered for the comfort of a child—not because she had one shred of belief in him. Spencer grimaced and joined the Coopers.

They were a pleasant upper-middle-class couple, both obviously distressed by the situation and eager to put it behind them. They sat perched on the edges of the two chairs before his desk, hands gripping at each other's. Spencer assumed his chair, not letting any emotion escape him. He would play the neutral observer, here. He had no other choice—for the moment. On the other side of the glass, he could see Mercy's gaze fixed upon him in a dazed sheen of panic and prayer. Damn, why couldn't she have come to him sooner? Then he could have found some leverage to get out of this back-against-the-wall position.

"Mr. Cooper, why don't you fill me in."

Cooper pressed his wife's hand and assumed a confidential pose. "I want you to know right up front, Sheriff, that we're not interested in pressing charges, here. We've got Cassandra back safe and sound and that's the important thing. I don't see that there's a need to have Mercedes punished as long as she promises there will be no further... willful behavior on her part."

Spencer felt a throb of tension build along his jaw. What exactly was it about Jeff Cooper that had his teeth grinding? It was more than his callous dismissal of Mercy and his all-too-sincere smile. It was what he wasn't saying. And Spencer had listened to all the half-truths from this particular family that he cared to.

"Maybe you'd better lay out the situation for me first, then we can discuss consequences."

The Coopers exchanged nervous glances. Then the slick front was back as Jeff Cooper directed his words to Spencer.

"As you probably know, the child's parents were killed not too long ago. It was a devastating shock and I dare say not all of us handled it well. Mercedes had been estranged from the family for some time and I'm afraid she took the loss of her brother quite hard." Cooper leaned forward in that intimating pose once again to murmur sympathetically, "She's had problems with emotional stability before."

Spencer held to his impartial face, but inside he was seething. What kind of father spoke of a daughter's private failings with the clinical detachment of someone discussing the inability of a car engine to run smoothly?

"Because there was no will providing for Cassandra's care, she was placed in our temporary custody until an official hearing in August. We've applied to have it made permanent, of course. There is really no one else who could provide her with a stable family environment. Her mother had no close family."

"Except Mercy."

Cooper's look grew patronizing at Spencer's bland suggestion. "As I said, she hasn't done very well managing her own life. I can't imagine any judge granting her guardianship of a child."

Then, why was a nervous tick pulsing at the corner of his mouth?

"From what I've observed, Ms. Royce, er, Pomeroy—has been a model caregiver. The child is happy and provided for in a warm, loving environment—"

"Then how do you explain the fact that she kidnapped the child?" Cooper interrupted tersely, apparently far from pleased to hear of the scene of familial bliss Spencer was drawing. "Is that the act of someone stable and trustworthy enough to be responsible for a little girl?"

"Kidnapped? That's a very strong word, Mr. Cooper. One you, yourself, have been unwilling to use—officially. Do you intend to change your original statement?"

"Jeff—"

"It's all right, Cindy. My wife has had an understandably trying time. We just want to put all these unpleasantries behind us."

"For Casey's sake?" Spencer drawled.

Cooper blinked in surprise, then murmured, "Yes, of course. The fact of the matter is, Mercedes took the child without consent from her lawfully appointed guardians. We could make this an ugly scene but prefer not to."

"For Casey."

Cooper tensed at Spencer's obvious contempt. "For all of us, Sheriff. I really don't know what your degree of involvement is, here"

"I'm their neighbor, and I consider myself a friend," he clarified succinctly.

"But you're a man sworn to uphold the law and you know your duty."

Spencer fixed him with a piercing stare until Cooper squirmed in discomfort. "My duty, as you've so aptly pointed out, is Casey's welfare."

"Sheriff, please," Cindy Cooper petitioned quietly. "We've been through so much. All we want is Cassandra back."

"You hired this man, Sweeney, to find your daughter and grandchild?"

"Yes." Cooper sighed in exasperation. "We didn't know what else to do. We didn't want to involve the police in any great degree, which was why the missing-persons report instead of a kidnap charge."

"You knew Mercy had her and that she'd be safe."

"Yes, of course," Cooper muttered impatiently. "It was a misunderstanding, a misjudgment on Mercedes' part. I know how much she adores the child, but she can't just snatch her from her rightful home and run without notice. Can she, Sheriff Halloway?"

"No," he admitted with regret.

"Then you will, of course, do your duty and return the child to us?"

"I can't see that I have any other option in the matter, do I."

Cooper's smile grew condescending, that smug boa-constrictor look, as the loops began to tighten. "No, you don't."

But Spencer didn't have to like it.

Mercy's gaze was riveted to Spencer's face. She sat with a coiled-spring tension, straining to decipher the shut-down look on his face on the other side of the glass wall as he conducted his interview with her parents.

It wasn't going well. Jeff Cooper was as smooth as they come. Who would disbelieve a word he said? He was going to paint her as dark as they come: unstable, emotionally distraught— What were some of the other words he'd used to dilute her mother's love? But was Spencer buying into that same slick spiel? She watched him as he took it in, but his controlled features gave nothing away.

Why shouldn't he believe the respected Jeffrey Cooper, with his sterling reputation in an upscale banking firm?

Even her mother had.

"Mercy?" Casey's fright trembled in the speaking of her name.

"Shh, sweetheart. It's all right."

"Spencer won't let them take me, will he?"

Before she could answer with some placating vagueness, Spencer got up and started from his office. Mercy fixed her desperate hope and wild gaze upon his hard, angularly drawn features. It didn't look good. She stood and sheltered Casey with one arm, waiting anxiously to learn what that taut expression meant.

He came to them with a slow, reluctant step and she knew the results before he said anything.

"Mercy, I'm sorry—"

"No."

"They have legal—"

"No!"

"Mercy, I want to go home," Casey began to whine as she burrowed against her, clutching both her and Mr. Stubbs for all she was worth. "Can Spencer take us home?"

That wish burned in her uplifted gaze. "Spencer, please. You can't let them take her."

Never having felt so damned helpless in his whole life, Spencer reached out to the confused little girl, slipping his palm over her shoulder. She was quaking beneath that supporting press. Then he spoke quietly to her aunt.

"Mercy, there's nothing I can do. You had to know that already. They have the signed court order giving them temporary custody."

"I don't care!"

"But I have to." He knelt down so he and Casey were eye-to-eye. Her panic and despair forced so many emotions through him, he didn't know which one to grab on to. His throat cramped up on him as he tightened his hold on her but there was nothing he could say to override the pain in her eyes. "I have to do my job."

How lame that sounded, even to him. Especially to him. After all his big promises, after all his pleas for them both to trust him. And this was the best he could manage, a weak excuse for an apology while a child's features filled with a "My life is over" bleakness.

Just then the Coopers came out into the waiting area and the tension multiplied.

"It's time to go, Cassandra," Cooper began a bit impatiently, as if he'd wasted all the time he cared to on emotional displays. "Let's get your things. We've got a long drive."

"Mercy—"

The child's whimper had Spencer's heart going down for the third time. He clenched his teeth against those pathetic *I'm sorry* words that didn't mean a damned thing at a time like this. At a time when action, not resignation, was what

Mercy needed from him. And he couldn't supply it. There was nothing he could do...except fail her.

"Come on, Cassandra."

Then Cooper reached for the child. And it was Mercy who exploded.

Her hand flashed up, striking his away with a surprising violence. "Don't you touch her!" The words snarled from her as she hunched over the child like a mother wolf protecting its young from a sly and dangerous predator.

And it was then that Spencer understood.

It was Jeff Cooper. He was the one who'd viciously taken Mercy's innocence. As ugly and shocking as such a notion was, Spencer hadn't the slightest doubt that it was true.

He was handing Casey over to a monster.

"I'll take her," Cindy Cooper suggested with an interceding gentleness. "Come on, Casey, dear. It's time for us to go home."

"But I want to stay here! I want to live with Mercy and Spencer!"

Cindy gave the two of them a gauging glance, questioning their relationship. Then she cooed, "That's not possible, dear. Come on."

"No-o-o! I won't go-o-o! Mercy! Spencer!"

With a stark look that said the battle was lost but not the war, Mercy stood, grappling with her control long enough to say, "Casey, go with your grandmother for right now. But I'll see you soon. You can count on it." And she speared the older man with a look of frosty warning. *Don't you dare try anything.*

Cooper bristled, ready to make trouble with a growl of, "I don't think so—"

"Jeff!" Cindy Cooper's single word cut off his angry protest. "Not here." She extended her hand to the child. "Come on, honey."

And Casey's hand eased out gingerly to slip inside it. Then, almost immediately was pulling back. "I don't want to leave! Why do I have to go?"

"Because the law says you have to," Mercy bit out frigidly even as her eyes pooled with liquid misery. "For now, it says you have to."

With one hand imprisoned by her grandmother, the only way the little girl could reach out for Mercy was to drop Mr. Stubbs. The toy fell to the floor as her hand waved frantically. Jeff Cooper stepped between them to catch those groping fingers in his big hand.

"Say goodbye, Casey," he instructed severely. Then he gave Mercy a long, promising stare that was full of control and menace, one that crippled her resolve and cost her all hope. A glare that carried her back to the terrors of childhood and left her helpless. He wouldn't let her forget who held the power. Who had always held the power.

Then she stood with every tendon quivering as her parents led the weeping child away.

Chapter 16

Mercy could garner no resistance when Spencer took hold of her arm and led her into his office past the wide-eyed May Walker, then closed the door for privacy. She dropped into the chair he backed her up to, her legs suddenly like over-cooked noodles, and sat there in a stupor of anguish. Spencer pulled the other chair around so he could sit facing her, their knees touching.

"Tell me everything."

She stared at him through swimming eyes. Her gaze was dull, drenched with desolation. "It's too late. Like you said, there's nothing you can do."

"The hell there isn't." That ground out through gritted teeth and Mercy's attention gathered with a slight curiosity. "He's the one, isn't he?"

Mercy didn't have to answer. Shadows, stark and terrifying, clouded her expression. Spencer gave a low curse.

"And I just handed Casey over to him."

"It's not your fault, Spencer," Mercy said weakly. Her hand slid over one of his knees and was quickly captured in the tight curl of his fingers. "I should have told you what I was running from."

"Tell me now, sweetheart."

The endearment slipped out quite naturally, a low, throbbing reflection of all the frustration and tenderness he'd guarded so stingily for so long. Now there was no point in trying to hide it. Not when his one driving passion was to make her feel safe and loved. She was going to need every scrap of his strength to get through the telling of what massed in a huge ache behind her glittering gaze.

And he was going to be there for her in every capacity: friend, partner, confessor, lover—mate. Whatever she needed. Anything she needed.

But instead of reaching out to him, he watched her withdraw into herself without ever physically moving. It was something in her eyes, the way they dimmed and grew unfocused, distancing herself from the pain with a disassociating numbness of spirit and mind. But she didn't try to hide anything from him; not one nightmarish, unsettling detail.

"My father died when I little. I was Casey's age when Mom remarried. I never liked Jeff. I don't know why. I guess it was that special radar kids have when something makes them uncomfortable, even when they don't understand what it is or why."

Spencer nodded, encouragingly. How could a six-year-old understand an animal like Cooper?

"He made a big deal about us being close. 'The best of friends,' he'd say. Mom was thrilled that he was so fond of her children, though he never paid much more than a surface attention to Terry, who was almost eight years older than I was and busy with his own friends. I was 'Daddy's Little Angel.'

"He'd have me sit on his lap while we watched TV and he insisted on tucking me into bed at night. Mom never thought to question what he was doing up there for so long, and for the longest time, I had no idea that it was anything wrong. Just a lot of cuddling and touching while he'd make up stories. Back then they didn't teach children the difference between good and bad touching. He was my mother's husband, my new father. I never dreamed he could be doing anything to hurt me.''

"The son of a bitch."

Mercy didn't react to Spencer's fierce summation. She was sitting bolt upright in her chair with her arms banded tightly across her breasts. There was something defensive and heartbreakingly vulnerable in that insulating self-hug, as if she were used to comforting herself when no one else suspected anything was wrong.

"As I grew older, I started to dread his coming upstairs with me. His games had become our secret. I wasn't to tell anyone or they might think I was a bad girl and they might take me away from my house and my toys and my friends. They would think I was a liar, trying to make trouble for my new dad. I wouldn't want to hurt my mother, would I? If I told, Jeff would have to go away and my mother would hate me. I loved my mother. She was so happy with the relationship Jeff and I had together. Of course, she had no idea just what that was. I'd like to think she would have done something about it if she knew, but I was a good girl. I never told a soul."

She went on in that same flat voice, reciting the horror of her growing-up years, telling of how she'd spent a wonderful two weeks at a girls' camp only to come home and find Jeff Cooper was interested in other kinds of games. Games that hurt. Games that went on late at night while the rest of the family slept.

And the threats grew darker, more cruelly explicit. And the terrorized girl had nowhere to turn.

"I don't know what happened exactly," she continued in the lifeless tone that made Spencer's flesh creep upon hearing it. "I was sitting down to breakfast. I was about thirteen and I remember Terry was away at ball camp. Dad—he insisted that I call him Dad—came up behind me and put his hands on my shoulders and I just started screaming. I just snapped. I couldn't stop. I heard myself spilling all his nasty secrets while my mom just sat there staring at me from across the breakfast table as if I were insane.

"And when I'd calmed down, I remember her calling my doctor. He was a golf partner of my stepfather's so he was willing to make a house call to avoid any loose talk. 'Hormonal hysteria,' I think is what he decided I was suffering from and he prescribed a mild sedative—just the thing for the overly sensitive daughter of one of our city's most influential citizens."

"Your mother didn't believe you." Spencer's whisper echoed the amazement felt by a child who'd just had every thread of safety torn from her.

"Either she didn't or she was afraid to. She must have suspected something when I refused to be in a room alone with Jeff from that point on. If he came into my bedroom, I'd start shrieking. If he touched me in public, I'd threaten to make a scene. And we couldn't have Jeffrey Cooper's little girl making an ugly scene.

"That fall, I was sent to a private boarding school and I never went back home, not even for holidays. But it didn't matter how far away I was. I still carried the stain of what he'd done to me; the guilt, the shame, the certainty that I was to blame for what had happened."

"He is a sick man, Mercy, and you were a child. He took advantage of you in the most despicable way possible."

She looked up at him almost as if surprised to see him sitting there. And she managed a thin smile that tore him in two. "I know that, Spencer. But a teenage girl with no one to confide in didn't. I grew up believing the fault was mine, that I was that bad girl who tried to break up her parents' happy home."

The muscles worked along Spencer's tight jaw but he didn't say anything to try to talk her out of those feelings. Words wouldn't erase them. "Didn't your brother ever ask questions? Didn't he guess what was going on?"

"Terry was a wonderful brother, but he was so much older than I was. We didn't even go to the same school or share any of the same friends. We weren't really close until

I was in college and he got married. My parents told him I was jealous of Jeff's relationship with my mother and that was the reason for my rebellion and estrangement from them. I never told him any different. I guess I was afraid that if I did, he'd look at me the way Mom had over the kitchen table. It was easier for me to pretend those early years never happened.''

"But hiding the pain didn't make it go away."

"No," she admitted in a small voice. She was wringing his hand between both of hers in an unconscious show of agitation. And trust. "Thank God for Amy. I think she saved my life. She was my college roommate. I guess I told you that. I never dated, and one night she asked me why and it just came out. Only she believed me. She convinced me to start therapy, to get back in touch with my brother, to get on with my life. They don't make friends better than her.

"Seeing my brother and his wife and their little girl together was one of my greatest joys. They were the family I wished I'd grown up in. Terry even had me named Casey's godmother, and I swore to that little baby and to myself that she would have the happy childhood I was denied."

But all that had changed when Mercy received the news of Terry's and his wife's deaths.

"The court placed Casey with my parents. It was hard, but I made myself go over there after the funeral, to see for myself that she was all right. I had a long talk with Casey about her mom and dad and that's when she asked if she could come live with me. She didn't like the way her grandfather touched her. She said his kisses made her feel 'icky.' And from that second on, I was living the nightmare all over. He was going to do it again and by God, I was going to stop him this time."

It had been hard to go through legal channels when she was sure Casey's innocence was in the balance but Mercy put up with the frustration and delays because she didn't want to make any mistakes. She'd looked up Amy Cheswick, who was now a respected lawyer specializing in abuse cases, a direction she'd chosen after witnessing her old roommate's pain. Though Amy had urged her to expose her stepfather for the child molester he was, Mercy was determined to win custody of her godchild without a scandalous open-court battle. When Amy filed, Mercy's parents refused her visiting rights; then began the long, agonizing wait for the end-of-the-summer hearing.

"I couldn't stay away, Spencer. I was sure Casey was in danger. I convinced my parents' housekeeper to let me have a few secret visits with Casey and each time I saw her, the evidence of my stepfather's abuse was more and more apparent.

"And then one day, Casey called me, crying. When I asked her what was wrong, she told me that in her school, they said it was wrong for anyone to touch her any place her bathing suit covered and that if anyone tried to touch her there, she should tell. I was the one she told.

"I didn't know what to do, Spencer. Amy was out of the country on her honeymoon but she'd asked me to house-sit for her and told me I could have the use of her family's cabin if I needed someplace to get away from it all. The only thing I could think of was getting Casey away, someplace where I could keep her safe until I could reach Amy. I didn't care if it would damage the chances of gaining custody. I just knew that if I didn't act right then, something terrible, irreversible was going to happen to that child. So I took her, even if it was against the law."

Spencer leaned forward to catch up both her cold hands in his. "Sometimes laws protect the wrong people, honey."

She nodded jerkily. "I told the housekeeper I had my mother's permission to take Casey for the weekend. I left Mom a note telling her I had Casey...and why. And we ran. Casey's such a smart little girl. She may not have understood everything that was going on but she knew enough to trust her feelings about Jeff. And she knew she could trust me to see that everything turned out all right. I promised her we'd be a family. And I let her down, Spencer." Her gaze grew all wet and bleak with self-blame. "I promised that I would keep her safe and I let her down."

"No, sweetheart, it was the whole system of justice that let you down."

And she looked up at him with her heart exposed, having trusted him with her secrets and her shame and now so terribly vulnerable because of it.

Until he said, more softly still, "I let you down."

She caught herself, ready to say that it wasn't his fault, and suddenly realized that it wasn't her fault, either. There was no blame, just an injustice too long ignored, waiting to be righted.

Flushed with courage and a renewed sense of purpose, she stood.

"Where can I rent a car?"

Spencer was immediately suspicious of her crisp tone. "Why? You're not thinking of going after them, are you?"

"Someone has to, Spencer. Someone has to be willing to break those rules if the rules are wrong. I'm responsible for that little girl. I made her a promise, and I'm not going to break it."

And from deep in his own past, Spencer heard another promise being made, a promise made to a boy named Toby that life could be good if he would just have faith in an idealistic Detroit police officer.

Maybe this was his one chance to make good on that broken vow.

He took Mercy by the shoulders, just holding her still, forcing her to think. "What are you going to do, honey?" he asked her reasonably. "What do you think will happen if you go charging after them blindly? Especially when they have the law, such as it is, on their side? What kind of good do you think you can accomplish for Casey? They'll get a restraining order. They'll use it to ruin any chance you have of gaining custody. That's not the way."

She stared at him as if confused and her shoulders quivered as her breathing grew rapid and less controlled. She dropped back into the chair, numbly. Finally, in a low, fractured voice, she said, "I don't know what the right thing to do is, Spencer. But I have to do something. I have to."

"I know, sweetheart."

Then she was in his arms, the most natural place in the world for her to seek comfort. She sagged across his lap, her face lost in the fabric of his shirt, her tears making dark splotches the way raindrops had upon their first meeting.

"He—he hurt me, Spencer" came the raw pull of pain from a wounded soul. "He stole away my ability to trust, my right to grow up safe, the joy of a childhood. I won't let him do that to Casey. I won't!"

"We won't, sweetheart. We won't let him."

And he held her, the way the child she'd been had needed to be held. His hand stroked the rippling brightness of her hair and he spoke to her in soothing sentiments, telling her how brave she'd been, how strong she was and how much he admired her for both things.

And it wasn't until she was limp and drained of the ragged need to cry that Mercy realized he'd said *We*.

She sat back, fumbling for a tissue, taking one from him with a husky murmur of thanks. She blotted aching eyes and gave her nose a thorough blowing. And surprisingly, she did feel stronger. Not alone.

"Better?" he asked with a gruff tenderness as his thumbs sought out the spots of dampness she'd missed upon her face. When she nodded and risked a watery smile, he smiled back but the intensity in his eyes held her. She waited to hear what was on his mind.

"I want to help you, Mercy."

"I'd like to have you on my side."

"And by your side. You're going to have to get used to that idea, too."

She nodded, willing to start.

"We need to make some plans. Legal plans that they can't protest. No more foolish gestures that could end up causing more harm than good. All right?"

She gave him a slight, supportive smile.

He smiled back. "I've got to make some calls and I don't want to do it from here. This is personal business, not professional."

Mercy liked the sound of that.

"I know it's going to be hard for you to be patient and wait, but I don't think Cooper would be stupid enough to try anything right away. He's got to know we've got our eye on him, just looking for any mistake. He's got to prove himself to be Mr. Upstanding Citizen when he appears in court and he's not going to give us any proof to the contrary. It's the long run we're going to have to concentrate on, not the 'right now.' And right now, I'm taking you home."

Mercy let Spencer guide her back through the station, hearing him tell May he was taking the rest of the day off but could be reached at his cabin. For once, she was grateful that he was a take-charge kind of man. She couldn't have managed another decisive thought if she'd had to.

Especially when she saw Mr. Stubbs discarded on the floor like innocence tossed away.

And after Spencer helped her up into his Blazer, then climbed in himself, he hesitated a moment, puzzled by the way she was bent over double, her arms wrapped about her middle.

Wondering if she had taken ill, he asked, "Mercy, are you all right?"

She gave a weak little moan and then he saw she was clutching something to her breast. He recognized the fuzzy patch of monkey fur peeking out against the curve of Mercy's cheek.

Casey's Mr. Stubbs.

That was the last straw in his struggle to maintain control. He was a judicious man, careful never to jump headlong into anything without being sure of where he was going to land. But this time, he was emotionally overboard without a thought of where his two feet would be planted.

Spencer clenched his teeth and fired up the four-by-four. In the darkness of his mind, he pictured what he'd like to do to Jeffrey Cooper.

And if the waters of commitment he'd just plunged into were suddenly dangerous, it wasn't because of an undertow.

It was because a shark had just entered them.

A man-eater.

From where she sat, Mercy could see Spencer in his office loft making another telephone call, his umpteenth since he'd told her to make herself at home.

They'd picked up something to eat at a drive-through on the way out of town and had eaten everything out of wrappers in the front seat of Spencer's truck as he headed north along 37. He'd planted her on the sofa the minute they got inside and he'd been overhead on the phone ever since. She could hear the comforting drone of his masculine tones but not his actual words.

Calling in favors, he'd told her. He must have been owed by everyone in the downtown Detroit phonebook, she decided as the hours of the afternoon slid by in a daze.

With Mr. Stubbs still cuddled in her lap, Mercy looked around idly, trying to keep her thoughts from straying back to what was foremost in her mind and heart. The room's warm, earthy embrace was a calming influence, just like the man who lived in it.

Spencer Halloway was better than a prescription for what ailed her. Kind, empathetic, a doer, a fixer. And gorgeous. She couldn't forget gorgeous. If a woman could do better, she was at a loss as to how. When she thought of all the effort and energy she'd thrown into keeping him at bay, into keeping him out of her affairs, afraid he'd lose all respect for her if he discovered the truth...

Worse, afraid he wouldn't believe her...

What a fool she'd been.

She'd been fighting the wrong enemy. It hadn't been Spencer. Her own worst enemy had been her own lack of faith. In men. In love. And in her lack of trust. If she'd just come to Spencer a few days earlier...

She surged off the couch and started to pace. What was the use? How could she think of anything else when Casey was in the hands of that... creature. Taking the child and running hadn't been the smartest move. Amy would have her head when she found out about it. Talk about making the Coopers' case for them! The impulsive act would make her look desperate and flighty and emotionally...unstable. Not the picture of security that her parents presented.

What if she couldn't convince the courts to give her Casey? The thought of snatching her up for another ill-advised disappearance held no appeal. Not when it meant leaving Pine Creek. This was her home now, win or lose. She couldn't imagine ever leaving it for anywhere else.

That left only one alternative: exposing Jeff Cooper for what he really was.

Who would believe her? Not even her mother would support her claim of abuse.

Things didn't look good and she was a knot of anxiety when she heard Spencer pad down the spiral stairs. He took one look at her rigid expression and tugged her into his arms.

"None of that, now," he warned her gruffly. "It's too early to hang out the white flags."

"I'm not giving up," she mumbled into consoling curve of his shoulder.

"Attagirl."

"I'm going to fight for Casey the way I wish someone had fought for me. No more running. I'm not that helpless, scared little girl any more."

"And you're not alone," Spencer added.

Mercy went still in his arms. He'd said *We.* He'd talked about the long run. She had to wonder if the two were linked together. She, Casey and Spencer for the long run. The idea seduced with promise.

Spencer knew the moment the mood changed between them. A sudden thrum of energy quickened where her softness melted into him, a sense of restless expectation he tried to rein in, fearing the time wasn't right. He didn't want her to think he was just going through the motions to serve his own shallow purposes. God knows, the woman had been used enough for one lifetime. He didn't want her to believe his own desires took precedence over her worry for Casey. Because they didn't. He couldn't love the child more if she'd been born between the two of them.

But the way she felt in his arms, like a swirl of caramel-fudge topping, all rich and sinfully inviting. It was hard to resist . . . just a taste.

He nuzzled her hair—a slight thing—but then her face lifted. He saw an instant of surprise in her eyes; as if she couldn't believe he'd want her after all she'd told him. He'd have to set her straight on that in no uncertain terms. She was the most desirable, beautiful, deserving woman he'd ever known and he was more than a little bit concerned that maybe he was the one not good enough for her.

But then her arms lassoed his neck, drawing him down to the soft part of her lips. And there was no denying the wild, sweet sense of right stirring between them.

And Spencer committed the rest of his life at that moment to making her believe it.

He'd planned for things to move slow and easy but Mercy was the one to shake things up. She took his mouth with an urgent pressure, her tongue stabbing deep, plunging him into sensory overload. Her body slid against his, her hips rolling, her breasts rubbing, her whole manner eager—a little too eager—to prove she wanted him.

Spencer levered a sanity-saving distance between them and evaded her determined kisses. He could feel her confusion and the insecurity that had it turning inward.

"I'm sorry," she began with a self-deprecating flush. "I'm not very good at this."

He chuckled as he sketched her hot cheek with a fingertip. "I wouldn't say that."

She risked a shy glance upward. The gesture was so innocent, so hopeful, he had to smile. And that made her frown.

"Then what's wrong? I thought you'd want—"

"Oh, I do," he interrupted quickly, not allowing her to work up to any grand self-sacrificing speech. "But it has to be what you want, too. And when you want it. That's what makes it right. I just want to be sure you're not pushing this because you think you have something to prove to me. You don't, you know.''

She studied him, perplexed, then a sly, feminine smile curved her just-kissed lips. ''It felt pretty right to me just then.''

His arms tightened a notch, his smile starting to spread. ''To me, too.''

And she coaxed him back down for a kiss that managed to be both winsome and wicked.

From there, they took it one step at a time, like a complex tango for two. Her fingers were at the buttons of his shirt, his were nudging beneath her pullover. Hers played along his belt buckle and zipper, his shimmied her jeans over her hips and down that long, long stretch of legs. The fact that it was daylight, the fact that they were standing in the center of his living room escaped them. The time and place were perfect for two people too long alone and lonely. The desire to please each other absorbed them after a day of desperate tension. The need to find solace in the act of sharing intimacy breached any argument.

Long, hot kisses and savoring caresses covered each section of skin that was bared until there was only touch, only skin. Mercy moaned with a beckoning urgency as the sultry, twining steps of their dance found a matching rhythm. She was scarcely aware of being swept into the bedroom until the cool sheet bunched beneath her and Spencer's heat and masculine weight became her covering. She experienced a brief instant of uneasiness as he settled over her, then his head dipped down to catch the budded tip of one aching breast and the momentum of delight overtook her. Pleasure pulsed through her in a hot liquid surge and she arched up for more, his name becoming an increasingly urgent litany upon her lips.

When he filled her, she couldn't remember a time when she'd been empty. All her senses expanded until there was nothing but him, nothing beyond the two of them together, linked as one until she was shuddering from the inside out.

She'd had no idea, no idea at all, that loving a man could feel so good, that her vulnerability and fear could evolve into such a magnificent strength that it let the soul soar free. With Spencer, she soared. And then she slept hard, knowing that she was exquisitely, infinitely loved.

With Mercy slack and sated in his arms, Spencer knew a moment of complete bliss. The same compulsion he felt to reach for a cigarette was now satisfied by the sound of her soft sigh.

Mercy was his second chance, the kind a man rarely got and never walked away from unless he was a total idiot. Spencer was no fool. This one incredibly, delightfully disturbing package had brought him back the joy of life and Casey was going to be his chance to heal a ragged wrong; the chance for him to salvage a life to replace the one he'd let slip away.

The sudden shrill of the phone startled him from his musings. Quickly, before Mercy was jarred from slumber, he flipped off the ringer on his bedside phone and hurried to catch the third ring in the living room.

"Halloway."

"I've got a ship-to-shore call from an Amy Cheswick. Will you accept the charges?"

"You're damned right I will."

Mercy stirred languidly, aware of warmth and the heaviness of total relaxation. She stretched like a cat and opened her eyes to survey her surroundings. Recognizing them, she gave a sleepy smile and let herself drift off again.

After a lazy moment, she felt the mattress dip and the indescribably wonderful sensation of male heat as Spencer slid under the covers with her.

"Where did you go?" she murmured.

"Just some business to take care of, sweetheart." His arm slipped beneath her shoulders, curling to coax her into using his chest as her pillow. And as she nestled in with a purr of contentment, she had a bittersweet wish that she could be as sure of the rest of her future as she was of Spencer Halloway.

Just as she surrendered her vaguely troubled musings in search of a reviving sleep, she heard a rumbling assurance spoken against the top of her head.

"I love you, Mercy. Whatever it takes, sweetheart, we'll get Casey back."

Chapter 17

When it came right down to it, Mercy couldn't have made the trip without Spencer's supporting presence.

She awoke to the smell of coffee and breakfast on the table, further enticed from the covers by Spencer's soft kiss on her lips. A splendid way to get the day started. He was determinedly cheerful as they ate; unquestionably a morning person, while her mind was firing with a few cylinders missing. He was the smugly smiling cause of her lethargy and proud of it. The one thing that managed to slip through the fuzz surrounding her brain was how impossibly sexy Spencer looked in the morning with a dark burr of whiskers on his lean cheeks and nothing on but a pair of form-hugging sweatpants.

All designed to distract her from the inevitable—the sinking sense of despair that came over her when she looked at the third empty chair.

When she loitered over the last swallow of coffee, her unfocused stare beginning to blur with tears, Spencer got up and circled behind her chair. She could feel the heat of him at her back, and like to a powerful magnet, was drawn to lean back against those rugged contours with her eyes closed.

His big hands fell on her shoulders, massaging with a gentle strength, thumbs stroking the sides of her throat with an insightful brevity. Quickening rivers of longing. And a deep current of contentment. Trust.

"I'm going to leave you with the mess if you don't mind while I grab a shower and shave. Then what do you say we go pick up Casey?"

Go pick up Casey. Just like that?

She twisted around so fast, the momentum kept her heart spinning in crazy, hopeful revolutions. "What?"

He gave her that slow full-of-hell grin. "I like a lot of chatter at the breakfast table and since you're about as conversational as a stump, I guess I'm going to have to go get my other girlfriend to keep me company."

She stared at him through a deepening bewilderment, her pulse sprinting with anticipation. "How? Spencer, what are you planning to—"

He kissed the tip of her nose. "Just trust me, okay? Rinse the plates and load the dishwasher. I'll take care of the rest later. I'll take care of everything." And he disappeared into the bathroom, leaving her teetering on the edge of an emotional abyss.

Go pick up Casey.

Spencer made it sound so simple. Like picking up a loaf of bread. Trust him. Easy words to say. Harder words to follow when put to such an extreme test. Her excitement faltered when put up against the cruel facts.

Spencer didn't know her stepfather.

Jeff Cooper wasn't going to make it easy. He knew everything there was about taking control, about manipulating, about making things...unpleasant.

And she was going back there, to that house where a nightmare of shadows lingered. Where a young girl's terror still hung on the edge of a silent scream. She didn't know how she could face it again. Except that this time, she wouldn't be alone.

If Spencer had something in mind, she could be sure it was backed with the full force of the man he was. If there was one thing she'd learned about him in the past weeks, it was the depth of his determination and his uncanny ability to carry through on things he started. If this new plan that had him humming in the shower involved getting Casey back, her trust was a small price to pay.

And she did trust him. Without question. Without explanation.

That was all the encouragement she needed to begin hurriedly clearing the table.

They rode in silence. Mercy was afraid to question Spencer's confidence, fearing it would prove groundless. She hugged Casey's Mr. Stubbs to her and clung to the unspoken hope he offered.

Trust him. Trust him.

It was hard. She'd never had anyone but herself to depend on before. Except Amy. And now Spencer. A select-but-priceless group.

Mercy tried to muster some of her bravado from the other night, that Rocky-meets-Rambo assertiveness, but the closer they got to her old childhood home, the harder it was to pretend calm. Feelings of intimidation and panic began to seep in like a cold fog, smothering her optimism.

Until Spencer reached out without glancing her way to scoop up her hand in his.

"You're not alone in this, kiddo," he reminded her.

He said it casually, as if it shouldn't mean the whole world to her. As if it was no big deal. After all, he'd pushed his way into her life like a bulldozer, refusing to take no for an answer, refusing to demonstrate a rational caution, refusing to be scared off by her dark secrets and the overwhelming consequences of her past. He deserved what he got.

Her.

Mercy swallowed nervously at the thought of her being any kind of prize. A man like Spencer Halloway—a man of unequaled good, of limitless loyalty, of unbelievable generosity, and with too darned much raw masculine appeal for any one man—deserved better. But he was so insistently stubborn, so determined to have her. He didn't have a lick of sense. A sane man would have gone running at the first hint of trouble, but he'd stuck around long enough to have a whole truckload dumped on him. And from all indications, he planned to stick around a whole lot longer.

He was crazy. That's what he was. A glutton for punishment.

"I love you, Spencer."

It just sort of slipped out, that one elemental truth that made all the frustration, all the aggravation, all the expectation worthwhile.

For a long second, she was deathly afraid she'd said the wrong thing. What if he'd done everything because of some Good Samaritan debt he felt he needed to fill in order to give his own past a clean slate? She'd heard him say words of love the night before, but words whispered in bed weren't always words with a long-term guarantee. Had he meant them?

Then he glanced at her, just a brief flicker of his eyes off the road. The intensity of love flaring in that gaze burned away all her doubts. He gave her his slow, lopsided smile and said, "Good." Then his attention went back to the road, but she noticed the smile remained.

All the guarantee she needed.

The Coopers lived in an upscale suburban neighborhood where everyone belonged to an association, paid for a private security patrol and was a member of the same society clubs. Lawns were uniformly green and all the vehicles parked in the driveways were new.

"Nice," Spencer murmured sarcastically as he pulled into the long, sloping drive of a two-story white brick home with a columned front and sculpted hedges.

Mercy said nothing, silently agreeing with his mild distaste for sameness. She'd long ago lost the appreciation for surface affluence. It was a nice, luxurious front for something cold and ugly. But unfortunately, few saw beyond that carefully cultivated facade. Few wanted to look, as long as that carefully groomed image was maintained.

Before turning off the engine, Spencer angled toward her. His expression was steeped in care as he asked, "Are you sure you're ready for this? You don't have to go one-on-one with them, sweetheart. I know they're not going to make it easy on you. If you don't want to do this, I'll understand. I can go in alone and then we can let the courts do your talking for you later."

Mercy took a breath, discouraging the small, cowardly part of her that begged to accept the easy route. But the stronger part knew it wouldn't be enough. "No. I want to do it face-to-face. I need to."

The truck wound down to silence. In it, her breathing, even her heartbeats, sounded unnaturally loud. It was the rapid tempo of fear.

"Are you going to go in with me?" she asked in a fragile voice.

"Let them try to keep me out." He sounded like he hoped they would. A small, noticeable tic had started at the corner of his mouth the moment they left Pine Creek. A pulse of warning. He was no one to mess with in this particular circumstance. Mercy was glad.

The comfort she took from his protective growl and bristly stance was astronomical. She wanted to kiss him. She wanted to break down into tears and babble about how much it meant to her, him being with her. But he was already out and jogging around to her door, issuing her out like she was a princess.

"Let's go get Casey," he said as he curled her hand into the crook of his elbow. He couldn't have mistaken the brittle tension that came over her, yet she marched up the flagstone walk with more grit than most soldiers heading for the front lines. He smiled grimly, with pride.

Cindy Cooper received them coolly at the door. Casey wasn't home, she claimed in a frigid little voice. Her grandfather had taken her out for a fast-food lunch at her favorite restaurant. Then, as she showed every intention of closing the beveled-glass door in their faces, Spencer wedged in his foot.

"We'll wait."

She stared at him with a mixture of indignation and upset, her breeding allowing her a fine, starching control. "I see you are not in uniform, Sheriff. Can I assume this is not an official call?"

"Not yet it isn't." And he let the implications settle deep and dire while he stood half in, half out, and as immovable as five tons of concrete.

"Have you a warrant?" She requested that stiffly as if she'd heard it on TV but was uncertain if it applied in this instance.

"Would you like me to get one for you, Mrs. Cooper? It wouldn't take long."

"We need to talk, Mom."

Cindy Cooper's gaze darted to her daughter in wary anxiousness. "I don't know, Mercy. I shouldn't let you in without Jeff being here."

"Who are you trying to protect, Mother? It was never me, was it?"

With an exasperated sigh, Cindy threw open the door. "Come in, but don't expect me to listen to any more of your wild stories."

Mercy advanced with a slight coaxing pressure from Spencer's palm at the center of her back. A chill swept over her the moment she crossed the threshold. It was like stepping back into the insecurities of a child, crossing into their austere house. Where the baseboards were never dirty but the family laundry was soiled beyond redemption. Spencer kept his arm firmly hitched around her.

"Wild stories?" she questioned her mother as they followed her into a tastefully decorated living room. As children, she and her brother had never been allowed to walk on the white carpet. Out of habit, Mercy started to slip out of her shoes, then stopped herself. In a form of subtle defiance, she stepped into the room and felt the thick pile give satisfyingly beneath the poke of her heels. "That's what you called them when I was little, so you didn't have to believe the truth. Is that what you're going to call them when Casey starts telling you the same things? Wake up, Mom. The only stories are the ones you've been telling yourself all these years when you wanted to convince yourself that everything was normal."

Cindy confronted her, her ivory cheeks stained brightly with agitation. From anger. From fear. Her gaze flickered to Spencer uneasily before returning to her daughter. "How can you persist in telling these same lies about your father? You're not a child anymore. You realize the consequences of what you're saying. You know what kind of damage such accusations could do to his position at the bank. Just the hint of something like this going public would ruin him."

"Is that all that matters to you, Mother? That Jeff's earning potential might suffer? What about Casey? What about Terry's little girl? Don't you care that another child is going to be ruined at the hands of that monster you married? Are you going to let him molest her, too? Or worse?"

Cindy went dramatically pale and whirled away. Her footsteps faltered as she hurried past them on the way to the front door. "I want you to leave. I want you to leave right now."

"But it's not going to go away, Mom. It never goes away. Believe me, I know. You made the wrong choice defending him when I was little. Don't make it again. I'm begging you. Don't turn your back on this last chance to make it right."

But she was jerking open the door.

And on the front steps stood her husband, with Casey's hand clutched firmly in his.

"Spencer! I knew that was your truck! Mercy!"

The child wiggled with unexpected vigor, managing to slip the tight cuff of her grandfather's fingers. She raced across the foyer to fly into Mercy's open arms.

"Did you bring Mr. Stubbs? I couldn't sleep a wink without him. They wouldn't let me go back for him."

That small voice with its hitch of anguish was enough to steel Mercy for anything. Even her stepfather's cold, assessing glare.

"Of course we brought him, honey. We know how much he means to you."

"Just can't stop making trouble, can you?" came Cooper's sinister claim.

Mercy looked at him over the top of Casey's head. And for once, she didn't flinch away from the coldness of his glare. Hers bit right back at him. "Oh, you don't know what trouble is, mister."

Her bold tone took him aback a bit, then he stepped purposefully aside to clear the doorway. "You were just leaving, weren't you?"

"Yes," Mercy agreed tartly, settling the suddenly anxious child on the floor. "Casey, get your things. You're going with us."

"Really? Can I?"

Casey cast a fretful look at the glowering figure now blocking the exit, then she moved in tight against Spencer's side, tucking her tiny hand inside the huge surrounding safety of his. An unspoken gesture of faith and trust.

"You're going to leave," Cooper restated. "Without the child. Right now. Don't you think enough damage has been done already?"

"Yes, more than enough," Mercy replied in full agreement. Then she let loose with some purposeful intimidation of her own. "And I won't keep quiet about it anymore."

"Are you making some sort of threat?" Cooper snarled in disbelief.

"Not just 'some sort.' Consider it the real thing. With all the ugly little details brought out in full, nasty color in front of all your business partners, clients, neighbors...everyone."

He laughed harshly. "Who's going to believe your word over mine? The word of a powerful and respected businessman over an obviously overwrought young woman who's been in and out of therapy to deal with some imagined trauma?''

"Does it matter?" she asked with an icy calm. "Does it really matter whether anyone believes it once it's brought out into the open? The victim is the one who always bears the scars. Believe me, I know.''

"I believe her" came Spencer's deep affirming drawl. "And I'm going to do my best to see a judge does, before awarding Casey into Mercy's care.''

"That's absurd!"

Spencer smiled. "That's a fact that you can, if you'll pardon the pun, take to the bank with you.''

"You don't know who you're dealing with, Sheriff. You have no authority here. If you don't leave my home right now, I'll have you arrested for trespassing and harassment. If you were smart, you'd forget this whole thing and slink on back to that hick town of yours before I have you up on charges of complicity in a kidnap case. You have no idea what you're getting into. These are all lies, you know. Everything she's told you. But I don't blame you for believing them. She tells a convincing tale.''

"Try selling it someplace else, Cooper. I never doubted her for a minute.''

"I'll have your badge," he seethed, not one to take insubordination lightly. And in his mind, everyone was accountable to him. "Do you understand me?''

Mercy did. She knew they weren't idle threats. She'd seen what Jeff Cooper could do when he got the powerful machinery behind him moving. It would crush anyone foolish enough to stand in its path. And the last thing she wanted was for Spencer to get hurt.

She put her hand on his forearm in a beseeching gesture. "Spencer, maybe we should—"

He gave her a quick smile. "Sweetheart, don't let him get to you. That's his game, intimidation. Trust me. I didn't come here unprepared. But what he doesn't know is that I've dealt with slicker scum than him from the criminal cesspool and he doesn't scare me at all with his impotent threats. As a matter of fact, I don't think he can bully anyone but little girls and weak women."

Cooper had gone a deep crimson. Veins bulged in his neck and forehead.

And Mercy was deeply, thoroughly scared. Her first thought was to reject the reassurance that Jeff Cooper presented no danger to them. She knew he was. She'd experienced it firsthand. When she was a child. But Spencer Halloway was no easily threatened child. And she trusted his judgment. She used her faith in him as a shield to stand behind so she wouldn't retreat into silent terror as she had when she was young.

In fact, she stood even bolder at Spencer's side to claim, "We're taking Casey with us. If you think I'd let her spend another minute alone with you in this house, you're crazy—even crazier than I already know you are."

"Why you little b—"

"Excuse me. I'm sorry I'm late. Traffic from the metro airport was terrible."

They all turned in surprise to see a slight woman clad in a red tailored business suit push her way into the Coopers' home. All but Spencer, who was grinning.

"Amy! I thought you were in the Caribbean," Mercy stammered as her old friend hugged her in a brisk embrace.

"I was, until this…very attractive sheriff…contacted me. We had an interesting conversation and he had some, I must say, compelling reasons for me to come home early. Don't you know by now that I'd drop anything for you, Mercy? But don't tell my new husband that. He thinks he's the center of my world." The tiny whirlwind took a breath and fixed a severing stare upon Cooper. "Is this him?"

"Who is this woman?" Cooper demanded in a rage.

"I'm sorry I forgot to introduce myself. I'm Amy Cheswick, from the Wayne County prosecutor's office. And I have a writ here prepared by Judge Miles Webster granting temporary custody of Miss Cassandra Pomeroy to Sheriff Halloway."

Cooper stared at the folded document, not taking it. "What is this? Some kind of joke?"

"I don't joke, Mr. Cooper—not about things of this nature. This is official," she continued brittlely. "Sheriff Halloway is court certified to provide emergency foster care in cases involving a threatening domestic situation. A new hearing to determine permanent custody has been scheduled for next Monday. Is that soon enough for you, Sheriff?"

"That's fine," Spencer said amicably.

"I guess we'll see you in court, Mr. Cooper."

"Threatening?" His astonishment finally ended with thoughts of self-preservation. "What kind of garbage have you been hearing, lady?"

Amy Cheswick drew herself up to her significant five feet two inches of female outrage and squared off in front of the much bigger man. "Don't get in my face, Mr. Cooper. What I've been listening to is the cries for help from a little girl caught in a vicious, predatory home life—cries her own mother refused to hear. And if you make one bit of trouble for us, I'll make sure not only the court hears them, but every newspaper, radio and television reporter I've had the privilege to meet hears them, too. Are *you* listening, Mr. and Mrs. Cooper? Do we have your full attention now?"

"You—you can't do this," Cindy Cooper protested, finding her voice at last. "What about Casey? My daughter isn't fit to raise a child. She's single. No court could possibly give her any credence. What Casey needs is the security of a traditional home—"

"What Casey needs," Spencer interrupted smoothly, "is love and respect and security—something she'd never get here. Mercy is recognized as Casey's godmother and the judge I spoke to seemed to think that would have a lot of pull in his decision to award custody. As for a traditional home, I'm sure Mercy would do fine on her own but I fully intend to take a very active role in Casey's upbringing. I'm an officer of the law. I make a damn stable impression. And believe me, Mrs. Cooper, that's a hell of a lot of credence."

Mercy trembled hearing that claim, realizing he'd just committed himself completely to her and Casey and to that "long run" they'd discussed earlier.

"Jeff...?"

Cooper paid no attention to his wife's whimpered plea. He was too aware of the dangerous situation he was facing with the feisty attorney and hard-eyed sheriff against him. "So if we give in to these blackmail demands, no other charges will be filed?"

Amy glared at him. "Don't you wish. As far as I know, Mr. Cooper, there is no statute of limitations on cases of child abuse. My suggestion is that you retain a very good lawyer because your stepdaughter already has one that's eager to drag your respectable butt up before a jury of your peers. But that's up to Mercy. Right now, Casey is our main concern."

Casey had been listening intently but most of the conversation went over her head. In her mind, all the big angry words trickled down to one thing.

"Does this mean I get to go home with you?"

Her big eyes lifted hopefully to Mercy.

"That's exactly what it means. Go gather up all your things, honey. You won't ever have to spend another night under this roof."

Without a second of hesitation, the child rushed to comply. The sound of her small feet pounding up the stairs echoed huge in Mercy's and Spencer's hearts.

Now it was just a matter of escaping the situation gracefully, when all Spencer could think about was how good Cooper's neck would feel within the span of his two hands. Let him know what it felt like to be helpless and see how he liked it. Not much, Spencer guessed. And he'd like the loss of his reputation even less. That got Spencer smiling.

"How could you?" Cindy Cooper demanded of her daughter in shrill despair. "How could you do such a—such a terrible thing to this family?"

"Mom," Mercy began quietly. "I wasn't the one who did the terrible thing."

"So this is how you get even with me for not believing you? By ruining my life?"

"I'm not doing it to spite you, Mother. I'm doing it for the sake of a child I happen to love and for the sake of the child I once was."

Just then, Casey came bounding down with a hastily stuffed overnight case in hand. She grinned up at Spencer when he took it from her and immediately possessed herself of a hand from both Spencer and Mercy to make a firm announcement.

"Let's go home."

And without a backward glance at where all those old memories resided, Mercy led the way outside.

In the driveway, she and Amy embraced for a long, tearful moment and her oldest, dearest and most trusted friend said, "You done good today, kid. It gets easier from here on out, as long as you don't forget what you're fighting for."

"I won't. I've got you to thank for that."

"Me and that good-looking hunk of lawman over there who probably ran up the national debt in long-distance calls paving the way for this moment of triumph. Hang on to him, girl." And she winked knowingly.

"I plan to, Amy."

"As the saying goes, we'll have our day in court." Amy sank down into her BMW. "Until then, I've got a honeymoon to get back to."

Spencer handed Mercy and Casey up into his Blazer. Casey had a tearful reunion with Mr. Stubbs, then, as he followed Mercy's directions to her apartment, there was a long silence. Not uncomfortable, but pensive. Because he was going to be dropping them off there and heading back to his own life in Pine Creek alone. And that was the last thing in the world any of them wanted.

Finally, Spencer broke in to ask, "Casey, how'd you like to live with Mercy and me as a family in a little north-woods hick town once everything is settled?"

"Just fine!" Casey bubbled as she and Mr. Stubbs hugged him enthusiastically. "We've got fireworks to go to.

And all those fishing holes.'' Then the child cast a look in the other direction. ''Won't it be fine, Aunt Mercy?'' Her six-year-old brows rose with her imperious command.

Mercy smiled at her, then met Spencer's questioning gaze over the top of Casey's bright head. ''Just fine,'' she repeated with a confident smile. ''I love you, Spencer. Let's go home.''

Grinning wide, Spencer Halloway turned his four-by-four around. And headed north.

* * * * *

COMING NEXT MONTH

INTIMATE MOMENTS®
Silhouette®

Blood *is* thicker than water...

a new Silhouette Intimate Moments miniseries by

DALLAS SCHULZE

They have a bond so strong, *nothing* can
tear them apart!

Read the second book in this heartwarming series,
coming in June 1995:
ANOTHER MAN'S WIFE, Intimate Moments #643

Gage Walker's best friend's widow and child
desperately needed his help. And Gage was not the
kind of man to turn his back on responsibility. Trouble
was, his "friendship" with Kelsey was stirring up all
kinds of emotions that Gage had long ago buried
and *definitely* didn't want to feel—such as passion,
commitment and pure, raw *need*. And those feelings
could only lead to one thing....

Look for future books in this delightful series.

Silhouette® ...where passion lives.

He's Too Hot To Handle...but she can take a little heat.

ANNOUNCING THE

PRIZE SURPRISE
SWEEPSTAKES!

This month's prize:

L-A-R-G-E—SCREEN
PANASONIC TV!

This month, as a special surprise, we're giving away a fabulous FREE TV!

Imagine how delighted you and your family will be to own this brand-new 31" Panasonic** television! It comes with all the latest high-tech features, like a SuperFlat picture tube for a clear, crisp picture...unified remote control...closed-caption decoder...clock and sleep timer, and much more!

The facing page contains two Entry Coupons (as does every book you received this shipment). Complete and return *all* the entry coupons; **the more times you enter, the better your chances of winning the TV!**

Then keep your fingers crossed, because you'll find out by July 15, 1995 if you're the winner!

Remember: The more times you enter, the better your chances of winning!*

PRIZE SURPRISE
SWEEPSTAKES

OFFICIAL ENTRY COUPON

This entry must be received by: JUNE 30, 1995
This month's winner will be notified by: JULY 15, 1995

YES, I want to win the Panasonic 31" TV! Please enter me in the drawing
and let me know if I've won!

Name_____

Address _____ Apt. _____

City   State/Prov.   Zip/Postal Code

Account #_____

Return entry with invoice in reply envelope.

© 1995 HARLEQUIN ENTERPRISES LTD.   CTV KAL

PRIZE SURPRISE
SWEEPSTAKES

OFFICIAL ENTRY COUPON

This entry must be received by: JUNE 30, 1995
This month's winner will be notified by: JULY 15, 1995

YES, I want to win the Panasonic 31" TV! Please enter me in the drawing
and let me know if I've won!

Name_____

Address _____ Apt. _____

City   State/Prov.   Zip/Postal Code

Account #_____

Return entry with invoice in reply envelope.

© 1995 HARLEQUIN ENTERPRISES LTD.   CTV KAL

OFFICIAL RULES
PRIZE SURPRISE SWEEPSTAKES 3448
NO PURCHASE OR OBLIGATION NECESSARY

Three Harlequin Reader Service 1995 shipments will contain respectively, coupons for entry into three different prize drawings, one for a Panasonic 31" wide-screen TV, another for a 5-piece Wedgwood china service for eight and the third for a Sharp ViewCam camcorder. To enter any drawing using an Entry Coupon, simply complete and mail according to directions.

There is no obligation to continue using the Reader Service to enter and be eligible for any prize drawing. You may also enter any drawing by hand printing the words "Prize Surprise," your name and address on a 3"x5" card and the name of the prize you wish that entry to be considered for (i.e., Panasonic wide-screen TV, Wedgwood china or Sharp ViewCam). Send your 3"x5" entries via first-class mail (limit: one per envelope) to: Prize Surprise Sweepstakes 3448, c/o the prize you wish that entry to be considered for, P.O. Box 1315, Buffalo, NY 14269-1315, USA or P.O. Box 610, Fort Erie, Ontario L2A 5X3, Canada.

To be eligible for the Panasonic wide-screen TV, entries must be received by 6/30/95; for the Wedgwood china, 8/30/95; and for the Sharp ViewCam, 10/30/95.

Winners will be determined in random drawings conducted under the supervision of D.L. Blair, Inc., an independent judging organization whose decisions are final, from among all eligible entries received for that drawing. Approximate prize values are as follows: Panasonic wide-screen TV ($1,800); Wedgwood china ($840) and Sharp ViewCam ($2,000). Sweepstakes open to residents of the U.S. (except Puerto Rico) and Canada, 18 years of age or older. Employees and immediate family members of Harlequin Enterprises, Ltd., D.L. Blair, Inc., their affiliates, subsidiaries and all other agencies, entities and persons connected with the use, marketing or conduct of this sweepstakes are not eligible. Odds of winning a prize are dependent upon the number of eligible entries received for that drawing. Prize drawing and winner notification for each drawing will occur no later than 15 days after deadline for entry eligibility for that drawing. Limit: one prize to an individual, family or organization. All applicable laws and regulations apply. Sweepstakes offer void wherever prohibited by law. Any litigation within the province of Quebec respecting the conduct and awarding of the prizes in this sweepstakes must be submitted to the Regies des loteries et Courses du Quebec. In order to win a prize, residents of Canada will be required to correctly answer a time-limited arithmetical skill-testing question. Value of prizes are in U.S. currency.

Winners will be obligated to sign and return an Affidavit of Eligibility within 30 days of notification. In the event of noncompliance within this time period, prize may not be awarded. If any prize or prize notification is returned as undeliverable, that prize will not be awarded. By acceptance of a prize, winner consents to use of his/her name, photograph or other likeness for purposes of advertising, trade and promotion on behalf of Harlequin Enterprises, Ltd., without further compensation, unless prohibited by law.

For the names of prizewinners (available after 12/31/95), send a self-addressed, stamped envelope to: Prize Surprise Sweepstakes 3448 Winners, P.O. Box 4200, Blair, NE 68009.

RPZ KAL